Detroit City Mafia

Detroit City Mafia

INDIA

www.urbanbooks.net

Urban Books, LLC
300 Farmingdale Road, N.Y.-Route 109
Farmingdale, NY 11735

Detroit City Mafia Copyright © 2020 INDIA

ISBN 13: 978-1-64556-111-8
ISBN 10: 1-64556-111-9

First Trade Paperback Printing November 2020
Printed in the United States of America

10 9 8 7 6 5 4 3 2 1

Distributed by Kensington Publishing Corp.
Submit Orders to:
Customer Service
400 Hahn Road
Westminster, MD 21157-4627
Phone: 1-800-733-3000
Fax: 1-800-659-2436

Prologue

"911. What's the emergency?" the young operator asked after the second ring. She sounded perky and cheerful, like the heaviness of her job hadn't yet weighed her down.

"Help! I need help!" I screamed as loud as I could into the blood-covered phone I was clutching for dear life. "Please, help me." Using what felt like my final breaths, I begged this stranger with every ounce of energy I could muster to send help my way. Internally though, I could sense the end was near. My toes were turning cold, and it was becoming harder and harder to get air.

"Everything is going to be okay. Calm down, please, and tell me what your emergency is," the operator said.

"I've been shot in my stomach, and I . . . really . . . can't . . . breathe." As I ended the sentence, I started to cough up chunky bits of blood. On cue, my body began to tremble. I knew death was around the corner.

"Help is on the way. Just hang on. Keep talking to me. Are you alone?" Now, fear had consumed the young operator's voice. Gone was the perkiness. Now she was panicked. "Hello. Are you there? Stay with me."

Although I wanted badly to reply, I just couldn't. My attention was focused on the large hole in my stomach. There was so much blood you'd swear I'd been covered with gallons of dark red paint. This shit looked like the scene of a horror film, and I was the unlucky victim.

"Hello. Please say something," the 911 operator begged frantically. She wanted me to give her some indication that I was still alive, but I just didn't have the strength.

As I tried to press a button on my call screen to at least let her know I was still alive, the room started to spin. My eyelids opened and closed uncontrollably. Suddenly I felt extremely tired. Fighting with everything I had, I forced myself to stay awake. I knew if I closed my eyes now, they would probably never open again.

Fuck! This was really it. The curtains were finally about to close. All my life, I thought I would die of old age, in a hospital, surrounded by my loved ones. Yet, here I lay, dying young and all by myself. Silly me for thinking that God would look out for me this one time. *Shit!* My life had been hell for as long as I could remember. Why would today be any different?

Right on cue, the phone slipped from my bloody grasp into the large pool of blood flowing from my midsection. I tried hard to reach for it, but it was no use. *Fuck!* I couldn't believe today had turned into such a tragic occasion. It was my wedding day, and to make matters worse, I was expecting my first child soon. How would my seed survive in such an ugly world without me? Nobody would love my son or daughter like me! No one could teach my child the game like me! *Fuck!* I thought again as the severity of this situation hit me like a ton of bricks.

Just then, I heard the sirens approaching from outside, and things began to look up. Maybe I was going to be all right after all. Silently I prayed the Lord would spare me. God knows I'd done some dirt! Nevertheless, I was just beginning to figure my life out, and then some shit like this happened. I'd heard the saying, "Tomorrow ain't promised," plenty of times. I just never knew how true the shit was until this very second.

Knowing that help was only seconds away, I used the time to ponder the situation. I needed to keep my mind focused on something to prevent myself from closing my eyes. Who could've done this? Who was that fucking crazy? Not only had the bastard sniped me in the church, but they had also come for me in a venue filled with all of my soldiers. Whoever did this shit was brazen. They had no idea of the war they were starting, or maybe they did. Either way, there was going to be some smoke in the city once word got out that this shit had happened to me.

In addition to being on the rise as one of the top narcotics distributors in Detroit, I literally had the projects on lock! Once my niggas found out the hand that was feeding them had been laid to rest, they were bound to go bananas. No doubt, shit would be dry on the streets without me for a while.

As these thoughts ran through my mind, I began to transition from feeling helpless to pissed off. Impulsively, I wanted to get up from this cold floor and grab my gun to retaliate. I knew the perpetrator was probably still in the church, hiding among my family and friends who were waiting in the sanctuary for the wedding to start. If I had to die today, I at least wanted to take that bitch-ass nigga with me. Yet when I tried to move even my fingertips, my body betrayed me, forcing me to lie still and wait for assistance to arrive.

Finally, I surrendered and closed my eyes to calm my rapid breaths. While doing so, I decided to go ahead and make peace with God. We had never really seen eye to eye, but I knew things were out of my hands and now in His. Quickly, I recited a short prayer in my head that I'd learned in Sunday school and decided then to let the chips fall where they may. If I died, I died, but if the Lord saw fit to let me see another day, I promised to give up the game, but only after I'd gotten revenge on the person who tried to end my life. It sounds crazy to think about killing someone as you're dying, but that was me: a hothead from the east side of Detroit, with a trigger finger that was always on go.

My days on earth hadn't always been the easiest, but instead of seeing myself as a victim, I always saw myself as a victor. I had fought many battles and slain several giants in my short life, and today was no different. Seconds felt like days before I finally heard the sound I'd been waiting for.

"My name is Bryan, and this is Elizabeth."

I opened my eyes to see an older male EMT introduce himself as he and his partner dropped down to the floor beside me. After they ripped my clothes off and poked me with several needles, I was wrapped with some gauze, then lifted onto the gurney and rolled toward the waiting ambulance. With weak eyes, I caught a glimpse of a few spectators in the hallway of the church. They all had tears running down their faces. I knew they could see death riding shotgun with me on the stretcher, because I saw his punk ass too! Still, I fought.

"It's going to be okay. You will pull through this," someone yelled out.

I wanted to encourage everyone not to worry. I wanted to tell them that it was all going to work out in the end, no matter which way it went, but I was way too feeble. Instead, I managed to muster up the strength to at least give the onlookers a halfhearted smile. If I had to go out like this, I at least wanted the last thing on my face to be a smirk. I needed niggas to know that I wasn't scared and that nobody could get the best of me, even in death.

"What happened, baby? Who did this?" my fiancé asked while running up to the stretcher. This caused a tear to form in the corner of my eye. Not for me, though. I was too G for that shit. The tears I was shedding were simply for the loss of what could've been and the loss of love unexplored to its fullest potential. These tears were falling because we were losing the forever that we'd promised each other.

"Please step back! We need to clear a way to the door. Our patient needs to get to the ambulance," Bryan hollered.

"Don't you fucking die on me! Do you understand? I love you. I need you. Baby, I need you!"

"I love you too." I tried to mumble the words for what I felt would be the last time. My heart began to break into a million pieces. Death for me was inevitable, and I knew it.

Finally, we made it outside into the cool April air and into the waiting emergency vehicle with flashing lights. Elizabeth jumped behind the wheel and took off, pushing the large vehicle to at least eighty miles per hour. I shrieked in pain as we hit several unavoidable potholes. Unfortunately, these were a permanent fixture on all Detroit roads.

Bryan placed an oxygen mask over my face and hooked me up to some white machine. I listened as he called over to the local hospital, telling them about my grave condition. He advised them to assemble a surgical team and to have them at the door stat.

"Elizabeth, drive faster!" he yelled. She punched the gas so hard that Bryan must've lost his balance. I saw him fall toward the back door, then quickly regain his footing. "Stay with us. We won't lose you tonight." Bryan sounded like he felt confident, but I didn't feel the same. I knew my time was up.

Within twenty minutes, we had arrived at Detroit Receiving Hospital. It was the number one trauma center in Detroit. Bryan and Elizabeth pulled my gurney off the back of the ambulance and flew through the emergency room doors like it was their lives that were on the line. From there, I was then handed off to a team of doctors and nurses. At this point, all I could see were blurs of faces. I couldn't make out anything. They anxiously went to work on my body all the way into the operating room, which was lit up with so many white lights it could've almost been mistaken for heaven.

"Come on, people, we have a life to save here!" someone yelled. I assumed he was the doctor in charge.

The operating room was freezing cold. I was numb yet shivering uncontrollably. When the staff transported me from the gurney to the table, my entire body went limp. I couldn't feel a thing, not even my face. The light above my head was so blinding that I had to ponder if it was the surgical lamp or the Lord Himself.

"Who shot me?" I randomly mumbled while peering at the anesthesiologist, who was injecting something into my IV line. Naturally she didn't respond, but it didn't matter. Out of nowhere, an array of scenes began to play out in front of me like the movie of my life. Maybe this was God's way of giving me the answer to my question before I took my last breath. Maybe He wanted my soul to have eternal peace . . . even if I was going to hell.

"Goddammit. We're losing this patient!" the doctor screamed.

Beeeeeeeeeeeeeeeeeeeeeeeeeeeeeeeeeeeeeeeeeeeeeeeep! Right then, right there, I flatlined.

Chapter One

"Okay, Mrs. Johnson, I'm done for the day. If you don't need anything else, I'm going to head home." The time on Murdonna's watch told her that it was almost ten o'clock p.m. She'd been working since eight o'clock a.m. at Johnson Family Cleaners, trying to make a little money to buy groceries tonight. School was back in session tomorrow, and she didn't want her siblings to go to bed hungry.

Though she absolutely hated working for Mrs. Johnson's bougie ass, she desperately needed the money. Murdonna wasn't a full-time employee, she was just someone Mrs. Johnson liked to call when she needed the bathrooms cleaned, the floors scrubbed, and the merchandise pressed whenever she'd gotten behind on her work. Murdonna basically worked for next to nothing because she was desperate, and Mrs. Johnson capitalized on that.

"Okay, dear, take this." Stepping from the office, wearing a fly Chanel pantsuit, Mrs. Johnson held out a brown paper bag from Eddie V's Steakhouse for Murdonna to take.

With confusion on her face, Murdonna didn't reach for the bag. "What's that?" She knew the old lady liked to play games from time to time with how she paid for labor, but Murdonna seriously hoped today wasn't going in that direction. When Mrs. Johnson had called her today to work, they discussed her rate being $8 an hour.

By Murdonna's calculations, she knew twelve hours multiplied by $8 should have put her pay in the range of $96, give or take a few dollars because Mrs. Johnson sometimes took out taxes.

"These are some leftovers from my dinner last night at the steakhouse. I'm not going to eat the rest, so you can have it." Evelyn Johnson nudged the bag forward, but still Murdonna didn't take it.

"I don't want your leftovers, Mrs. Johnson. I want the money we discussed on the phone before I caught the bus over here."

"What we discussed was the rate I was going to pay you. I never said that rate would be in cash, darling." Evelyn folded her arms like she was irritated. "The food in this bag cost me a hundred thirty-seven dollars last night. I figured since I ate a little already, the rest is worth about a hundred. So really, you're getting a little more than what you were expecting," she stated matter-of-factly.

Murdonna wanted to call this woman all kinds of bitches, but she decided not to. She couldn't believe that Evelyn even thought that pulling a stunt like this was okay. "Mrs. Johnson, I don't want your leftovers. I need the money we discussed."

Before Evelyn could respond, the back door to the cleaners opened, and in walked Evelyn's spoiled son, Thomas. "What's up, Ma. I need some cash for this new game that comes out in the morning." He barged right into the conversation without excusing himself, which was something he often did.

"Wait for me in the office," Evelyn replied, but Thomas wasn't having it. With his hand out, he demanded to get some cash pronto, and she obliged. Reaching into her bra, she pulled out five $100 bills and handed him two.

"Thanks, Ma. I appreciate it." After planting a kiss on his mother's cheek, he exited the building just as abruptly as he'd entered.

This exchange was nothing new to Murdonna. For the past two years, she'd watched Mrs. Johnson give her ungrateful son the shirt off her back time and time again. Evelyn loved that boy with all of her heart, yet he only seemed to love what she could do for him. Murdonna wished she were in his shoes sometimes. Her life was a far cry from that, though.

"Murdonna, I've got to head out. I don't have time to argue with you today. Either you want the food, or you don't," Evelyn said, turning her attention back to the matter at hand.

"How could you possibly think what you're doing is fair?"

"Baby, life isn't fair," Evelyn scoffed. "Didn't your mother teach you that as a child?"

"Don't bring my mother into this." Murdonna's blood was beginning to boil. Already irritated about the situation, the last thing she wanted to hear was something about her mother, especially from a woman who, she knew, looked down on her.

"I'll tell you what. If you come back on Friday and work for a few hours, I will have cash for you then. Or you pick from the pile of clothes that haven't been claimed in six months." Evelyn presented her final and best offer while balling up the steakhouse bag and tossing it into the trash.

Murdonna wanted to holler and scream. She wanted to cry and tell this woman how badly she needed the money right now. She wanted to explain how she and her siblings had nothing, but she didn't. There was no reason to bring this bitch into her business, because it wouldn't matter anyway. Evelyn wouldn't feel compassionate.

"Have a good night, Mrs. Johnson." Without another word, Murdonna took the invisible blow to her chest but didn't flinch. With her head held high, she left the cleaners and headed to the bus stop.

Chapter Two

During the forty-minute ride, she sat in silence as she pondered her next move. She was tired, hungry, and fed up with the direction her life was heading in. Never had she thought things could be this bad, yet here she was.

"Excuse me, miss, do you got a dollar or some change you can spare?"

Murdonna looked up to see an older woman dressed in a pair of dingy gray sweats and a torn white T-shirt. She was holding a baby in her right arm and a cup of loose change in her left hand. Murdonna wanted to tell this lady that, of the two of them, she was probably in the better financial position, but she didn't. After looking into the baby's eyes, Murdonna felt saddened. She knew this baby hadn't asked for the life he'd been given, just like Murdonna hadn't. Reaching into her pocket, she pulled out two dimes and dropped them into the woman's cup.

"Twenty cents!" the woman scoffed.

Murdonna couldn't believe the audacity of this woman. "Just so you know, I gave you my last. Be blessed!" Standing up, Murdonna walked toward the front of the bus because her stop was approaching.

Through the rearview mirror, the bus driver had seen the exchange and overheard the young woman's comments. Murdonna reminded him of his daughter, and he could see the sadness trying to hide in her eyes. After bringing the bus to a stop, he reached into his pocket and pulled out a $5 bill. "It's not much, young lady, but

I would love for you to take it." He held out his hand as Murdonna got closer.

Inside, she wanted to act proud and decline the hand-out, but without being paid by Mrs. Johnson tonight, her back was truly against the wall. "Thank you, sir. Next time I ride your bus, I promise to give it back."

"No givebacks. You just be safe out there." He nodded and watched her exit the bus. Silently he prayed that things would get better for the young girl.

Relieved to have something in her pocket, Murdonna started up the block toward her high-rise apartment building. Living in the low-income projects was something she wasn't proud of, but she wasn't embarrassed about it either. Over the years, the slums had provided her family shelter from the elements, and for that, she was grateful.

Just as she approached the end of the block, she decided to step inside of Terry's corner store to grab a few things. $5 wasn't much, but it would at least buy a few packs of ramen noodles and a liter of pop. Once inside the store, Murdonna walked up and down each aisle. Though she already knew what she was going to buy, that didn't stop her from staring at all the things she couldn't afford. She wanted a peanut butter and jelly sandwich so bad she could taste it. Quickly she contemplated stealing the items she needed, but when she looked up to see the store clerk staring at her like he was memorizing her face, she changed her mind.

After making her purchase, Murdonna stepped back out into the chilly night air. Though it was early September, the temperature in Detroit was forty-seven degrees. It was almost midnight, and the streets were nearly empty. No one was out except for some local dope boys standing on the corner selling rocks, and a few hookers selling ass and blowjobs.

As she walked the last two blocks to the low-income housing projects, Murdonna couldn't help but notice the various drug transactions happening. Silently she wondered how she could insert herself into the dope game. It looked so easy, but she knew it came with heavy consequences. Yet and still, Murdonna reasoned with herself that the rewards had to be better than the risks.

In her hood, most of the women only had two options. They could either find employment at the nearest strip club, or they could become some hustler's arm candy. Murdonna didn't like either option. Taking her clothes off for strangers was a no-go, and being one of many women, chasing after the same neighborhood dude was out of the question, too. She wanted a way to make her own money and create her own lane. All she needed was an opportunity, and once she got one, it would be all uphill from there.

Finally, she reached her high-rise building. The corridor that was usually filled with people hanging out was now empty. She knew this was partly due to school being back in session tomorrow and partly because of how late it was. Most people made themselves scarce in the projects after dark to avoid the seedy characters who came out at night. Murdonna wasn't fearful, though. She had too much on her mind to be afraid of what was lurking in the shadows.

After entering the lobby and pressing the button, she waited five minutes for the elevator to arrive. When it did, she stepped on and sighed. It had been a long day.

"Hold up," someone hollered before jumping on. He pressed the button for the tenth floor while conversing on his cell phone.

Murdonna recognized the young man as someone she'd gone to school with. His name was Payro. She knew he ran with the DCM, Detroit City Mafia, a small crew in their projects. Murdonna wanted to tap Payro's shoulder and ask him a question, but he was so engrossed in his conversation that he hadn't even noticed her. Murdonna was used to this type of treatment. She didn't have name-brand clothing, and she didn't have money to keep her hair and nails done. Therefore, no one ever looked her way, especially not boys her age.

After Payro stepped off the elevator, Murdonna rode the rest of the way in silence. Once she reached her floor, she trekked down the long hallway until she reached her door. After putting her key in the door and turning the knob, she was greeted by a quiet house. Her brother was asleep on a pallet in the living room, and her sister was asleep on the couch. Silently, Murdonna slipped off her shoes and placed her key onto the table. She placed the noodles onto the counter and put the pop into the fridge. Next, she walked to the back of the apartment and turned on the light in her mother's room. The bed was still made up the way she'd left it this morning.

So many thoughts flooded Murdonna as she stared at the empty bed. She wondered what the next day would bring. She wondered where the family's next meal would come from, and she wondered how long it would be before she would crack under all the pressure she was under to figure shit out with no guidance. Yet and still, without a word, she cut off the lights in the bedroom and headed for the shower.

Chapter Three

The next morning, without waiting for the alarm to sound, Murdonna rose from the bed, made it, and then headed for the bathroom to brush her teeth. From the sound of the chatter coming from the living room, she knew her brother and sister were probably getting ready for school. Though no one was really excited that school was back in session, everyone typically loved the first day of school. It was the perfect chance to catch up with friends you hadn't seen all summer, and it was the day everyone flexed their new school outfits. For the Carter household, though, today was just another day. The friends they had were each other, and none of them had any new clothes to flex.

After brushing her teeth and pulling her medium-length hair into a ponytail, Murdonna headed to the front of the small one-bedroom apartment to boil water for the ramen noodles she'd purchased last night, but they were gone. She didn't bother to ask her siblings what happened to them, because she already knew that they'd probably woken up in the middle of the night, seen they were there, and made themselves something to eat. Murdonna knew that food around the house had been scarce. Therefore, she didn't make a fuss.

Instead, she headed for the door of the apartment and walked down the hallway and into the trash room. This room was where all the tenants left trash bags when they were too lazy to throw them down the trash chute or walk them outside. Murdonna scanned through the findings, grabbed a bag that looked promising, and quickly ran back to her apartment before anyone could see her.

After setting the bag down on the kitchen floor, Murdonna stared at the State Farm calendar pinned to the cracked wall in the kitchen. "Day forty-two." She grabbed a marker from the drawer and placed a big red X over today's date. The image of all the red X's covering all the days she'd marked on the calendar made her stomach turn.

With a sigh, she took a seat on the folding chair in the corner of the galley kitchen and began going through the contents of the black trash bag that smelled like shit. Though she wanted to throw up, she tucked her face into her shirt and continued to rummage. She was looking for empty pop cans and bottles she could take to the stores and recycle for money. Though Murdonna hated to dig in the garbage, she knew the contents of each bag could sometimes provide a way to feed her siblings. Therefore, she rolled her sleeves up and went to work.

With her eyes closed, she fumbled around the bag until she felt the necks of two bottles. She pulled them out and saw that they were empty beer bottles covered in cigarette ashes. After rinsing them off and placing them into the sink, she went back to searching through the bag.

As she neared the bottom, her hand was met with something squishy. Instantly she knew what it was and felt even sicker. This bag of trash had come from the Walters' apartment. She knew this because they were the only people on the floor who used black trash bags with red strings. She chose the bag because the Walters always had pop cans and beer bottles. But they also had a set of twins still in diapers. With that in mind, Murdonna knew for sure that her hand was currently resting in a pile of shit.

Shaking as much of it off as she could, she ran over to the kitchen sink to wash her hands but was met with disappointment when nothing happened. "Come on." She hit the nozzle with her clean hand. Instead of free-flowing water, it only dripped out tiny drops.

"I hate it here!" she screamed. In all honesty, her apartment building probably needed to be condemned years ago. If it wasn't one thing, it was always three others. There were continuous water issues, heating and AC problems, as well as other things like mice and roaches.

"Donna, I'm hungry." Donzell walked into the kitchen wearing a wrinkled, dingy white uniform shirt that was two sizes too big for his seventy-pound frame. With eyes as big as his stomach, he swung open the old, rusted refrigerator, then frowned. "Man, we still don't have no food?"

Still trying to get the shit off her hand, Murdonna was irritated. She wanted to use this as an opportunity to ask his little ass what he thought had changed since the last time he checked the refrigerator for food, but she decided against it. She knew he was just being a kid. "Didn't you eat noodles last night?"

"Yeah, I had a pack, but that was last night. Today is a new day." His stomach was aching, and it was beginning to make his head hurt.

"Did you put deodorant on?" She changed the subject to keep him from thinking too hard about being hungry. This was a trick she'd been using all summer.

"I'm thirteen. You don't have to keep asking me silly questions like that." He smacked his crusty lips, hating the way his sister always treated him like he was still in elementary school. He was in the eighth grade, which was practically grown in his book.

"Well, did you?" Raising a brow, Murdonna waited for the answer, because she knew better. Donzell wanted to be treated like a man but consistently acted like a toddler.

"I'll be right back. I forgot something." He made a dash toward the back of the small apartment.

"Yeah, that's what I thought." Murdonna knew her little brother like the back of her hand.

Their mother had been an on-again, off-again heroin user since Murdonna was 5. Every time she relapsed, Murdonna would have to go stay with a family member or family friend. By the time Murdonna was 10, she had decided to step up and help raise her siblings so they wouldn't have to be separated. Every time their mother went on a binge or checked herself into rehab, Murdonna kept the house running. She made sure they all got to school or daycare, and she made sure everyone had something to eat. Although Murdonna had turned only 17 two months ago, she was probably 35 in the mind. She had seen more shit in seventeen years than most people would see in a lifetime.

"When is Mama coming back from rehab?" Mya, the middle child, waltzed into the kitchen, still wearing her mismatched pajamas from the night before.

"I don't know, but she'll be back soon," Murdonna lied. She wanted to tell her 15-year-old sister that their mother hadn't lasted a day in rehab before she'd checked herself out and gone missing with the food stamp card and whatever money she had in her possession.

After two days of their mother being gone, Murdonna noticed that the food stamp card was missing. Thinking that her mother had taken the card with her by accident, Murdonna called Yellowstone Rehabilitation Center. She was going to ask someone who worked there to grab the card from her mother and leave it at the front desk, and she'd catch the bus and pick it up. However, when she spoke with the receptionist, she was told that her mother had checked herself out the morning after checking in. At first, Murdonna didn't think much of it, thinking that her mother would be home shortly. However, that wasn't the case. A day turned into a week, and before long, forty-two days had passed.

As Murdonna looked at her sister, she decided not to tell her that she thought their mother was probably dead. Every day since Sheila had gone missing, Murdonna called the local precinct to see if she had been booked. By day five, when the officer on the phone informed her that Sheila wasn't there, Murdonna knew something was wrong. She knew her mother's patterns of behavior, and this was far off base. Though Sheila went missing often, she was never gone longer than two days unless she was locked up. As the days passed this summer, Murdonna went around and asked as many people as she could if they'd seen her mom, but not one person offered any leads. Though Murdonna could feel in her spirit that shit wasn't right, she remained hopeful.

"Well, when is she coming back exactly? I'm hungry, and we ain't got nothing, not even a box of crackers!" Mya made a show of opening and closing each cabinet in the kitchen. Their food supply had been completely depleted right down to the powdered milk and eggs. "What's next to go? The electricity?" Mya hit the light switch just to see if they had power.

Luckily they did, but Murdonna wasn't sure for how long. She'd gotten a past-due notice two weeks ago but had no money to pay it. Therefore, it went into the pile with the others.

"Do we even got running water around this bitch?" Mya turned the knob on the sink, and of course, the water didn't turn on. With eyes as big as saucers, she looked at Murdonna for an explanation.

"Girl, relax. We got water! Even though it's barely running today, it's not shut off." She couldn't help but laugh at the situation. Murdonna was happy that on her list of things to worry about, the water bill wasn't one of them because it was included in the rent. However, she had a funny feeling the landlord was about to come collect, and she didn't have a dollar to give him.

"Donna, I'm scared. We've been fucked up a couple of times, but we have never been here before." Mya held her stomach, which growled loudly right on cue.

"I'm scared too." Donzell looked pitiful when he reentered the kitchen. This time he was fully dressed in navy blue uniform slacks that flooded and a pair of old yellow Converse shoes.

Murdonna felt bad that her siblings were starving, but she felt even worse that her brother looked like a hot-ass mess. Although she'd done the best she could with what she had, it just wasn't enough. Over the summer, that boy had grown like a weed, and none of his old uniforms fit. Sheila hadn't purchased him a pair of shoes all year, but thankfully someone had left those old Converses behind on the city bus last week. They were a size twelve. Donzell wore a size eleven, but it didn't matter when that was all they had. "Can we stop at McDonald's?"

"D, you know I don't have any money for McDonald's. I'm sorry." Murdonna looked down at the floor. She hated to tell the kids no, but what else could she do? She had already spent every piece of change she could find. She'd also gone to bed hungry plenty nights just so they could get enough of whatever she managed to scrape up for dinner. Murdonna was losing weight, her hair, and her mind at a rapid pace. Things had to get better, but for now, all she could do was press on.

"Mya, go get dressed. If you're ready in the next fifteen minutes, I will be able to get Donzell to school in time for the free breakfast, and if Mrs. White still works in the kitchen, I'll get her to slide us some fruit out the back door."

"Oh, no. I'm not going to school with nothing to wear." Mya shook her head vigorously. She was just starting her sophomore year in high school. Her reputation would be ruined until graduation if she started on the first day wearing faded rags or her sister's hand-me-downs. She would also choose to die rather than be seen rocking the same old shit from last year.

"Skipping school is not an option, Mya!" Murdonna raised her voice, mother-like. "Now go get dressed so we can leave."

"Girl, bye! You are not my mama! You can't make me do shit," Mya shot back. It was a dagger meant to remind her sister that she wasn't the boss. Instead, it only fueled the fire that had been building for the past forty-two days.

"Bitch, I know I'm not your fucking mother! Do you see needle marks in my veins?" Murdonna snapped. "Do you see me out here sucking dick for dimes?" She really didn't mean to say all of that, but it slipped out.

She sighed after seeing the horror on Donzell's face. Though they all knew their mother was an addict, Murdonna and Mya always kept the hardcore truths about their mother to themselves. "Look, I know I'm not your mother, but I am really trying to do my best here, given the circumstances. If you start skipping school this early in the year, the truancy officers will be out here. Once they find out we ain't got no food or real adult supervision, they are going to take us away from each other." Murdonna laid down the facts and kept it one hundred.

"I don't want to be split up." Donzell spoke with fear evident all over his face. No longer was he the macho man he pretended to be. He was the scared little boy who wouldn't make it a day without his family. Donzell loved both of his older sisters, especially Murdonna. Although Sheila was his birth mother, he secretly wished Donna was the one who delivered him. She was the one who always fed him, dressed him, and nursed him back to health when he was sick. Donna was everything Sheila wasn't. Though he liked to give her a hard time, he silently loved that she was always in his corner. Murdonna was his rock, and Mya's too.

"We won't be separated. Don't worry about that." Mya wrapped an arm around her brother. Since he was the baby, everyone spoiled him.

"Are you going to get dressed and go to school then?" Donzell looked up at Mya.

She bit down on her bottom lip and hesitated to answer. Murdonna knew her sister's plight all too well, because she also had a reputation for being one of the poor girls at their school. Although many of her classmates lived in the same tenement as she, she was judged a little harder because of her mother's reputation around the neighborhood. Sheila was known for breaking into their neighbors' apartments, giving blowjobs for a score, and plenty of other unfavorable things.

"So, are you going or not?" Donzell repeated his question.

"D, I just—" Mya started.

"Look, Mya, I'll let you slide this one time, but that's it," Murdonna relented. "Go down to the cleaners this afternoon and see if Mrs. Johnson has any unclaimed stuff you can fit into. Tell her I'll be there when I get out of school on Friday to work off the debt." After last night's encounter, the last thing Murdonna wanted to do was go to work for that old bitch. She hated the way Mrs. Johnson operated her business, always flaunting her new shit and making slick comments about the less fortunate. But Murdonna didn't give two fucks right now. Her sister needed clothes, so she decided to bite the bullet and deal with the rude bitch one more time to make it happen.

That's just how Murdonna was, always making sacrifices to benefit those she loved.

"Thank you, Donna." Mya hugged her sister. They didn't always see eye to eye, but she did appreciate all Donna did for her, even when she didn't say it. "Can I ask you something?"

"What now?" Donna looked at her sister curiously.

"Why do you smell like shit?" Mya pinched her nose.

"I smelled it too, but I didn't want to say anything." Donzell laughed, and his sisters joined in. Murdonna broke the embrace with her sister and walked back over to the sink to try again to clean her hand. Thankfully, the water worked.

"Donna, can I get some new stuff too?" Donzell started in with his requests.

"Go get your bookbag. We'll talk about it later," Murdonna instructed, and Donzell followed orders.

Quickly she slipped into a pair of classic white Reeboks that she'd had for nearly six years. Luckily her feet had stopped growing, which meant she was able to hold on to her stuff. The shoes had been washed so many times the soles were yellow and the Reebok tag had come off, but Donna didn't mind. They still got her from point A to point B.

"Do you think she's dead?" Mya blurted out once they were alone in the kitchen.

"Who?" Murdonna asked, though she already knew.

"Mom, who else?" Mya smacked her lips. "We should call the police and report her missing."

"No, don't call the police," Murdonna insisted. "If they show up here, it'll only cause more trouble for us."

"Well, what are we going to do in the meantime?"

"We're going to do what we've been doing. Survive!" Murdonna grabbed two notebooks and a pen from the kitchen counter. Thankfully, the grocery store ran a

$0.10 sale on certain school supplies, or she would not have been able to afford them. "Sheila will be back. Don't trip."

Murdonna grabbed her key from the table, then headed for the door with Donzell on her tail. "Don't forget to go see Mrs. Johnson, because your ass will be in school tomorrow. Lock up and don't let anybody in here, and I mean nobody." After she gave the warning, Murdonna and Donzell headed on their way.

Chapter Four

"Thanks for walking me to school," Donzell mumbled while following closely behind his sister down the block. Although Donzell's school was only down six short blocks and across the street from their building, it seemed like it always took them forever to get there.

He didn't vocalize it, but he hated walking past all the homeless people, junkies, and drug dealers by himself. One time when he was in the fifth grade, someone approached him and asked if he wanted to try a sample of something. Donzell was too young to know that what the man had in the small baggie was cocaine. However, he was wise enough to run from the stranger back into the apartment building to tell his mother.

Sheila yelled at him and insisted he march his ass back outside and get to school, but he was afraid. She told him that he was being a bitch and laughed in his face. He asked if she would at least walk him halfway, and she told him he had five fucking minutes to get back outside before she beat the brakes off him. Donzell left the apartment but didn't go back outside. Instead, he waited on the stairwell alone for six hours until he heard the other children returning from school. Though the stairwell was a treacherous place itself, Donzell liked his odds there better.

"Did you hear me?" Murdonna nudged him. "I asked what you want to be when you grow up."

"Oh, that's easy." Donzell had known what he wanted to be for quite some time. "I'm going to be a police officer with the homicide division." He loved crime shows and was strangely fascinated with how detectives used certain techniques to catch criminals.

"That's cool." Although Murdonna had no love for the police, she wasn't one for crushing dreams. "You can be anything you want to be in life. Just apply yourself, and the rest will work out."

"You sound like my teacher. That's what she said last year." Donzell laughed. Even though he was almost 14, he still had a young, childlike innocence about him. Murdonna often wondered if the drugs their mother took while pregnant affected his development. Yet and still, she loved that her brother was in no rush to be in the streets, and she wished he would stay that way for a little while longer. She'd seen too many young men in the projects grow up too fast and end up dead or in jail before their sixteenth birthday. Mya, on the other hand, was a different story. Her ass was too grown for her own good. Murdonna hated the backtalking, smart-mouthed little wench sometimes, but she would kill any nigga or bitch about her.

"D, I'm going to stop right here, but I'll watch you the rest of the way." Murdonna pressed the button for the light to change.

"You should come over and get some fruit from Mrs. White like you said this morning." Though he hadn't said anything, Donzell wasn't oblivious to the fact that Donna had dropped nearly twenty pounds this summer. He knew she wasn't eating properly, and that didn't make him feel good at all. He needed his sister to be okay, because if Murdonna went down, they all would go down.

"Nah. I'm good, little brother, but thanks for thinking of me. Have a great day in school, okay? Learn something good and tell me about it later." She patted his nappy head, then watched him cross the street. After he blended in with the other children heading toward school, Murdonna made her way around the corner, where the city bus would pick her up for school.

As soon as she approached the bus stop, she noticed a group of boys from her building. She hadn't ever really said much to any of them, but one face in particular stood out. It was Payro, the guy who was on the elevator last night. He was a low-level drug dealer who worked under a guy named Sysco. Sysco used to serve Sheila regularly before she left for rehab. Murdonna figured, after checking herself out of rehab, Sheila would've probably ended right back trying to score some heroin from Sysco. Therefore, she wanted to find out if they knew anything about her whereabouts.

Nervously, she approached the group and cleared her throat. "Hey, Payro, can I talk to you for a minute?" She tried to act cool.

"Minutes cost money, shorty." Peering into her eyes, he continued, "Do you have any?" Payro was trying to flex for the large crowd, and Murdonna didn't like it.

"Look, I really don't need you anyway! I'm just trying to find Sysco. He is the man in charge, right?" She rolled her eyes.

"I'm the man in charge. Any questions you got for Sysco go through me. What's up?"

"I need to ask about my mother, Sheila. Have you seen her?" Murdonna asked just as the bus pulled up.

"Sysco don't fuck with crackheads, ma," one of the boys in the crew teased Murdonna. "You probably need to check in the gutter. She might be down there with the rest of the rats."

Everyone laughed at the joke except for Payro. No one knew it, but his mom was once a junkie, addicted to narcotics too. She died of an overdose when he was 2 years old. That was why he had a soft spot in his heart for this situation. It also helped that the short, light-skinned, slim-thick shorty standing before him was easy on the eyes. Though she could've used a trip to the mall and the hair salon to get her shit tight, Payro appreciated her natural beauty.

"Nah, baby. I don't know where your mom is at, but when I see Sysco later, I'll see what's up, all right?" Payro licked his full lips.

Murdonna had never been this close to him before. As a result, she never noticed how smooth his ebony skin was or how perfect his teeth looked. She was also intrigued by the smell of cologne drifting off his body. It smelled expensive. She was impressed by the boy but didn't let on, because she knew someone like him would never be into her.

"Thank you, I really appreciate that." Murdonna smiled before going over to stand in line for the bus.

"Bitch, don't be standing next to me all close, looking like you got bed bugs and shit!" another boy in Payro's crew taunted.

Over the years, Murdonna had become accustomed to being the butt of everyone's jokes. Luckily, she was in her last year of high school, counting down the days before she could tell everyone to kiss her ass. "I guess if anybody knows about bed bugs, it's you, nigga. Didn't I see the maintenance man fumigating your apartment last month?" Murdonna didn't miss a beat in the roasting session. Usually, she tried to avoid conflict, but today was not the day, and she was not the one.

"What the fuck was that for, P-dot?" Payro frowned. He knew Murdonna's feelings were hurt even though she played it cool. "Apologize now!" he demanded.

"You must be out of your rabbit-ass mind if you think I'm about to apologize to this broken-down bitch!" P-dot shook his head vigorously and smacked his lips.

"Who are you calling a bitch?" Murdonna bucked, ready for action. Being a project girl had taught her to always stay prepared to fight at a moment's notice. She was nice with her hands, too.

"I'm talking to you, bitch!" P-dot put his finger right between Donna's eyes.

"Chill out with all that!" Payro jumped in between them. "You don't even know her, so why are you calling her a bitch?" After his mother died, Payro, aka Lawrence Tucker, was raised by his grandmother, Frances. She taught him to respect all women unless they disrespected him.

"I don't have to know her!" P-dot hollered. "All I know is her mama is a dick-sucking, pipe-smoking, dirty-pussy bitch!" The minute P-dot let the words fall from his lips, he knew he'd fucked up, and so did everyone else.

By instinct, Murdonna picked up the biggest piece of broken pavement she could find on the sidewalk and smashed it into his head. Blood splattered everywhere, including on Murdonna's face. She was sick and tired of people talking shit, especially about a mother who she didn't know was dead or alive.

"Goddamn!" Payro nearly jumped from his Mauri gator shoes. He couldn't believe shorty had just cracked this nigga's shit like that.

"Say something else about my muthafucking mama and it's lights out for you, nigga." Raising the weapon again, Murdonna went to strike P-dot, but Payro stopped her.

He grabbed her arms. "Look, baby, you don't need to be catching cases and shit over this dumb fuck. Take a minute and breathe." Gently he removed the piece of concrete from her trembling hand. "Get on the bus and go to school. I'll take care of him, and I'll call Sysco and see what's up with your mom, all right?"

Murdonna snapped out of her trance. She could see P-dot bleeding profusely from the small gash in his head.

"Go ahead, get on the bus. I got him," Payro insisted.

"Thank you." Wiping her face with the back of her hand, Murdonna got on the bus, produced her bus pass, which allowed her to ride for free, and took a seat. Several people were staring at her on account of what they'd just witnessed. However, when she made eye contact with them, they all looked away. She couldn't believe what she'd just done, but that bitch-ass nigga deserved it. Hopefully, he would learn his lesson and leave her the fuck alone next time.

Looking out the window, Murdonna watched as Payro and one other boy tried to help P-dot to his feet. The way homeboy was staggering, she knew he probably had a concussion. Instantly she worried about going to jail, then quickly got over it. For one thing, she knew the neighborhood niggas didn't snitch. She also didn't think jail would be so bad right now. "Three hots and a cot sounds good to me anyway," Murdonna thought aloud before laying her head against the window and closing her eyes.

She wasn't tired, but closing her eyes was the only way to stop her stomach from aching. There was so much shit on her mind that she appreciated the mental break. Her brain felt like it weighed a million pounds, and her shoulders felt as though they were going to cave in. The stress of not knowing where her mother was or where their next meal was coming from was really weighing on her. Things would've been easier if she were alone, but having two extra mouths to feed really put pressure on her to figure shit out rather quickly.

Thirty minutes later, the bus stopped in front of Cass Tech, one of the most prestigious high schools in the city. Murdonna was a very smart kid. Therefore, she passed the high school's entrance exam with flying colors. In the ninth grade, she entered school with big dreams and high hopes for the future. Now she was just ready to be done.

After filing off the bus with the other students, she made her way toward the school. While everyone else ran to their cliques of friends in the courtyard to reunite and discuss their summer activities, she continued to walk alone. Though she had never been one for cliques, she often longed for at least one or two solid friendships. She wished she had someone to share her secrets with, have sleepovers with, and do what other girls her age were doing, but that was impossible. For as long as she could remember, she'd been pushing people away for fear of exposing her homelife. She didn't want anyone at school who didn't already know to know that her mother was a junkie and they were broke.

"Good morning, students. All metals go in this tray." A female security guard shook a tray in front of the students as they proceeded through the metal detectors. This was mandatory in almost all Detroit public high schools. Many people hated them and felt like having metal detectors was ghetto. Donna actually appreciated them. In fact, she credited them as the reason there had been no school shootings in Detroit, compared to other places like Florida.

Beep! Beep! A student named Ray set the alarms off the same way he had every morning last year. He almost always forgot to remove his belt.

After grabbing her spiral notebooks from the tray, Murdonna headed to the second-floor bathroom. She wanted to wash her face good to remove the blood before class. As soon as she stepped in, she was met by three girls from the cheer team. They were applying makeup, freshening up their hair, and chatting about nothing in particular.

Paying them no mind, Murdonna grabbed a paper towel, wet it, and then ran it under the soap dispenser. It felt so good to wash her face and her hands with fully functional hot water. A few seconds later, the cheerleaders left the bathroom, and Murdonna noticed that one of them had left a half-eaten breakfast sandwich lying on a napkin on the windowsill. She stared long and hard, contemplating picking it up and eating it. She was extremely hungry, but she didn't want to be reduced to eating someone else's food. Then again, she'd been reduced to digging through shitty garbage lately, so why would this be an issue? Just as soon as she decided to go for the sandwich, the bathroom door swung open, and the cheerleaders walked back in.

"See? I told you I left it in here." A girl grabbed her food before Murdonna could get to it.

"Well, obviously you can't eat that now. It's been sitting in the bathroom too long," one friend chimed in.

"Yeah, Taylor. Having food in the bathroom is like dropping it on the floor. There's a five-second rule."

"You're right!" Taylor, the owner of the sandwich, took her perfectly good food and threw it away.

Murdonna could've cried. She wanted that food so bad, but there was no way she'd be retrieving anything from a high school girls' bathroom. There was no telling what could be lurking in the trashcan, like bloody pads or tampons. Furthermore, she would never be able to live down the embarrassment if she were caught.

Feeling deflated, she grabbed her things and walked down the hallway toward her first class. Upon arrival, she was greeted by her least favorite teacher.

"Ms. Carter, I see we both have the unfortunate task of having to deal with each other again this year." Mr. Hendricks smiled as Murdonna entered his classroom. Last year he taught AP English to the juniors. This year he was teaching it to the seniors. He wasn't a bad teacher. He just joked too much and didn't know when to shut the fuck up. For that reason alone, Murdonna despised being in his class again.

"How was your summer, Mr. Hendricks?" Murdonna asked without really wanting to hear the answer.

"It was wonderful yet short. The wife and I traveled to Amsterdam." Mr. Hendricks pretended that he was smoking a joint and laughed. "Just kidding. I don't do drugs." He stood behind his desk. "How is your mother?"

"What?" Murdonna didn't know if he was being a smartass by mentioning drugs and then her mother, or if she herself was jumping to conclusions because she was still on ten from this morning. She didn't want to hear shit else about her mother, especially from someone she knew didn't really care.

"I was asking how your mother was," he repeated, oblivious to her irritation. "I know she was dealing with some things last year, and I was wondering how things were going."

Though he sounded sincere, Murdonna knew it was bullshit. She knew this was another one of his "I don't know when to shut the fuck up" moments.

"Mr. Hendricks, if I'm not asking you about your wife,"—Murdonna pretended she was drinking a bottle of booze—"then please don't ask me about my mother."

"Ohhhh." Several kids in the class made the childish noise just to perpetuate the drama.

"Have a seat, Ms. Carter!" Mr. Hendricks adjusted the blue tie on his neck before taking his own advice. Murdonna took a seat next to the window just like she always did. She loved being able to look out on the vacant lot behind the school and let her mind drift away. She was a good student by nature, schoolwork came easy, but lately, it had been hard to concentrate on anything with everything going on at home.

Even though her mother had just recently come up missing, for the last few years, her addiction had been getting the best of her. Murdonna knew it was only a matter of time before everything exploded. She just wished that nothing blew up before she could turn 18. Then she'd be able to legally care for her siblings as well as graduate school and be able to work full-time. Though she had dreams of going to college, she wasn't holding her breath.

Six minutes later, the first bell rang, indicating that class was starting. Mr. Hendricks grabbed a piece of chalk and stood. He wrote a few words on the board, then began to lecture the class. Although Murdonna loved English, she was hardly paying attention. Outside in the distance, she noticed a black-on-black Chevy Impala sitting on twenty-four-inch rims with a crowd of boys gathered around it. Payro emerged from the passenger seat wearing a fresh new outfit to go with the Mauri gators he was wearing this morning. The outfit was different from the one he was wearing earlier. Murdonna knew he changed clothes because P-dot's blood was on his first outfit.

While peering through the window trying to see what the men were doing, her stomach began to ache a very familiar ache that showed up like clockwork every month. Suddenly a wave of cramps hit her stomach full blast. "Fuck!" she whispered, knowing exactly what was about to happen. It was her goddamned period. It always attacked like a thief in the night without warning. One minute she was fine, and the next minute her stomach was hurting like a muthafucka and she was flowing like crazy. "Damn."

"Is everything okay back there, Murdonna?" Mr. Hendricks asked, noticing her distress.

"Can I go to the bathroom?" She knew if she didn't get up now, this day would go from bad to worse. Within the hour, her pants would be saturated with menstrual blood, and she would never be able to live down that shame.

"No, Ms. Carter, you may not," Mr. Hendricks dismissed her and kept on talking about the lesson. While Murdonna tried to squeeze tight and sit there for a few more minutes, she once again glanced out the window.

By now, Sysco had gotten out of the car from the driver's seat and was conversing with the younger men. He was a tall, muscular brown-skinned man with deep dimples and curly black hair. His eyelashes and eyebrows were thick but sexy. There was also a keloid running from his right ear to the middle of his chin.

Murdonna watched closely as he reached into the window and retrieved a Jordan shoebox from the back seat. From the box, he retrieved a few small banded bundles of money and distributed them to the crowd. Murdonna knew he was paying his dealers for selling dope to the high school kids.

Instantly she was fascinated by what she'd seen, and she knew she needed to find a way to get that money. It didn't matter that what they were pushing was what had her mother fucked up in the head. What mattered was that her family could eat tonight if she could somehow get her hands on some dough. Without hesitation, Murdonna decided that she needed to talk to Sysco now! This was probably her only opportunity to catch him. Waiting any longer was not an option. Standing, Murdonna collected her things.

"Where are you going?" Mr. Hendricks asked.

"I'm going to the bathroom."

"If you leave my class right now, don't bother coming back until tomorrow."

"If that's what it is, then I guess I'll see you tomorrow." She shrugged her shoulders, completely unbothered.

"Murdonna, if this is any indication of how the remainder of the year will be, then I don't think you'll be walking across that stage." Mr. Hendricks shook his head in disgust. Murdonna was by far one of his brightest students, but she didn't apply herself. She always seemed to be preoccupied with something. Mr. Hendricks didn't exactly know all of what she was dealing with on the home front. However, that didn't stop him from making the assumption that she would be just another wasted mind of today's generation.

"Mr. Hendricks, let's remember that you get paid to teach, not think, so keep your thoughts to yourself, please!" Murdonna was tired of his bullshit.

"Before you leave, just answer my question." Mr. Hendricks pointed to the board. The sentence he'd wrote said, "What will become of you after graduation?" Coincidentally, it was almost the same thing she'd asked her brother this morning. "Ms. Carter, whatever you decide you want to be in life is determined by whether you walk out that door. So tell us, what will become of you after graduation?"

Murdonna looked out the window, then back at the blackboard, before carefully choosing her response. She was tired of being poor. She was tired of living in the projects. She was tired of going to bed hungry and having to fight the rats and roaches for leftover crumbs. Murdonna was sick and tired of being sick and tired.

Mr. Hendricks sighed, tired of waiting for an answer. "What are your ambitions?"

"I want to be the biggest goddamn drug dealer in Detroit!" Murdonna didn't so much as bat an eyelash.

The look on Mr. Hendricks' beet-red face was priceless. For once in his life, he didn't have any comeback line for her response. A few people in the classroom chuckled. One boy even ran up to slap five with Murdonna. He thought she was ballsy to make such a statement to a teacher.

"That was a good one," someone hollered.

"Y'all be easy. I'll see you when I see you." With those words, Murdonna Carter chucked up the deuces, leaving Mr. Hendricks and the students in the senior AP English class with their mouths open wide.

Mr. Hendricks knew she was serious. Therefore, he didn't chase after her. Instead, he could only shake his head in disbelief at the wasted potential and return to teaching his lesson for the morning.

Murdonna didn't care one bit about what she'd done as she walked out of the classroom with her head held high. She knew she was making the right decision for herself and for her family. Instinctively she knew Sheila wasn't coming back. Therefore, she had to be the glue to hold her family down, even if it meant jeopardizing her own life and freedom to do so. It was what it was. She knew that pressure could burst pipes, and going another day without food in her stomach was surely going to break her.

She never wanted to be a criminal. In fact, she used to judge some of the boys in her neighborhood growing up. Whenever she saw them slinging dime bags on the corner, she would roll her eyes. However, she realized now that many of them were just like her: trying to survive and make it another day.

Chapter Five

After leaving Mr. Hendricks' class, Murdonna stopped in the bathroom. Just as she suspected, blood had already ruined her panties and gotten on her jeans a little. To prevent her jeans from becoming more saturated, she stuffed her underwear with wads of tissue. It was sad—she didn't even have a quarter to grab a pad or tampon from the dispenser.

Once Murdonna was loaded down with tissue, she approached the sink to wash her hands. There she paused to stare at herself, something she hadn't really done in a while. The person staring back at her was unfamiliar. This girl looked unhappy and tired with reddish-yellow eyes and bags. This girl felt helpless with no one to turn to for help and stressed about what would happen once she was all out of moves. Though she always wore a brave face, deep down, she was scared to death of what life would be like when she didn't have any more fight left in her.

Several times in the last week, she contemplated buying some sleeping pills and taking the whole bottle. She was ready to go from this place, but she knew Donzell and Mya needed her. Besides, she didn't have any money to buy the pills anyway. "Just hold on, girl. Things are about to change." Placing her palm on the glass, she continued with the pep talk. "You got this! Hold your head high. This storm is almost over."

With those motivational words in her head, Murdonna crept through the school, carefully avoiding teachers and security guards until she finally approached the back door. There she stopped and thought about the choice she was about to make. On the one hand, if she left school today, she knew there was no turning back. However, if she stayed, then she knew it would be only a matter of time before someone reported her family to Child Protective Services. After three seconds of deep thought, Murdonna tossed her school supplies into the trash. Her mind was made up. She was ready to jump off the porch and run with the big dogs.

Exhaling a sigh of relief, Murdonna smiled when she saw who she was looking for across the street. Thankfully, Sysco and Payro were still chopping it up. The other boys were gone. This gave Murdonna the opportunity she needed to approach them without a crowd.

"Man, this motherfucker got to go, P!" Sysco barked with his raspy voice while pacing back and forth beside his car. "He tried to come for me at the goddamn grocery store! He damn near shot the old lady parked next to me. This nigga is out of pocket, P!" Sysco was so mad that Murdonna could practically see smoke coming from his head.

"That shit ain't cool. Chains is a bitch for that for real!" Payro spat.

"Hell yeah, he a bitch," Sysco agreed, completely oblivious to the young woman crossing the street and heading their way. "I need his neck for that shit, but can't nobody find his marked ass."

"I'll find the nigga, fam. Don't even trip." Payro dapped his cousin up. Though he wasn't really excited to pull the trigger, he did want to prove to Sysco that he was ready for a higher role within the organization.

As the little cousin, Payro kind of got put on by default. Most of the crew didn't respect him, but they tolerated him because he was the boss's family. Payro knew the crew felt like he hadn't earned his position. Therefore, he had to put in some work and change the way people saw him.

"Nah, don't worry about that. I already put the goons on his trail." Sysco knew what his cousin was, and a killer wasn't it.

"Man, fuck that. Chains came at you, which is like coming at me. I'm taking that shit personal." Payro elevated his voice to sound serious.

"Yeah, all right. Whatever then. Do you." Sysco playfully slapped his cousin's shoulder. "I'm gon' tell you like I told the goons. Whoever finds Chains and brings him to me first will get twenty stacks for him dead and thirty for him alive, just so I can kill his ass my damn self." Sysco hawked up a wad of mucus and spit it on the grass.

Murdonna's stomach twisted as she approached the men. The closer she got, her heart probably skipped three beats, and the lump in her throat made it hard to speak, but she did. "Excuse me."

"Yo, we ain't serving nobody right now. Come back later." Sysco dismissed the girl with a wave of his hand. After tucking his hands into his heavily starched 501 jeans, he continued conversing with his cousin.

"I ain't no fucking junkie." Murdonna smacked her lips. She knew she was looking a little rough these days, but never had she been mistaken for a fiend.

"Who the fuck is you then?" Sysco was growing irritated with this bum bitch. Given the situation with Chains, it didn't take much for him to lash out.

"Sys, this is the girl I was—" Payro started the introduction but was cut off by Murdonna, who cut right to the chase.

"I'm the bitch who knows where Chains is. You say you got twenty grand if I do him, right?" Murdonna was originally going to approach Sysco about selling some work and then asking about her mother, but when she overheard the conversation about Chains, a local jack boy with a bad temper, the plans changed. She'd never killed anybody before, but $20,000 sounded like $20 million right then. She was down for anything, including murder.

"Who the fuck is you?" Quickly Sysco reached beneath his shirt and grabbed a 9 mm handgun. Without blinking once, he pointed it straight at Murdonna's dome. He didn't care that he was outside and could've been seen.

"What the fuck are you doing?" Payro jumped in front of his cousin's gun but faced Murdonna. "You must have a death wish or something."

"You know her?" Sysco was ready to do her right then and there.

"Yeah, she cool, man. Don't shoot." P turned to face his cousin.

"Who the fuck is she?" Sysco lowered the gun but didn't put it away until his question was answered.

"She ain't nobody. Just some junkie's daughter, that's all." Payro didn't mean to say it like that, but it slipped out. Quickly he fixed it, though. "This is the girl who I told you split P-dot shit at the bus stop this morning. Sheila is her mother. Have you seen her?"

"Word, this is the girl out here putting the mash down on my soldiers?" Sysco paused with a smirk. He was impressed.

"Have you seen my mother?"

"Nah, I ain't seen Sheila in a minute." Sysco stared down at the girl who desperately needed a comb and a brush. Although he thought she was a pretty girl, with slanted eyes, a button nose, and full lips, the girl looked dingy. He wanted to run her ass through the car wash or something. "If I hear something, I'll shoot word back to you through Ro, though," Sysco finished with the girl, then tucked the gun back into his jeans and started talking to his cousin.

"I wasn't done talking," Murdonna spoke up.

"I was!" One thing Sysco hated was a female who didn't know how to stay in her place.

"You want Chains, right?" Murdonna completely ignored that he was trying to blow her off.

"You know where he at?" Sysco turned to face her.

"For the right price, I do." Murdonna exuded nothing but confidence as she casually talked about murder for hire.

"Look, this ain't what you want, shorty." Payro tried to send Murdonna away, but she wasn't having it. She had come too far to back down.

"You know what? I'll make it easy on you, little lady. I'll give you ten stacks just for telling me the location." Sysco rubbed his goatee. He doubted the girl was capable of murder. However, he could tell that she needed some money, and he needed Chains, so he made an offer he knew she couldn't refuse.

"Nah, I want twenty stacks for the body!" Murdonna's mind was made up, and the scary part was that she wasn't even afraid of committing murder. In the hood, niggas died every day. In her book, Chains would be just another face on a T-shirt.

"You ever killed a nigga before?" both Payro and Sysco asked at the same time.

"That doesn't matter," Murdonna replied with a straight face.

"I should kill you right here just for wasting my time." Sysco was dead serious. He didn't like people playing with him.

"Go 'head! You'd be doing me a favor anyway." Murdonna chuckled lightly. "I lie down every night praying I don't wake up anyway, so do it, nigga. Make my day."

"You better get lost," Sysco warned.

"He ain't joking," Payro added. "I suggest you leave." Even though he didn't know Murdonna personally, he didn't want to see her die today.

"Do you want Chains or not?" Murdonna really needed that money. She wasn't trying to leave without an arrangement. She was not going to fall back until she got what she wanted.

"You better get the fuck out of my face!" Sysco barked. Yet and still, Murdonna didn't move.

It wasn't until a loud screeeech could be heard coming down the block that everyone broke their gazes, looking up to see a squad car. Without another word, Sysco jumped into his Impala and sped off like a bat out of hell. Payro ran for the back door of the school, and Murdonna ran down the street away from the school. She didn't know what else to do. There was no way she could return to school now, so she kept running.

Quite naturally, the police car pulled up alongside her. "Hey!" the officer hollered after rolling down the window. "What's your name?"

"Murdonna Carter," she replied while slowing her pace.

"Why are you running away from school? Shouldn't you be in there?" said the lady officer on the passenger side.

Murdonna stopped and looked at the officer. Though she was afraid, she didn't have anything to hide. It wasn't like she had drugs on her or anything. "I came on my period. I need to go home and change my pants," Murdonna replied half truthfully. The female cop looked skeptical until Murdonna opened her legs and revealed the small trail of blood beginning to spill down the seam of her denim jeans due to all that running.

"Damn. Okay, I guess I'll let you slide this time." The female cop rolled the window up, and the squad car pulled off.

Murdonna exhaled a sigh of relief, then continued toward the bus stop. Even without receiving a verbal agreement from Sysco, she still headed straight to Chains' neighborhood like she hadn't a care in the world. She needed that money and would die trying to get it before she left it on the table for someone else to collect.

Chapter Six

During the forty-minute bus ride, Murdonna contemplated exactly what she was about to do. Every time she tried to talk herself out of it, she remembered there was no food in the refrigerator. She wished there was an alternative method to come upon some quick cash. However, she knew selling pussy wasn't an option. Murdonna wished she had a relative or someone to turn to in her time of need, but her mother's family wasn't shit, and the only thing she knew about her father was his name, Murdock Carter. Mya's and Donzell's fathers were long gone, too. All the siblings had were each other, yet they depended on her! That thought alone was what willed Murdonna to reach up and pull the stop cord above the bus window as the bus approached her destination.

Still bleeding and cramping like crazy, Murdonna made her way up the long block toward the small one-bedroom townhouse with stained glass windows and a red door. She knew this was where Chains was sure to be, because she'd made the trip over to his townhouse nearly a dozen times for Mrs. Johnson to pick up supplies for the cleaners.

Thomas Johnson, aka Chains, was the only son of Evelyn and Darryl. He was a spoiled middle-class American who wasn't satisfied with being the good little boy his mother pretended he was. Instead, he decided to create a street persona, buy three large chains—hence the nickname—grow out his hair, get a gun, and start jacking people in the hood. He would hit the urban communities at night and then escape to his hideout like nothing happened. Chains was living a lie, and Murdonna knew sooner or later, someone would pull his ho card. Even though she had a huge disdain for his mother, she never thought it would be she.

Approaching the door, Murdonna could hear a video game going. She paused before knocking just to give herself time to be sure this was what she wanted to do. Never did she think she would be capable of murder, but then again, desperate times called for desperate measures. All out of options and running low on patience with her situation, Murdonna willed herself to continue.

Boom! Boom! She knocked loudly to overpower the noise inside the house.

"Come in, Mom. It's open," Chains yelled in his proper voice instead of the hood voice he used in the streets.

Murdonna used the tail of her shirt to twist the knob, and, voilà, she was in. Cautiously she tiptoed inside and looked around. Chains was sitting on a brown leather sofa staring at the seventy-inch television with his back to her. There was some sort of helmet on his head being used to simulate the features in the game.

"Dang, you said you would be here in a few minutes. I didn't know you meant five." Chains talked freely to the person he thought was his mother. She'd just called and told him to get dressed. She wanted to take him to a job interview at a country club where her friend was the general manager. She thought it was time for his 20-year-old self to get off the couch and stop living off of her and his father. Evelyn could see the path her son was taking and decided that he was not about to become a statistic. "Let me beat this level really quick, and I'm going to get dressed, all right?"

Murdonna didn't respond. Instead, she quickly scanned the area for a weapon. Up until this point, she was so focused on the task at hand that she'd completely forgotten that she didn't have a clue what she was going to use to kill this bastard. *There it is!* In the kitchen, she spotted a knife set next to the butcher block sitting on the granite counter. Hurriedly she grabbed the fillet knife and crept up behind Chains.

"Give me five more minutes, okay?"

"Nah. Time is up!" Quickly Murdonna slid the thin blade used to gut fish across Chains' neck. Though his bones felt tough against the knife, the way his flesh split so effortlessly caused blood to spill from that nigga like a bottle of red wine. As Chains dropped the game controller to the floor, he silently stood and grabbed his neck.

Murdonna fearfully watched him frantically gasp for air. Although she couldn't see his eyes, she knew he was dying. She'd never been this close to death before. As gross as the image was, she couldn't help but watch it play out with fascination.

Within seconds he fell backward into the flat-screen television, causing it to fall from the wall mount and crash loudly on the floor. Murdonna knew then it was time to go, but her feet wouldn't move. Instantly her mind went blank, and she felt as if she were floating. The scene didn't seem real. However, as blood continued to pour from the lifeless body, before she knew it, it was as real as it could get.

Finally, she was able to gather herself and regain her composure. It was time to go, but before she left, she decided to go through his pockets and came out with $200 and a unique gold engraved lighter. Stuffing the money into her pocket, she ran for the back door, but then she remembered that she needed proof of what she'd done if she was going to get paid.

That was when she saw something lying on the black end table that caught her attention. It was his three large gold chains. One was yellow gold, the second was rose gold, and the third was white gold. All three of them had blinged-out medallions with the city skyline hanging from them. Murdonna knew Sysco would know without a shadow of a doubt that she finished the job his goons were sent to do when she presented him with the goods. With the chains, money, lighter, and the fillet knife in her possession, she slipped out the back door into the backyard and made a clean escape down the alley.

With her head down, she walked back the way she'd come. Carefully she held the knife away from her body. When she reached the end of the block, she wiped the knife off with her jeans to remove any prints as best she could. Next, she dropped it into the sewer and let the dirty water remove the rest. From there, she walked the rest of the way to the bus stop and waited like she hadn't just committed murder.

Mrs. Johnson arrived at the townhouse moments later to find her son DOA lying in a massive puddle of warm blood. While she sobbed on the phone with the 911 dispatcher, she silently wondered who in the world would've done such a thing to her precious boy. She knew he was no saint, but she definitely didn't think he deserved to be killed like this.

Minutes seemed like hours as Murdonna anxiously waited for the bus to arrive. Typically, city buses were on schedule, but right now, it was at least fifteen minutes behind. She hated being so close to the crime scene, but what could she do except wait?

As time passed, Murdonna tried to process what exactly she had become once she decided to put the knife in her hand. At that very moment, she felt powerful and fearless. At that very moment, she'd become a part of the streets, and there was no turning back. She now had blood on her hands, but her heart refused to feel bad. Doing what was necessary always came naturally to her, and this situation was no different.

"Hey, you got a light?" an older woman asked after taking a seat on the broken bench beside Murdonna.

"No, ma'am."

"Good, you shouldn't be smoking anyway." The woman chuckled to herself.

Truthfully Murdonna did have the lighter in her pocket, but she was too nervous to pull it out for fear it could be linked back to the murder.

"Baby, you've got some blood on your pants." The lady pointed.

"Yes, ma'am, I know. I started my period, and I don't have a pad." Murdonna shifted positions in her seat. Just then, a police car sped past, and then another. Shit really began to get uncomfortable when the third police car zoomed by, then a fourth and a fifth. Pretty soon, the block was swarming with homicide detectives.

"I wonder what in the world done happened down there," the lady said, though she was talking more to herself than Murdonna.

Silently Murdonna began to second-guess what she'd done. However, as soon as she saw the bus rounding the corner, the feeling passed. "Thank God!" she mumbled.

With no remorse, Murdonna stepped onto the public transportation just as cool as a block of ice. It didn't matter that she'd just taken a life. What mattered was her family would be able to eat tonight and for many nights to come once she received the $20,000 payoff from Sysco. Speaking of whom, she vowed to find his ass the minute she hit the slums of her neighborhood and collect her money. For now, though, Murdonna got comfortable in the seat on the bus and let her mind relax for the first time in a long time.

Chapter Seven

After getting off the bus, Murdonna stopped at the CVS on the corner near the bus stop to grab a few sanitary items along with tissue, paper towel, and laundry detergent. They had run out of those things a while ago and were making do with what they had. When the cashier announced that the total would be $32.76, it felt good for Murdonna to be able to hand over a crisp $100 bill, even though she knew it was blood money.

Once she collected her things, Murdonna headed down the block to Mr. Wu's, a popular Chinese spot in the hood. As usual, the place was packed, and the line was almost outside the door.

"Let me get a number seven, eight, and ten," she said through the small holes in the bulletproof-glass window when it was finally her turn.

"You show me the money first." Mr. Wu shook his head rapidly. He didn't know her name, but he knew her face all too well. Murdonna was known for placing large orders, tasting some of the food when she came to pick it up, and then complaining, which meant she either got the food for free or left it there and skipped out on the bill. One time she even went so far as to put a dead roach she'd collected from her apartment into one of the orders and then make a fuss. Mr. Wu never went after her for the money or called her out on her shit because he knew her situation due to neighborhood gossip. However, he wasn't falling for it this time.

"What's the total?" Murdonna asked politely. She didn't want to cause any problems. Besides, she knew she owed him for all of her shenanigans in the past.

"$49.19," Mr. Wu replied, knowing damn well this poor girl didn't have it.

With a smile, Murdonna slid $60 into the money slot. "Put the extra on my bill from last time." It wasn't much, but she wanted to make things right. Though she'd just killed a man, she wasn't a bad person.

"Ah, how nice of you to repay some of your debt." Mr. Wu's facial expression softened. "You will have good karma." He smiled, having no idea he was talking to a cold-blooded murderer.

As soon as the food was done, Murdonna practically ran to her block and blew through the courtyard of the projects like a breeze. The middle of her pants was now completely saturated in blood, and she needed to change clothes ASAP. However, the moment she reached the front of her building, she was stopped by Tricks, a well-known gossiper.

Even though she and Murdonna didn't usually talk, that didn't stop Tricks from wanting to be the one to tell her the news. "Hey, girl, what's up?" Tricks stood in front of Murdonna, popping some bubblegum and sporting a twenty-four-inch lace front, a face full of makeup, and a pair of pink glasses with thick lenses.

"What's up?" Murdonna nodded and tried to pass by.

"You heard what happened to Chains, didn't you?" Tricks jumped right into it.

"Who? No. What happened?" Murdonna felt sick to her stomach. How in the hell had the news of what she did on the other side of town spread to the ghetto so fucking quick? *The nigga probably isn't even cold yet.*

"Girl, somebody bodied that nigga!" Tricks leaned in like it was a secret, although she'd already told everyone who would listen for the past hour. Her girl Pumpkin was one of the EMTs dispatched to the scene. As soon as she realized who the victim was, she sent out a text blast to everyone in her phonebook. This was something she often did.

"Damn, that's fucked up." Murdonna felt faint but kept her head in the game, or so she thought. "Do they know who sliced him up yet?" Though she was fishing for information, immediately she wanted to cut her own throat when she realized the grave mistake she'd just made.

"Girl, I never said how he was murdered." Tricks raised a thick eyebrow. Her suspicions were running high. "Who told you that?"

"Huh? Oh, I overheard Monica say something about someone getting sliced when I was waiting for my food at Mr. Wu's." Murdonna raised her carryout bag to add some truth to her story. "I didn't know she was talking about Chains though until you just said something, and I put two and two together," Murdonna lied.

"That bitch gets on my fucking nerves, always trying to upstage me with information. She knows I'm the real *TMZ* of the hood. The police haven't even released that shit yet. Monica better watch out before she ends up on my hit list." Tricks smacked her lips and walked away with an attitude. Monica was another bigmouth in the hood, who lived in one of the townhouses. She and Tricks were always competing to be the first one to spread gossip. Therefore, Murdonna's cover story sounded very plausible.

With a sigh of relief, she wiped the sweat from her brow, then continued inside of the apartment building. Besides someone's toddler riding a two-wheeler up and down the hallway, the lobby was unusually quiet for this time of day. After pressing the elevator button, Murdonna leaned up against the wall and waited. Seconds seemed like an eternity before the dinted silver doors opened up.

"Hold that please," someone called out.

Murdonna looked behind her to see two white men in police uniforms approaching her in a hurry. No longer was she worried about the blood on her jeans. Instead, she prayed like hell she didn't pee on herself.

"Which floor are you going to?" the taller officer asked after taking the spot nearest to the buttons.

"Eight," Murdonna mumbled nervously.

"That's where we're headed, right, Jones?" the other officer asked his partner, who nodded.

"Hopefully this son of a bitch doesn't resist. I don't have time for that shit today," the taller officer replied.

Murdonna could feel the lump in her throat getting bigger, making it difficult to swallow as the elevator slowly ascended. Ding! They reached the eighth floor, and the doors popped open.

"After you, miss." the short officer held the door for Murdonna, who slid out of the elevator nervously.

Step by step, the officers followed her down the hall. She contemplated running down the stairs but decided against it. She realized if they were there to arrest her, she would've been in cuffs already.

"Here is 809," one of the officers said before stopping and knocking on the door. "Weren't we here last week for a domestic?"

"I don't fucking know," the officer's partner replied. "We're down in this shithole so much that I started losing track years ago." He laughed.

809 was the residence of Sherry and Robert Hampton, an African couple who always got physical with one another when one or both of them had too much to drink. The police came out to their apartment at least once or twice a month after one of the other tenants on the floor got tired of hearing them fight. However, no black eyes nor busted lips could keep the Hamptons from each other.

Murdonna exhaled, finally able to breathe again after realizing the police had not come for her. However, as soon as she approached her door, the tightness in her chest returned. Just as she'd suspected, there was a big pink eviction notice taped over the peephole for the world to see. The notice basically said that she and her siblings had ten days to get the fuck out, or they would be put the fuck out. Murdonna snatched the paper down then slid her key in the hole. She made a mental note to call the rental office and pay their past-due amount tomorrow with the money she'd be getting from Sysco. For now, all she wanted was a hot shower. Hopefully the water was working.

As she entered the apartment, Tee Grizzley's music could be heard coming from the bedroom. After setting the bag of food down on the table, Murdonna slipped off her shoes, unzipped her pants, and headed to the back of the apartment to go clean herself up. She still had an hour before it was time to pick Donzell up from school. Sniffing the air, Murdonna knew something wasn't right. The smell of weed coming from her mother's bedroom had gotten her full attention. With a frown, she flew down the hall and opened the door with such force that it hit the wall and left a small hole.

"Murdonna!" Mya damn near choked on the blunt she was smoking with some random nigga who was lying on the bed dressed only in his boxers and mismatched socks.

"What the fuck is going on?" Murdonna hollered, completely irate. Never had she expected Mya to do some shit like this.

"This is Gordon. You know, Mr. Landing's grandson," Mya tried to explain while covering her exposed B-cup titties.

"Little nigga, you got three seconds to start moving be-fore we both end up on the six o'clock news!" Murdonna hollered while watching the boy scramble to his feet and run from the room like it was catching fire. "Mya, I let you skip school, and this is what you do?" Murdonna smacked her lips. "I thought you were supposed to be going to get some clothes from Mrs. Johnson, but instead, you're in here fucking?"

"In my defense, I called up to the cleaners, but they were closed. The voicemail said there was an emergency," Mya explained while putting the blunt out in the ashtray resting at her mother's bedside.

Murdonna knew she was telling the truth about that part, but still, she didn't let up. "Okay, that explains why you're not there, but explain to me how this random-ass little boy ends up in here with you?"

"Please don't be mad." Mya stood from the bed.

"I'm not mad. I'm pissed the fuck off!" Murdonna barked. "I can't believe you were up in here fucking! You're only fifteen!" she screamed while undressing and heading into the bathroom. She wanted to whip her sister's ass, but the blood oozing from between her legs took priority. "You are too young for that shit, Mya."

"I know it was wrong, but I thought I could get some money from him. Please don't be mad." Mya followed her sister into the bathroom, which proved to be the wrong move.

Whap! Whap! Murdonna hit her sister with a two-piece combo that sent her flying backward into the wall.

"So you're a ho now? Is that what you're telling me?" Murdonna snapped with her hand raised for another hit.

"No!" Mya cried with her hands held in the air. She was trying to block the attack.

"Well, fucking for money makes you a ho!" Murdonna shouted. "Do you wanna be like Sheila? Do you want to be out here sucking dick for dollars?"

"No." Mya cried like a baby. She was so embarrassed. In her mind, she was taking one for the team and doing something to ease the burden off her sister, but now she felt stupid and nasty.

"Don't ever do no shit like that again!" Murdonna was so mad that she was shaking. She couldn't believe that her baby sister would stoop so low.

"Donna, I know you haven't been eating. I just wanted to get a few dollars for dinner, that's all. I'm sorry."

Mya cried harder, causing Murdonna to also break down into tears. She knew her sister was merely trying to survive the best way she knew how. After the low Murdonna had stooped to today, she of all people understood what a person would do when their back was against the wall.

Although Mya was naked, Murdonna pulled her sister up from the floor and hugged her tight like a big sister should. "Listen, as long as I'm around, you don't ever have to worry about that. I got you." Murdonna sniffed. "I got us always, believe that."

"I know you do, Donna." Mya hugged her sister back. "I just wanted to show you that I got you too."

"You are a beautiful girl whose value extends way beyond what's between your legs. If you start fucking for dollars now, all you're doing is telling the world that your shit ain't priceless! Know your worth, Mya." Murdonna released her sister. "Wipe your eyes, put some clothes on, and go eat. There is food on the table."

After Mya walked away, Murdonna stepped into the bathroom and ran some hot water. As she waited, she took a seat on the toilet and shed a few more silent tears. For the first time in forty-two days, she cried. She cried for her mother, she cried for her siblings, and she cried for herself. For she knew the path she had to take in order to keep her family afloat. Hearing Mya say she was fucking out here for food made the thought of slicing Chains' throat even easier. For the love of family, Murdonna would cross over to the dark side without a second thought. She knew now there was no turning back. It was game on!

Chapter Eight

Feeling refreshed from the bath, Murdonna slipped on a pair of black jeans, one of her mother's T-shirts, and her old, faithful Reeboks. After noticing a drop of blood on one of the shoes, she cleaned it with some peroxide. Next, she grabbed a trash bag and bagged up her bloody clothes. She knew she had to get rid of the outfit because it had her victim's DNA on it.

After taking one last look at the chains she'd stolen from him, she tucked them under her mother's mattress and joined her sister in the living room. "Put your shoes on and walk with me to get Donzell."

"I can go get him for you if you want." Mya looked up from the notebook she was writing in.

"Let's go together. I bet he would like that." Murdonna really wanted Mya to go with her because she had a hidden agenda.

Within minutes, Mya had on her shoes, and they headed out. As they walked to the school, Mya apologized again for what she'd been caught doing. She didn't want her sister to think badly of her. Murdonna told her that all was forgiven as long as she promised never to do that again, and Mya agreed.

When they reached the school, Donzell was just coming outside with a group of boys. At first glance, it looked as if they were engaging in horseplay, but then Murdonna noticed that Donzell and three of the boys were fighting. In fact, Donzell was being jumped.

Before she could do or say anything, Mya went into attack mode. She took the biggest boy, pulled him off her brother, and commenced punching him in the face repeatedly. Her removing the biggest boy allowed Donzell the opportunity to regain his composure and give the other two a run for their money.

Once Mya was done with her victim, she joined Donzell, and together she and Donzell whipped ass on the other two until they got tired. Murdonna didn't bother jumping in because she knew Mya had it covered. Besides, she was way too old to be fighting some kids.

As the fight was nearing an end, an older male teacher came outside and intervened. "What happened?" he addressed the group, but no one said a word. "Okay, cool, I see no one wants to talk. I guess we need to go in the office and call your parents, Le'Chez, Donzell, Marshawn, Henry, and . . ." He squinted to get a better look at Mya, whom he didn't recognize. "Do you attend this school?"

Unsure of what the outcome was going to be regarding this altercation, Murdonna decided to walk over. "No need to call home. These two are with me."

The minute the teacher looked up to address Murdonna and took his gaze off the group of fighters, Le'Chez, Marshawn, and Henry took off running down the street. For a second, he contemplated running behind them before remembering that playing the role of security added nothing to his paycheck. Besides, since the fight occurred after school, it wasn't that big of a deal. Therefore, he chose to send the remaining fighters on their way with a warning.

"Are you good, D?" Murdonna smiled with pride as she and her siblings walked away from the school. She knew Donzell was a timid child, and she often wondered about him being able to protect himself. However, after seeing him hold his own today, she knew he'd be all right.

"Yeah, I'm cool. I skinned my elbow, that's all." He flexed his bloody arm for his sisters to see. "Thanks for having my back, Mya."

"You know I always got you. What was that shit about anyway?" Mya licked the blood off the back of her knuckles.

"That nigga was talking shit about my clothes." Donzell didn't usually curse, but today he was in rare form. The fight probably had him turned up. "He and his boys have been calling me a slave boy all day, so I told them I'd beat their asses like a slave as soon as school got out."

"Well, beat that ass you did!" Murdonna geeked him up. She was so proud to see him handle his business.

"Where are we going?" It took Donzell five minutes to realize they weren't walking in the direction of home.

"I ran into something good today, and I want to share my blessings with y'all." Murdonna was so excited. It wasn't very often that she was able to do unexpected things for her family, but she loved putting smiles on their faces.

"What happened? Is that why you came home early?" Mya asked. She needed all the details.

"Well, I decided today that I'm officially done with school for now." Murdonna knew there was no point in lying. Tomorrow when she didn't get on the bus with Mya, the cat would've been out of the bag anyway. "I left school and went and got a job that pays decently."

"You dropped out of school?" Donzell was appalled. His sister was always the one preaching about getting an education, yet she was dropping out.

"For the time being, yes, but I'll get my GED one day and probably go to community college. For now, though, I got to do what I got to do."

Mya tried to shoot her shot. "Can I drop out too? That way, I can go to work with you."

"Girl, bye!"

"For real, Donna, what's good for the goose should be good for the gander." Mya shrugged.

Donzell added his two cents. "I don't take her side often, but she does have a point."

"Listen, I am the oldest. That means I'll make all the sacrifices in the world if it means that you two will succeed. I need y'all to go to school, get good grades, go to college, and make something of yourselves. That's the only way my sacrifices will make sense. We will be the last of our bloodline to live in poverty, believe that! Now enough about school."

Murdonna stopped in front of Kara's Candyland, a small mom-and-pop market that sold quarter candy. It was their favorite store in the neighborhood. All summer, they'd talked about what snacks they would buy from the market if they had the chance to go. "I got a small advance from my new employer. It ain't much at all, but I figured we all deserve a treat." Handing Mya $10 and Donzell the same, Murdonna watched with joy as her siblings went into the store and shopped for candy like they were spending a million dollars.

She wasn't much of a candy eater, but she'd been craving a grape Faygo pop and some Better Made potato chips. As she grabbed her things, she couldn't help but smile, seeing the happiness in her siblings' eyes as they shopped. Life wasn't about money. It was about moments. Though she hated what she had to do to create this moment for her siblings, she'd do it again without hesitation.

Later that evening, after they returned home, Murdonna, Mya, and Donzell sat down at the dining room table and ate until they couldn't eat anymore. Once again, the apartment was filled with life and laughter. It was almost as if someone had turned the lights on in the dark situation. After dinner, they played a few hands of Uno, where the wager was candy. Donzell ran the table and took all of Mya's Mike and Ike's. Murdonna didn't have any candy to lose, but she did have to forfeit a few pops.

Hours later, once everyone was asleep, Murdonna went to the back of the apartment and lifted the mattress. She slipped Chains' jewelry into her pocket and prepared to head out. She didn't know where to find Sysco, and for that reason, she hoped to run into Payro. He was always hanging around the projects, so it shouldn't have been hard.

"Donna, where are you going?" Donzell looked up from his pallet on the living room floor. He was supposed to be asleep an hour ago. That sugar probably had him wired.

"I'll be right back in thirty minutes. Go to bed so you won't be tired for school tomorrow," Murdonna whispered before opening the front door and stepping out. Nervously she locked the door behind her and headed down the hallway. Silently she surveyed the area and noticed how dingy it was. The walls were painted a stale yellow, which reminded her of puke. The carpet appeared to be a combination of green, gray, and brown. Murdonna couldn't tell if that was intentional or if it was caked-on dirt. She'd never really given the appearance of her hallway much thought, but the idea of coming into some money and having better living options made her notice everything, including the blinking light over the elevator. "One day we're going to blow this Popsicle stand," she said to no one as she pushed the button.

As she waited, she pondered what to say when she ran across Sysco, but she quickly decided that it didn't matter. Once he saw the jewelry, he had to pay up. At least that was what Murdonna hoped as she anxiously pressed the button again and again. For nearly ten minutes, she paced back and forth, hoping the elevator was working and would arrive soon because she really didn't want to walk down the stairwell alone at night. Just as she was about to hit the stairwell, she heard the sound she'd been waiting for. Ding! The elevator had arrived. Quickly she turned back around and tried to catch it.

"Ay, shorty, I was just coming to see you." Payro stepped off the elevator, looking happily surprised to see Murdonna. He didn't know which apartment was hers but was prepared to knock on doors until he found out.

"What are you doing here?" Murdonna was glad to see him too, but she wondered why in the hell he would be looking for her, especially at this time of night. As she asked the question, the elevator closed, leaving them to once again play the waiting game.

"Shit got a little crazy earlier. I just wanted to make sure you were good." He licked his lips and looked her up and down. "I didn't see you in school for the rest of the day."

"I'm good. Thanks for checking." Murdonna looked down at the ground. For some reason, he was making her nervous.

"That's no problem." Payro nodded. "Where are you headed this time of night?"

"I was actually about to go looking for Sysco. Do you know where I can find him?" She pressed the button rapidly.

"Girl, you just don't quit, do you?" Payro shook his head. "You better quit barking up that nigga's tree before you fuck around and catch some hot shit. You lucky he didn't do you right there behind the school."

"I told you earlier I'm not afraid to die." Murdonna was as serious as a heart attack.

"Be that as it may, I still don't want to see you dead for wasting that nigga's time."

"Once he finds out what I got, then he'll know I'm for real." Murdonna was becoming annoyed that no one was taking her seriously. She was willing to bet that if she were a man, there wouldn't be all this conversation.

"Tell me, what you got, my baby?" Payro asked while leaning up against the wall.

Without saying a word, Murdonna pulled the stolen jewelry from her pocket just enough to be recognized, and then she put it back quickly. "This is what the fuck I got!"

Payro's eyes damn near fell from their sockets. "What the fuck is that?" He stood straight up.

"Now you're the one playing games. Come on, you know what it is." Murdonna smirked, knowing that everyone knew what Chains' jewelry looked like. "Now the question is, are you taking me to Sysco?"

"Fuck, girl!" Payro laughed hard and loud, utterly intrigued. "You're cute, and you a savage. You're my type of bitch."

"Who are you calling a bitch?" Murdonna bucked up playfully.

"Don't hurt me please," Payro played along, then rubbed a hand across his face. "Nah, for real though, that shit right there is gangster as fuck. I never pegged you to be that type of chick, though." Payro was thoroughly impressed.

"What can I say? Pressure bursts pipes! When your back is against the wall, you're capable of anything," Murdonna replied. "In case you haven't noticed, I really need that damn money," she said, stating the obvious.

"You deserve that shit. Let's go get you paid." Payro pressed the button on the elevator twice, and they waited in silence until it came. He'd underestimated Murdonna but saw now that she was not to be fucked with. She could prove to be valuable to him. He wasn't sure where he could use her, but he decided to keep her close just in case.

Once they were outside, Murdonna followed Payro through the corridors to a vacant townhouse located at the back of her project building. The place looked to have been in a fire previously. The windows were boarded up, and black soot covered the red brick. Payro hit the back door three times before it opened. Some big black man stood there with his arms folded.

"What up, Wiz. Is my cousin here?" Payro dapped the man up then proceeded inside.

"Yeah. You already know he's in the back," Wiz replied.

"Bet." Payro nodded for Murdonna to come with him.

"Hello." Naively she waved at Wiz, then bypassed the large man who stared her down. Nervously she grabbed Payro's hand. He looked down at their joined body parts and smirked but didn't say a word. Later he would tease her about being a killer who still needed her hand held, but for now, he liked it, so he let it ride.

Loud music could be heard coming from the living room where Sysco was laid back on a red sofa, throwing dollars at a buck-naked female. She was dancing to one of Trey Songz's joints in slow motion. Though her eyes were closed, she looked as if she was high or drunk off something. Sweat dripped down her face, and her body seemed to drag. When Sysco looked up to see his cousin with the girl from earlier at the school, he grimaced before grabbing the remote and muting the wireless sound system.

"Ro, please tell me you didn't bring her here." Sysco sat up on the couch, fully prepared to go the fuck off. Even though he was only four years older than his cousin, he always scolded him like he was a child.

"I did, but it's only because she got something for you," Payro replied nervously. He knew Sysco was a hothead. Therefore, he wasn't sure how this was about to go.

"This little girl couldn't possibly have shit for me." Sysco shook his head vigorously. The curly hair on his head moved wildly as he continued tossing dollars into the air.

"It's about that thing we discussed earlier," Murdonna said, stepping up. Payro may have tiptoed around Sysco, but she wasn't about to follow suit. After all she'd been through in life, Sysco was hardly scary.

"In case you haven't heard, baby girl, the shit's already been handled." Sysco was trying to remain calm. However, it was taking all he had to remain seated instead of going upside both the bitch's and his cousin's heads for interrupting his relaxation time.

"I know, nigga. That's because I handled it," Murdonna admitted boldly and then relaxed her shoulders. "Now, I need for you to excuse your goddamn company so we can sit down and talk about this business." She watched Sysco's eyes shift from hers to Payro's, who nodded his agreement with what she was saying.

"Take five, Bambi!" Sysco yelled at his personal dancer, who stopped mid-twerk, grabbed her money off the floor, and then strutted past them, still looking as high as a kite. "So where is the proof?" Sysco finally asked once they were alone.

"First things first. Where is the money?" Murdonna wasn't a fool. She knew how the hood operated. Everybody was scheming, and she wasn't about to get played.

"Ro, go get the bag from under the bathroom sink," Sysco instructed without removing his eyes from Murdonna.

On cue, Payro hurried off obediently. He loved and admired his older cousin to death. Secretly, he wanted to be him, but he knew he had to wait his turn for the throne. Sysco was the man in Detroit, and everybody knew it. Payro wanted Sysco's clout and respect, but for now, the 18-year-old was cool just being the apprentice.

"Here it is." Payro returned from the bathroom and set the bag down on the coffee table. He unzipped it for Murdonna to inspect. Her eyes widened with anticipation. She had only seen that amount of money on television.

"Go ahead and count it. I got all night." Sysco smiled, knowing this little bit of chump change probably meant the world to shorty.

"I'm sure it's good." In all honesty, it didn't matter how much money the bag contained because anything in it was a step up from where she'd started this morning. Immediately she began to daydream about how she was going to spend the first few dollars.

"Now, where's my proof?" Sysco made himself more comfortable in his seat as he watched the young girl with the baby face pull three chains from her pocket. "Holy fucking shit!" He smiled like the Grinch before standing abruptly. Suddenly he was intrigued by the girl and wanted her on his team. The shit she'd managed to pull off today was nothing short of amazing. "You did this by yourself?" He was in awe.

"Yeah." Murdonna nodded.

"Did you tell anyone what you did?" Sysco held his breath while waiting for her to respond. He knew she was a rookie, and oftentimes, rookies made mistakes.

"Nah. Never that," Murdonna replied in a cool tone. However, her mind drifted back to Tricks and her fuck-up earlier.

"Are you sure? Because if you did, then we got a problem!"

"I said no, didn't I?" Murdonna sounded sure, though she knew Tricks was a loose end who had to be dealt with before it was too late.

"So tell me, what's next for you?" Sysco questioned. He wasn't ready to let her go just yet. He needed to see where her head was at and how she could be of service to him.

"Funny, I was just wondering the same thing." Murdonna looked down at the bag then back at Sysco. "How much is a brick of coke?"

"I don't think you're ready to be pushing weight, my baby." Sysco shook his head.

"Just this morning, you didn't think I was ready for murder, yet here we stand."

"Facts!" He nodded his agreement before giving her question careful consideration. "I normally don't do business with people I don't know, and when I do, I charge sixteen. But on account of what you did for me today, I'll only charge you twelve grand if you want one."

Sysco could see where this was headed, and he liked it. The only thing missing from his squad was a down-ass chick! Murdonna appeared to be the missing link to Detroit City Mafia. It was Sysco's up-and-coming drug organization. The squad was small but solid. One day Sysco planned on taking over the world, but for now, he settled for the projects and a few of its surrounding neighborhoods.

Going over to the black duffle bag, Murdonna reached in and counted out $8,000. "I'll take this, you keep the other twelve, and I'll take a brick."

"You think it's that simple, huh?" Sysco laughed lightly. "Just like that, you're going to become a drug dealer?"

"Just like that, I caught a body, didn't I?" Murdonna knew she would excel at anything she put her mind to. "In the ghetto, you either eat or starve. I've been hungry long enough! Put me on, and you'll never regret it." She sold herself to Sysco like she was on a job interview.

Truthfully, she was hungry and wanted to learn more about the dope game. Ever since this morning, when she said she wanted to be the biggest dope dealer in Detroit, she couldn't think of doing anything else. She was tired of sitting on the sidelines while everybody else made money. Besides, she knew females were the best at everything. All she needed was the opportunity to get in the game, and she would surely, quickly become the most valuable player on Sysco's team.

He rubbed his head, then looked at Payro, whom he'd been training ever since he was a little nigga. He knew if anyone was capable of showing the newbie the ropes, it was him. "All right, bet. Ro, you take her under your wing and show her the way. If there is a problem, come to me. Don't let anything happen to her. Is that understood?"

"Yeah, I got her." Payro nodded. He wasn't fully comfortable with Murdonna joining his team without a sidebar conversation with his cousin first, but he knew there was nothing he could do to veto Sysco's decision, so he went with it.

"All right then, it's settled." Sysco smirked. "Bless her with a brick, and I'll see y'all tomorrow."

Murdonna wanted to thank Sysco profusely for the opportunity, but she knew better. She didn't want them to see her as weak, which was why, after stuffing the money into her pockets, she simply turned and followed Payro. He led her into the kitchen, where two men stood guard. Opening the refrigerator, he grabbed a brick, placed it into a black shopping bag, and handed it to her.

After Payro broke her off, Murdonna headed to the door. That's when Sysco appeared in the hallway. "Hold up. Before you go, I need to know your name, shorty." Sysco leaned against the wall and stared her up and down.

Murdonna paused. She knew giving her government name wasn't even an option. Thinking fast, she turned and replied, "Just call me Murda!" Though it was just an abbreviation for her name, it was the perfect nickname for her, given the day's events.

"Murda it is then." Sysco winked and watched the newest member of his crew sashay away with more confidence than he'd noticed this morning.

Chapter Nine

Murdonna felt like a boss bitch as Payro walked her back home to her building. Not only was she a few grand richer, but she had also been inducted into the number one crew in her hood. Murda was proud of all she was able to accomplish in one day. She knew this was just the beginning and that things would only get better from here. One day she would conquer the world.

"Hey, ma, are you sure you know what you're getting into?" Payro wasn't 100 percent sure about Sysco's decision to put shorty on with the crew. They didn't know shit about her. Was the bitch a problem solver or a shit starter? Was she a rider, or would she roll on her niggas the minute shit got hot? Most of the time, you vetted a nigga before you put them into your crew, but Payro knew Sysco had a gift with regard to the game and saw things in people that they sometimes didn't see in themselves.

"Honestly, no, Payro. I don't know what I'm getting into." Murda shook her head while spitting her truth. "But I sure as hell know what I'm getting out of, and that's poverty." Having the brick in her possession as well as $8,000 in her pockets meant things would finally start looking up for the Carter household. Murda couldn't wait to take her brother and sister shopping for new clothes and groceries either. "The dope game is going to be my way out. I want you to teach me everything so I can be the best to ever do it." Murda smiled as visions of luxury cars and custom homes invaded her mind. The possibilities were endless.

"The street life ain't for everybody, Murda." Payro hated to burst her bubble. Yet and still, he continued. "The shit is cool for a minute, but when some real trouble shows up on your doorstep, you either about it or you ain't. I done seen a lot of niggas find out they ain't about that life a little too late." Payro was trying to use the walk back to the high-rise building to kick knowledge to the girl, but she didn't seem too fazed by his speech.

"Look, I hear what you're saying, but when you come from nothing like I did, you seize every financial opportunity given to you. It doesn't matter if those opportunities come with harsh consequences. A bitch like me is just glad to be on." Murda spoke with assuredness because she meant every single word she said. She was about to get her family out of the slums one goddamn crack rock at a time.

"I come from nothing, so trust me, I understand."

"Well, then you know that nothing you say is going to change my mind."

"All right, since you're for real, I want you to have this." Payro stopped midstride then passed her a black gun he'd pulled from beneath his waistband. It was midsized and kind of heavy. Murdonna wasn't too familiar with guns and had only held one once. It belonged to Donzell's father. Murdonna had found it tucked into the couch one day when she was looking for the remote. She was young and knew playing with guns was bad, so she didn't hold it for long before she tucked it back into the couch. Though she wasn't used to the gun, for some reason, it felt comfortable in her hand.

"That's a Smith & Wesson, .40-cal. It's a fifteen shooter. If you are ever in a situation and you need to let loose, be sure to count your shots so you know how many bullets you got left," Payro explained.

"Is it dirty?" Murda asked, not wanting to be in possession of a weapon that had already been used to commit a crime.

"That doesn't matter." Ro looked from side to side. "Dirty or not, I'd rather have it and not need it than need it and not have it. Just don't get caught with that shit," he warned.

Murda took the cold steel and tucked it into the small of her back.

"Look, there are three rules you must live by in these streets." Ro started walking again. "Rule number one: there ain't no friends in this game," he said while holding up his index finger. "Rule number two: don't get caught slippin'. Rule number three: get what you can out of this game, and get the fuck out! This ain't no forever type of shit."

"You've been hustling for a while. What do you want from this game?" Murdonna picked his brain.

"I want to touch at least a million dollars, and then I'll bid the dope game farewell."

"That's all?" Murda frowned. "Your goals are too small, my friend."

"I said a million, not five dollars." Ro smacked his lips.

"You do realize that one million dollars ain't shit, right? You could probably buy a nice house, two nice cars, take a few exotic vacations, and live cool for about ten years, and then what? Your ass will be back at square one."

"So, what is your end game, genius?"

"Nigga, I want my children's grandchildren to be wealthy," Murdonna scoffed. "Fuck a million. I'm trying to create generational wealth. I want to do for my family what rich white people do for theirs all the time."

Payro was about to give Ms. Know-it-all a piece of his mind for shitting on his dream, but lucky for her, one of his customers had approached them.

"Hey, Ro, do you got what I need?" The fiend was lurking in the shadows. Her hair was pulled back into two nappy braids, her lips were extra dry, and she was scratching her arm so bad it was bleeding. Murda made a face and grabbed her queasy stomach. The customer's demeanor didn't bother Murdonna, but she reminded her so much of her mother Sheila that it was sickening.

"Don't make that face, baby girl." Ro smirked. "Despite what she looks like, that's money she got in her hands." Ro pointed. "She's the reason you'll be getting out of the ghetto, remember? And having all of that generational wealth, remember?" He reached into his pocket and produced a small baggy with a rock in it. After the customer slipped the money into Ro's hand, he slipped the vial into her other one.

Once the transaction was done, he wrapped up the conversation with Murdonna. "I'll see you in the morning. Bring the brick around on Fifth, and I'll show you how to cook it up. You'll be out here serving and making money in no time." Silently he couldn't wait for baby girl to get into the thick of things. Maybe then she would realize this shit wasn't as easy as she thought it would be. Right now, though, he decided to let her live in her fairy tale.

"All right, bet. I'll see you tomorrow." Murda waved goodbye, then leaned back against the brick exterior of her building and watched Payro until he and the fiend had both disappeared down the street into the darkness. She needed to take a minute before going inside to reflect on the day's events.

Murdonna wasn't sure if she was excited or nervous, but the butterflies in her stomach were fluttering like crazy. She knew without a shadow of a doubt that there was no turning back now. Though she didn't know where this new life of crime would lead her, she was certainly up for the challenge if it meant no more days of having to go to bed hungry. From today on, she made a silent vow to herself that her new motto would be, "Get rich or die trying." Death had to better than struggling. Therefore, no matter the consequences, Murda vowed to see this thing through until she hustled her way all the way to the top.

Just as she finished clearing her mind and was about to enter her building, Tricks was exiting, dragging a bag of trash behind her. As usual, she was busy on the phone, spreading more gossip. "Hey, let me hit you back." Tricks stopped chatting and looked at Murda like she wanted to say something.

"What's up?" Murda nodded after noticing that Tricks was looking at her sideways.

"Remember when you said you talked to Monica earlier today at the restaurant?"

"Yeah." Murdonna already didn't like where this line of questioning was going. "What about it?"

"Funny thing is, Monica ain't even in the city. Word on the street is that she was locked up last night for boosting at Somerset Mall." Tricks knew Murdonna was lying. "So how did you get the information about Chains?" She needed to know who her competition for gossip was in the projects.

"Girl, why does it matter? Just leave it alone." Murdonna was irritated.

Tricks wanted to press the issue, but her phone was ringing. Knowing it was probably someone with some fresh information on whatever was going on in the hood, she decided to leave the conversation alone for now. "This won't be over until you give me your source."

"Take your call and leave me alone." Murdonna didn't have a beef with Tricks, but if she wasn't going to let the issue go, then Murdonna had to do something before things escalated.

After giving Murdonna a skeptical look, Tricks answered the phone and continued on her way through the corridor, dragging the bag of trash behind her. "That nigga Nell been fucking Curtis's bitch for at least a month now." Smacking her lips, she continued, "What do you mean, how do I know? I knew that shit when I seen him pick her up from the nail shop."

Tricks was so engrossed in her discussion that she hadn't noticed Murdonna following her behind the building where the large trash bins were. Usually, tenants in the building used the trash chute on their floor to drop garbage into the large dumpster that was positioned in the basement. However, because some asshole had set the trash chute on fire this afternoon, everyone now had to carry their bags outside. It was a major inconvenience and scary as hell with all the rats and rodents outside. The garbage spot was a feeding frenzy.

"If Curtis found that shit out, he would beat the brakes off of both they asses." Tricks leaned back, then flung the garage bag into the large pile. During the motion, she dropped her phone. "Fuck!" It was too dark to see anything, but she was not about to leave without her most prized possession.

As Tricks frantically searched the dark area, Murda stood back and watched like a lion about to jump on her prey. Knowing that Tricks was a loose end, Murdonna had made the decision to close the chapter on her the minute Ro gave her the gun. Silently she surveyed the area for something she could use to muffle the sound she knew it was going to produce. That's when she noticed an old pillow cushion resting on the ground. Nervously Murda leaned down and swooped it up.

"Who is that?" Tricks could feel someone in her presence, but her eyes were too weak to see who it was without the pink eyeglasses she'd left in her apartment on the nightstand.

Hastily Murda inched closer, pressed the gun up against the pillow, took off the safety, and then pulled the trigger. Pow! Although the sound was much quieter than it would've been without the cushion, Murda knew someone in one of the apartments could've easily heard it. Therefore, she had to move fast. Thankfully the first shot had caught Tricks in the back, which made her drop to her knees. In this position, she was more accessible, so Murdonna walked closer.

"Please don't kill me," Tricks begged for her life. "I'll do anything, please. I'm pregnant." Tricks' revelation halted Murda, but only for a second. She wanted to turn around and run. Nevertheless, she knew at this point the job had to be finished. Quickly she sent two more shots into Tricks' body. The second one hit her shoulder, and the third one hit her in the neck, causing her to die almost instantly. Although Murdonna didn't actually lean down and check her pulse, she knew Tricks was dead the moment she stopped gasping for air.

Without a word, Murda took a few deep breaths, trying hard to keep her heart from leaping through her chest. Her adrenaline was on twenty.

"Hello."

The voice coming from a distance shook Murda to her core. The fear of being caught made her feet move deeper into the darkness behind the large trash bin. Though Murdonna was grossed out by the sounds she could hear the mice making in the bin, she remained silent.

"What the hell is going on?" the voice said.

Gripping the gun tight, Murda vowed she'd kill herself and the witness too before she ever went to jail for life. It was what it was. She had no fucks to give. It wasn't until the voice spoke again that Murda realized it was the person on the other end of Tricks' lost phone and not someone who'd seen what she'd just done.

Quickly she regained her cool, tucked the gun into the small of her back, then headed back around to the front of the building like nothing happened. Thankfully no one was outside. The streets were clear, and all was quiet.

Chapter Ten

Sleep hadn't come easy to Murda last night. Like clockwork, every fifteen to twenty minutes, visions of Chains and Tricks haunted her to the point where she was hesitant to close her eyes. Every time she tried, all she could see were their final images, which were full of blood and gore. Instead of dwelling on what she'd done to them, Murdonna had to constantly remind herself that it had to be done.

Hours passed in slow motion as she sat up in the middle of her mother's bed, staring at the wall until daylight. Though the images had her shaken, she still had no remorse for her actions. "How did I become a ruthless killer?" As she pondered the question, her stomach replied with a loud growl, reminding her of the answer. She hadn't eaten a decent meal in almost three months. Although she'd purchased the Chinese food yesterday, it didn't do shit to cure the hunger pains she'd been suppressing.

"Donna, are you ready to walk me to school?" Donzell asked after entering his mother's bedroom. Unlike yesterday, he was excited about school. Murdonna didn't even need to remind him about deodorant or brushing his teeth. She could smell the mouthwash from the door.

"No, little homie. Mya is going to walk you today." Murda slid to the side of the bed and pulled open the nightstand drawer. After reaching inside, she pulled out a $20 bill, then closed it again. "You take this to Mya, and tell her to get you both some McDonald's, all right? Tell her to give you the change in case you want to buy something from the snack line at school."

"You're giving us the whole twenty?" Donzell's eyes bucked. He hadn't seen that much money in forever.

"Yes, the whole twenty." Murda smiled as she watched her brother fly into the living room. No doubt he was telling Mya about the money, because seconds later she came busting in the room like a one-man SWAT team.

"Donna, where did you get that money from?" Mya asked with a hand on her hip. In her mind, she was the boss among the siblings.

"A friend." Murda stood, stretched, and began to make the bed.

"What friend? You ain't got no friends." Mya looked at her sister sideways. She knew better.

"Chill with the questions. Do you want the twenty or not?" After such a long night, Murdonna was not in the mood to be interrogated.

"Can you at least ask your 'friend' to buy us some school clothes, too?" Mya made air quotes when she said the word "friend."

"I'm going shopping today. I'll have some stuff for y'all this evening." Murda fluffed the flat pillows on the bed and made a mental note to buy some new ones, as well as a few other things for the apartment.

"Say you swear," Donzell demanded while jumping up and down. In his mind, Christmas had just come early.

"I swear." Murda raised her right hand to the sky. "When y'all come home, I'll have your shit waiting for you, I promise."

"See? I told you Donna would figure this out. You were worried for nothing," Donzell gloated. He knew his sister was going to come through for them just as she always did.

"Has anyone ever told you that you were the best sister ever?" Mya tackled her sister with a tight bear hug. Donzell joined in, and together they all fell down on the freshly made bed.

Murda was happy to see the smiles on their faces. It was a welcomed change from the norm. She was tired of watching them weep and having to wipe their tears. It was time to rejoice and live life the way they'd always dreamed.

"From today on, things will get better, I promise." Murda squeezed her siblings hard. "I mean that shit from the bottom of my heart."

"I know you do." Mya kissed Murdonna on the cheek. The gesture was something she hadn't done in years, but it felt right. Murdonna was the glue always holding the Carter family down for as long as Mya could remember. Silently she had more respect for her sister than she ever had for her mother. Even when they were little, before Donzell was born, Mya knew Murdonna was her protector.

"Bump that, do you know my size?" Donzell lifted his leg to show off the shoes Murdonna had taken off the bus. "Because this ain't it." On cue, the three of them erupted into laughter.

The family moment was broken up by the sound of hard knocking on the door. "Y'all need to grab your things so y'all can go."

Murdonna stood from the bed and approached the front door with caution. She looked through the peephole to see Payro standing there looking finer than ever in a green denim ensemble with a pair of matching Timberland boots. Quickly she unlocked the door and let him enter. "I thought I was coming to meet you."

"What's up, Murda? We gotta talk." He barged inside, practically knocking Murdonna over.

"Who is Murda, and why is he here?" Donzell asked his sister without removing his eyes from the stranger. Payro hadn't even seen the extra sets of eyes and ears until now.

"What's up, little man?" He nodded at Donzell. "What's up, miss?" He nodded at Mya, who smiled flirtatiously. They both stood patiently in the hallway, waiting to see why he'd come to their apartment.

"Donna, is this your 'friend'?" Mya made air quotes with her fingers again while looking on curiously.

"Y'all are about to be late for school. If you don't leave now, you won't be getting that McDonald's," Murda reminded them, and grudgingly, her siblings scurried out the door.

Once they were alone, Murda invited Payro over to the worn sofa to take a seat. It was stained badly with some of everything, and raggedy as hell. Needless to say, he didn't want to sit down, but he didn't want to offend her either.

"No time to sit. We need to be heading out anyway, but first, I need to holler at you about that shit you did last night." He looked Murda square in the face. He needed to get a good read on her.

"What did I do last night?" Though Murda didn't know what he was going to say, she had a feeling about why he was there at her door this morning. Therefore, her stomach doing backflips.

"Why did you put the heat on Tricks last night?" Payro frowned. "What did she do to you?" He was all for being about that life, but he wasn't down for killing innocent people. Aside from running her mouth too much, Tricks was harmless.

"What are you talking about?" Murda wasn't about to admit to shit. She knew better.

"Stop lying. I seen you behind the building, my nigga," Ro admitted. He'd just finished serving another customer and was about to take a leak behind the building when he saw the shit go down between Murdonna and Tricks. Not only was he pissed that it happened, he was pissed that it happened with the gun he'd just given her for protection.

"Ro, just let it go." Murda didn't want him any more involved than he had to be, so she tried to dead the issue.

"I'm not letting shit go until you tell me what the fuck happened! You're in my crew now. Whatever you eat makes the rest of us shit!" Payro was pissed. "Not five fuckin' minutes after I give you a gun, you draw down on some motherfucking body! Actions like that are questionable. Are you a hothead? Are you trigger-happy? I need to know what's up before I put you down with my crew."

"Honestly, I had to." Murda sighed while scratching her forehead. She didn't feel comfortable confessing to anything, but then again, she knew she had to say something if they were ever going to get past this.

"What do you mean, you had to?" Payro barked. He knew bringing Murda into DCM would present a problem, he just didn't want the bitch to start making trouble straight out of the gate.

"Yesterday, I slipped up and told her something about Chains' murder that I shouldn't have." Murda looked at Ro with lowered eyes. She felt like a child trying to explain something to a parent. "I was going to let it go, but then she brought it up last night, so I had to make sure she stayed quiet. The only way to do it was to lay her down."

Payro didn't say anything because he knew Murda was absolutely right. Tricks had a very big mouth. Therefore, he completely understood why she did what she did. "Did you tell anyone else what you did?"

"No. I learned my lesson." Murda shook her head. This time she was telling the truth.

"All right then." Payro nodded. "Give me the gun. I'll toss it and get you a new one. For future reference, keep your fucking mouth shut before somebody lays your ass down too." It was one thing for the girl to run her mouth about the dirt she did, but he didn't need her to implicate him or his crew in shit.

Murda wanted to check him about threatening her but decided to let it be for now. She didn't want to start any beef with him until she at least learned the game. Quickly she humbled herself. "My bad. I'm sorry. It won't happen again."

"Put some clothes on and let's go."

"Okay. Give me a few minutes," Murdonna obliged.

"Grab the brick," Ro added and made his way toward the door. "I'll wait for you in the hallway."

After quickly brushing her teeth and dressing in a simple pair of blue jeans with a white T-shirt, Murda slipped on her old, faithful Reeboks and met Payro in the hallway. He was leaned up against the elevator talking to Shana, a girl Murda hadn't liked since the sixth grade. Although neither girl knew where the beef stemmed from, the feeling was definitely mutual between them.

"Are you ready?" Murda asked with an attitude.

"Yeah, let's go." Payro reached over and pressed the button.

"Damn, Payro." Shana smirked. "I didn't know you was calling the bum bitches wife these days."

"Bitch, who the fuck are you calling a bum?" Murda snapped, ready to lay her paws on Shana, but she remained calm.

"I'm not calling nobody wife," Payro replied casually while looking from Shana to Murda. "But this is my homie, so watch that slick shit before I let her fuck you up. Shorty got hands." He laughed. If Murdonna was going to be in the crew, he would always have her back. That's just how it had to be.

"Nobody is scared of her, but I was just playing around." Shana grinned to hide her embarrassment. "Anyway, are you going to come back and see me tonight, boo?"

"I don't know. That all depends on what you're trying to do." Payro wasn't an ugly man by far, and the fact that he was Sysco's cousin meant that practically all the bitches in the projects wanted to sleep with him just off general principle. For that reason alone, he never felt the need to beat around the bush. If a chick wasn't trying to get down, it was no skin off his back. He just slid on to the next.

"We can do whatever you like." Shana licked her lips. Murda almost gagged. Ding! The elevator arrived right on time.

"All right, I'll call you." Payro smirked while hopping onto the elevator with Murda, who was utterly disgusted. During the entire ride down, she was awkwardly silent. "What's wrong with you?" he asked when they stepped into the lobby.

"Is that the type of woman you fuck with?" She frowned. "If so, you need to do better."

"Let me guess. You think I should be fucking with somebody like you?" Payro laughed. He was only teasing, but Murda was pissed. She was tired of being the butt of people's jokes.

"Nah, you could never fuck with me. My standards are too high," Murda shot back. She may not be a beauty queen at the moment, but she knew she had the potential. Now that she had a few dollars in her pocket, she planned on sprucing herself up to show everyone what they had been sleeping on.

"You're funny, girl. I was just playing, damn. Relax." Ro held the door open for Murda to exit.

"I am relaxed." Although Murda wasn't trying to get with him, what he said did hurt her feelings. Still, she played it off and kept her opinion inward. "One day, you're going to wish you had a down-ass bitch like me," Murda half-joked. Ro didn't reply.

Outside the building, Murdonna paused midstride and scanned the area with a confused look on her face.

"What's wrong?" Ro asked when he noticed she'd stopped walking.

"Where are the police? Where is the coroner?" Although Murda was relieved that no one was there to make a big deal about finding Tricks' dead body, she knew things weren't adding up. "Shouldn't they be here to claim the body by now?" she whispered, although they were alone in the courtyard.

"There is no body." Ro shook his head and continued walking down the street toward the spot.

"What do you mean?" Murda frowned. "I know the bitch didn't get up and walk away."

"No, she didn't walk away." Ro laughed. "I called my man Quan to handle that shit," he replied without a second thought.

The minute he saw what Murda did last night, he'd called Quan, the cleanup man whose mother owned a funeral home. For a small fee and a little dope, Quan would clean up the toughest situations and get rid of any evidence. Although Payro wasn't 100 percent sure what Quan did with the bodies, he imagined he either cremated them or hid them in the caskets of other dead bodies.

Though Payro could've turned a blind eye and let the body stay put, he'd promised Sysco that he was going to take care of Murda, and that was exactly what he planned to do.

"Thank you." Murda appreciated the gesture tremendously.

"Once I toss the gun, you're in the clear. Nothing will be able to tie you back to this shit."

Murdonna didn't know how she felt about giving Payro the gun that tied her to a murder. She wanted to think she could trust him. After all, he'd gotten rid of the body, but then again, she knew trust in the dope game could have deadly consequences.

The remainder of the walk to the spot was filled with conversation about random stuff. Payro used the time to pick her brain about certain things, and she did the same. The two really had a lot in common with regard to growing up rough. At least Payro had his grandmother and cousin. Murdonna could only depend on herself.

When they arrived at their destination, Murda noticed the townhouse was similar to the one they were at last night with Sysco, but the exterior on this one looked better. It looked like someone actually lived there. Seconds after Ro banged on the door, it opened. Standing there was a fat Puerto Rican kid with two braids in his hair and three braids in his long beard.

"What's up, Payro? Who is this?" He looked at Murda.

"Murda, this is Juan. Juan, this is Murda. She's the newest member of the squad." After Ro made the introduction, he entered the house with Murda at his side.

The place was well furnished with two leather sofas, a flat-screen television, two end tables, and a large area rug. It definitely had a woman's touch.

"What's good, Ro?" a young black man said from the floor. He was sitting between the legs of a pretty Puerto Rican girl, getting his hair braided. There were two additional men sitting in the kitchen playing dominos at a square card table. One of the men was none other than P-dot, the nigga Murda had split at the bus stop yesterday.

When everyone noticed the new face behind Ro, they stopped doing what they were doing to stare in their direction. P-dot was the first to speak. "What is this bitch doing here?"

"Chill out with that noise." Ro flexed his authority. "She's a part of the crew now."

"Man, what? Says who?" P-dot bucked. As far as he was concerned, shorty would never be a part of his crew.

"Says Sysco, nigga. You got any more fucking questions?" Ro replied. He already knew there was going to be some animosity behind the decision to bring Murda on, but honestly, it was too damn early in the morning for this shit. He just wanted to get down to business so that everyone could be on their way.

"I'm not working with no bitch, especially not this bitch!" P-dot didn't give a fuck who had decided to bring shorty into the Detroit City Mafia. He knew the dope game had no place for a female. In his mind, she would eventually get them all killed!

"P-dot, I love you, but if you can't get over yourself, then there's the door. My hands are tied." Ro didn't want to lose one of his closest friends, but he wasn't about to go against Sysco's wishes for nobody. In his mind, blood was and would always be thicker than water.

"Really? That's how it is?" P-dot stood from the table. "You've known me for ten years, and you've known her ass for ten minutes. You're choosing her over me after all the shit we've been through?"

"The call wasn't mine to make," Ro said, trying to explain the situation in a calm manner.

Murda was fed up with all the talking, so she decided to end the shit right then and fucking there. "Look, P-dot, I'm willing to work with you despite the ho shit you said to me yesterday. If you're willing to move past the situation we had, like an adult, then so can I. The sooner we do that, the sooner we can get to this money." Murda walked over to him and held her hand out.

P-dot looked down at her hand briefly before spitting a hefty wad of mucus right into her palm. Instantly Murda lost her cool! In a moment, her bad temper got the best of her, but whose wouldn't? With one swift motion, she snatched that nigga up by the front of his shirt and pushed his ass right on top of the coffee table. Raising her foot, she commenced stumping the dog shit out of his ass. Although P-dot was twice Murda's size, the fact that she was spazzing out like a savage beast had left him helpless against her attack once again. No one came to his aid, not even Ro. Everyone in the room could see that Murda wasn't shit to play with! Her hands were deadly, and for that reason, nobody wanted to get on her bad side, especially since Sysco was the one who had put her on in the first place.

Finally, after about ten minutes of being punched, kicked, and scratched, P-dot was able to reach into his jeans and pull out the small .22-caliber gun he carried from time to time. "Bitch, I will kill you!" he spat while pointing the gun right at Murda's chest. Everyone in the room froze with their breath held except for Murda.

"You bad, right? Then do it!" she hollered. "I've seen everything but God anyway!" Maybe it was the hand she'd been dealt in life, or maybe it was that she knew there was nothing to lose, but whatever it was made her not bat an eyelash while staring down the nose of the gun. Fear was a non-fucking-factor to her.

"I swear to God, if you don't get the fuck off me, I will blow your brains out!" Not only was P-dot embarrassed that this female had whooped his ass twice, but he was pissed that his boys didn't intervene. Clearly, sides had been chosen, and he was on the losing end.

"Murda, get up," Ro advised. Yet and still, she remained planted on top of P-dot. It was her way of provoking him to see what he was going to do. She knew he was a pussy, but she wanted everyone else to see it too.

"Five . . ." P-dot gripped the pistol, and Murda smiled. "Four . . ." He huffed, and she began to laugh. By the time he made it to "two," the front door swung open, and Sysco entered the living room. Everyone turned to look at him, including P-dot. Murda used the distraction as an opportunity to snatch the gun from his clutches and turn it on him.

"Boy, don't you ever, as long as you live, put another goddamn gun to my face unless you plan on using it," she screamed.

"What the fuck is going on? Ro, break this shit up!" Sysco pushed Ro toward his crew. He wanted his cousin to man the fuck up and get a handle on things before shit escalated.

"Enough. Neither one of y'all is shooting nobody. Get y'all asses up." Ro made a show of pulling Murda off P-dot. "Everybody just needs to relax before I bust a cap in both of y'all asses." He hated to look like he didn't have shit under control in front of his cousin. Situations like this made him look weak as a captain.

"Now that that's finished, can we get down to business, please?" Sysco walked farther into the living room, wearing a black and red Jordan warm-up suit with the matching retro shoes. He took a seat on the couch and crossed his legs at the ankle. "Angelina, would you mind making yourself invisible for an hour or so?" Politely he dismissed the girl from doing Chris's hair. She was the owner of the townhouse and Juan's older sister, but she understood her role. When Sysco told you to do something, you didn't hesitate to do it.

"Okay, baby," she replied in a sultry tone while making a show of getting off the couch so all the men in the room would look at her ass as she left. Murdonna rolled her eyes, knowing this would definitely be a constant downside to working with all men.

"Okay, now let's talk new business first." Sysco rubbed his hands together. "In case you haven't heard yet, or you simply need to hear it from the horse's mouth, this is Murda. She will be joining our organization under Payro's umbrella." Sysco looked around to see how everyone felt. Judging by what he'd walked in on and the look on P-dot's face, he directed his next question to him. "Anybody got a problem with that?" Sysco stared directly into P-dot's face.

P-dot looked at the ground without uttering a word. Truthfully, he wasn't at all scared of his boss. However, he knew better than to bite the hand that was feeding him. He didn't want any issues, so he decided to remain quiet for now.

"All right then." Sysco smirked. "Now that that's settled, from this moment forward, that beef shit between y'all is dead." He looked from Murda to P-dot. "If I hear that either one of y'all is on some bullshit, then y'all will have to deal with me. In the meantime, we are a family, and we will conduct ourselves as such. Detroit City Mafia is on the rise. We can't have division within the family when we're trying to conquer the streets. In the DCM, there are no I's in 'team.' It's all for one and one for all." He paused and waited for his crew to respond.

"All for one and one for all," everyone chanted back.

"Now let's talk old business. The profits from the last two months have been steady but not increasing. We've gotten a stronger product, we've run specials, and we've increased the number of soldiers we have on the ground, but nothing is raising our profits. Can anybody tell me why they think that is?"

"I think we need to holla at them Woodward niggas, Sys. I think they are selling to our customers for real," Juan added.

"Nah. Them niggas know not to step off into our terri-tory. They ain't crazy." Payro shook his head.

Murdonna thought for a second before finding the nerve to speak up. "I think we need to expand our clien-tele. From what I see, a majority of the customers live right here in the projects. No offense, but no matter how good the product is, or how many specials you run, they are only going to spend what they can afford to spend, which isn't very much around here. We need to find some prominent people like doctors and lawyers with expen-sive habits." Murdonna was very good with numbers and statistics. Therefore, it was a no-brainer to her that they needed more clientele in order to make more money.

The room was silent as everyone tried to get a read on how Sysco was taking her suggestion. Murdonna didn't know if that was a good thing or a bad thing until Sysco spoke up.

"We sell to consistent customers. This helps to mini-mize the risks. New customers are unpredictable. Not all money is good money." For as long as he'd been hustling, Sysco liked to keep things simple. He never had dreams of getting out of the projects. He never dreamed of retir-ing from the game. For him, hustling was a nine-to-five. As long as he made enough money to live comfortably, he was good. More money was accompanied by things like envy and jail time. Sysco wasn't interested in either.

"Yeah, I hear you, but consistent customers don't raise profits. Only new business does that. You've got to start thinking outside of the box." For Murdonna, it was simple: more business equaled more money. "Putting a hundred soldiers on the ground to sell to the same customers in the area just doesn't make sense. There are ways to gain new customers without drawing too much attention."

"Okay, genius, do you know any prominent people with habits?" He used her words to mock her.

"No, but that doesn't mean there are none out there."

"Okay, so your homework this week is to obtain one new client with bank, and we'll go from there." Sysco was open to her suggestion for expanding clientele but wanted to keep that shit to a minimum. Knowing that greed would almost always land you in hot water, Sysco preferred to do things low-key. Too much money would bring lots of unwanted attention. On the other hand, his supplier was always on him about expanding more, which was why he agreed to let her do her thing, but he would make sure to keep a tight grip on her.

"Okay, cool." Murdonna didn't know where to start, but she was definitely up for the challenge. This assignment was all she needed to get her feet wet in the game.

"All right, enough about business for today. Friday, we're going to take Murda out and show her how the DCM gets down. Until then, let's get back to this money." Sysco stood from the sofa and told the crew he'd catch them later. He left the young'uns with a smirk on his face and a newfound respect for Murda. Every time he saw her, she proved to have the heart of a lion. He loved that about her. Sysco knew if he groomed her right, she would one day be his biggest asset.

Chapter Eleven

After the meeting, everyone dispersed in their own separate directions, leaving Murdonna and Payro alone. He used the time to take her into the kitchen and give her the first lesson on how to cook crack. After placing the brick on the counter, he grabbed a face mask and handed her one. Then he went on to explain the reason for boiling the water as well as the process of cutting the brick with baking soda. "Depending on how strong your pack is, you may need to cut some batches more than others. If the shit is pure cocaine, adding baking soda would allow you to stretch it a lot further. If the pack is weak, then you shouldn't cut it, because basically, you'll be pushing some watered-down shit, you feel me?"

Murdonna nodded her understanding while mentally keeping track of everything he was saying. Once the powder was hardened, Payro put on two pairs of rubber gloves and grabbed a razor blade.

"What's the double pair of gloves for?" Murdonna asked while following suit.

"It's to make sure nothing comes in contact with your skin. Sometimes this shit can seep through your pores and sometimes into tiny cuts you don't even know you have. If that happens, you will get high!" After explaining the process, Ro took the razor blade and began breaking little rocks off and placing them into baggies. Some baggies had more rocks than others.

"Why are you putting more in some and less in others?"

"Doing this just gives you options. The ones with more are priced higher." Ro had thought that was self-explanatory, but then again, he remembered that she was totally new to all of this.

Fascinated with the entire process, Murdonna used her time with Payro to ask everything she wanted to know about the dope game and soaked up everything he was teaching her like a sponge. Her second-grade teacher once told her, "If you give a man a fish, you feed him for the day. Yet if you teach the man to fish, you'll feed him for a lifetime." Murda didn't know the meaning of that shit back then, but oh, how she comprehended it now. Knowing how to whip her own work and remix it was the first step in building her empire. Now that she understood the fundamentals of the game, she knew she was never going back to being broke.

After packing up the baggies, Payro and Murda left the townhouse and walked two blocks until they stopped in front of an abandoned two-family flat. Though the windows and the door of the house were boarded up, there were three folding chairs on the porch, an ashtray, and an empty bottle of Sprite. "This block is ours. We control here to Rosa Parks," Ro explained.

"What happens if I want to go past Rosa Parks?" Murdonna didn't like boundaries. She knew there was more money to be made beyond these limits.

"Then you'll be trespassing on someone else's territory, and let's just say there'll be some smoke in the city. So stay your ass on our turf," he warned. Payro knew there were rules that everyone in the game had to abide by. If you didn't, the penalties could be deadly.

For almost seven hours, Ro and Murda paced the lawn of the abandoned house. Though customers were steady, they weren't spending any real money. With an attitude, Murdonna flopped down onto the porch, reached into her pocket, and pulled out the money she'd collected all day. Flipping through the various denominations of bills, she was only at $465. "This shit is for the birds." She felt like she was wasting time.

"Girl, what are you complaining about now?" Ro was used to working alone. Though Murdonna provided company to pass the time, her constant questions and complaints were beginning to get on his last nerve. Real hustlers just did what they had to do.

"We have been out here all day, and I don't even have a stack yet."

"Some days it'll be like that. I don't know what to tell you." He shrugged. "You'll get used to it, trust me." Hustling was no easy task. It was not all glitz and glamour the way television portrayed it.

"I guess." Murdonna shrugged. She didn't think she could ever get used to standing around all day with nothing to show for it. Even though the money she made today was more than she'd made at any job she'd ever worked, she still knew there had to be a better way to hustle than this.

After checking the time on her watch for the hundredth time, she looked up to see a guy named Lanky Larry walk up the street. Larry stood at least six feet seven inches tall and weighed a buck fifty with rocks in his pocket.

"What's happening, captain?" Walking up to Ro, he slapped him five. "What you know, no good?" Larry always talked like a character from a seventies pimp movie. He dressed like one, too.

"What's up, old school?" Ro talked to Larry while at the same time watching the cars go down the street. When you were in the trap, you always had to have your eyes and ears open, never missing a beat.

"Old school?" Larry struck a pose in his plaid suit and pretended to be offended. "Boy, don't you know niggas like me never go out of style? Now, what's your problem? Pants hanging so far off your ass we can see that shit on your drawers."

"Yeah, okay." Ro laughed, and Murdonna did too.

"Now, who is this little tender right here?" Larry placed his hands over his eyes like binoculars.

"I'm Murda. You know me, Larry." She'd known him almost all her life. "I'm Sheila's daughter."

"Sheila?" Larry pulled a cigarette from behind his ear and tried to place her mother.

"Yes, Sheila. The one with the birthmark on her face."

"No shit. Sheila is your mama?" Larry smiled, exposing all seven of his teeth. "Where she been? I ain't seen her lately."

"I don't know." Murda shrugged. "She's been gone for a while now. I was hoping you might've seen her."

"Okay, sweet thang, don't worry. Ol' Larry will keep his eyes peeled. You got a number so I can call you if I do?" Larry was shooting his shot without shame.

"If you hear or see something, come back here. This is where I'll be." Murdonna didn't miss a beat. Besides, she didn't have a phone yet, so there was no number to give.

"Okay, cool. Well, I'm going to slide up out of here"—he lifted his leg and busted a dance move like he was a member of the Five Heartbeats—"but first, Ro, let me get a sample of something."

"A sample? Nigga, you got me fucked up." Ro laughed. "Hit your pockets. I know you got something."

"I don't have nothing on me. My check is late, but as soon as it comes, you're the first person I'm coming to see if you let me hold something."

"I know you got money. You keep a couple dollars in your pocket for them hoes you be tricking with." Ro knew if he fronted Larry anything, he would be ghost for at least a week.

The duo went back and forth like this for several minutes until Larry reached into his pocket and produced a $20 bill. Payro held the money up to the sky to check its authenticity. With Larry, you couldn't take chances.

"Aw, come on, you jive turkey! You think ol' Larry gon' give you a counterfeit?"

"Yes, the fuck I do. Remember that time your ass gave me a fake five?" Ro was laughing about it now, but back then, it was nothing funny. He'd tried to use the $5 bill on the bus, and it was rejected, and that was when the bus driver told him it was fake. Ever since then, Ro always checked Larry's money.

"Whatever, sucker. Just give me my shit so I can go."

After being serviced, Larry pimped off down the street like he hadn't a care in the world. Murdonna looked down at her watch again and yawned. Payro joined her on the porch, choosing a seat on the steps. For ten minutes, they sat in silence while watching the happenings of the neighborhood. Other than the occasional car passing by, the block was dead.

"Oh, shit, here comes my girl Bethany," Ro said as a newer-model white Jaguar pulled up in front of where they were posted.

"Who is she?" Murda immediately clocked the luxury car and wanted the rundown.

"She's a college student from around the way." Ro waved hello to the redheaded white girl just as she rolled down the window. "She's a tough customer, but she spends money," Ro mumbled under his breath, and Murda nodded her understanding. She knew Bethany was probably a spoiled brat in possession of daddy's wallet. Immediately she thought of ways to finesse her out of all the cash she brought today. That was the only way to make all this sitting around worth it.

"I got this one if you don't mind." Murda stopped Ro when he started walking toward the car.

"You sure?"

"Yeah. This is my last one for the night." Murda yawned. She was tired.

"You'll never be a millionaire if you keep closing down early." Ro shook his head. His new protégé had a lot to learn if she was going to have longevity in the dope game.

"Millionaires work smarter, not harder." Murda laughed while approaching the car. They had been on the corner selling cocaine all day. It was time to go home. There was no way she was staying at the trap after dark. With fifty rocks still in her possession, she was going to try to sell them all to Bethany and call it a night. "What's good, mama? What you need?"

"I need Payro." Bethany smacked her small, thin lips. She was unfamiliar with the new girl, which made her very uncomfortable.

"Payro is done for the day, so he sent me over here." Murda leaned down into the window with a smile. "Don't worry, I don't bite. Just tell me what you need, and I got you."

Bethany looked past Murda and tried to make eye contact with Payro, but he was now engrossed in a deep conversation with someone on the phone. Not wanting to be in the ghetto longer than necessary, she decided to give the girl her business. "Look, I'm having a party for my friends tonight. Give me two rocks." Bethany pulled out two crisp Benjamins.

"I got fifty vials left, and I think they all should go with you." Murda didn't even flinch as she spoke. She was on a mission.

"Fifty!" Bethany snapped. "I'm trying to fucking party, not kill them or myself. Are you crazy?"

"Sweetheart, please lower your tone before you draw even more attention to us than your vehicle already has." The expensive car Bethany was driving had no business in the ghetto, and they both knew it. "Look, you don't have to make use of them all at once. Use some tonight and save some for later. After the party there's always an after-party, right?"

Murda could tell by the look on Bethany's face that she wasn't sold, so she continued. "I know you don't like coming down here, right? Why not cop all this shit and save yourself from coming back in a few days? If you spread this out, you'll have enough to last you for a while." She paused and watched as Bethany pondered her suggestion.

"Fine. Give me fifty." Bethany reached into her Chanel bag and handed Murda $1,000. Murda handed over a black grocery bag. Inside was a freezer bag filled with the remaining cocaine bags.

"All right. Lock your doors and drive safe." Murdonna tapped the roof of Bethany's car, then watched her drive off. With a smile, she headed back over to Payro, who was wrapping up his phone call. "I'm done for the day. I'll catch you tomorrow. Same time, same place?" She rolled her eyes playfully.

"I told you, trap stars don't quit early." He laughed, knowing Murda had no idea what she was getting into. "This shit is a twenty-four-hour business. We still got product to move."

"I'm out of what we cooked earlier." Murda laughed. "Your girl bought everything I had left." Murda didn't miss the sour look on Ro's face.

He'd never been able to sell more than fifteen rocks at a time to Bethany. Instantly he regretted giving up his customer. "All right then, I'll check you out later." Ro still had twenty more of his own bags to move before he would call it a day.

Murda peeled off two Benjamins and handed them to him. "What's this for?" He was puzzled.

"I know she was your customer. That's just a little something to show you that I'm a team player, and I appreciate you hooking me up."

"That's dope of you." Ro was surprised. Nobody on his team had ever done any shit like that. As a matter of fact, he'd never done it to anyone on his team before. There was no real comradery among street niggas, but maybe with Murdonna around, things would change. "Do you need me to come over and help you cook the rest of your work tomorrow?"

"No. I think I got it." With a smile, Murda chucked the deuces and started off down the block.

It was nearly seven o'clock in the evening, and although she should've been going home to check in on her siblings, Murda had promised to lace them with clothes and shoes. For that reason alone, she wouldn't dare go home empty-handed. Anticipating the joy she'd be bringing them refreshed her as she headed to the bus stop. Just the thought alone had her smiling so hard that her cheeks were hurting.

As soon as she rounded the corner, the bus she wanted was just pulling off. "Fuck!" she spat. The next one would be at least thirty to forty-five minutes. Quickly she contemplated going home and trying again tomorrow or just waiting for a cab to pass by. She didn't have a cell phone or a debit card, so Uber wasn't an option. Before she could make a solid decision about what to do next, Sysco's black-on-black Chevy Impala pulled up out of nowhere.

"Where are you headed this evening? Shouldn't you be working?" he asked after rolling down the tinted window.

"I need to go to Walmart and grab a few things before I go home." Leaning down into the window, she couldn't help but notice how clean his car was. It smelled good, too.

"All right. Hop in. I'll take you." The nearest Walmart was a good distance away.

"Are you sure?" she asked cautiously. She didn't expect Sysco to offer her a ride, but his kindness surprised her. "I know you're a busy man with things to do."

"If I wasn't sure, I wouldn't have asked you to hop in." He smirked. "Come on, I got you." He unlocked the door, and Murda got in.

"Thank you. I appreciate the ride." She was nervous.

"What type of man would I be if I let you ride the bus this late? By the time you get out there, shop, and come back, it'll be after midnight."

"I have gas money for you." Reaching into her pocket, Murda thumbed through the stash and pulled out a twenty. She tried to hand it to him, but he looked at her crazy. Not knowing if he was offended by the small gesture or simply didn't want to take her money, she folded it up and placed it back into her pocket.

The ride started off silent as neither of them knew what to say. It wasn't like they were friends, and even though they'd lived in the same hood for years, until now, they'd never had a reason to speak. "So, your mom has been gone for a minute, huh?" Sysco asked to break the ice. He didn't really know or care for Sheila like that, but that didn't stop him from having compassion for her daughter.

"Yes. She's been gone for forty-three days, to be exact." Murda looked out the window, trying not to think about her mother because she didn't want to become emotional.

"Damn, that's a stretch." Sysco whistled. "And you've been holding it down all by yourself?"

"Yeah, that's right." Murda nodded. "We don't have any other options. I have to do what I have to do."

"I been there, and it's tough, but you'll make it through." Sysco turned on his blinker while swerving over into the left lane.

"What's your story?" Murda asked nervously.

"What makes you think I have one?" Sysco smirked.

"Everybody has a story," Murda insisted. "You know mine. Now tell me yours."

"Well, if you must know, my father killed my mother when I was sixteen."

"Really?" Murda turned to look at him, but he didn't return her gaze.

"Yeah, he suffered from depression and bipolar disease," Sysco continued. "He didn't get the help he needed, so I guess I can't really blame him, but I had to take care of my little brother, Orlando, who was ten at the time."

"Where was your family?" Murda was completely engrossed in Sysco's story. She saw similarities to her own.

"My grandmother was there, but there's only so much a woman can teach a man, you know?" Sysco merged onto the freeway. "She made sure we were fed and clean and had a place to call home. I was the one who defended us when other kids in the neighborhood tried to fuck with us, though. I was the one who put money in our pockets. I was the one who taught my brother to be a man." No doubt Sysco was proud of his role as the protector and provider of his family.

"I'm not a man, but I feel the same way about my siblings. I will make all the sacrifices if it means they end up better."

"No doubt. That's what the oldest do. We make shit happen."

"What happened to Orlando?" Murda anticipated hearing a success story. However, after several seconds of silence, she peered over and didn't miss the way Sysco stared off into the distance. She knew something bad must've happened.

"He died." Anxiously Sysco tapped the gear shift with his fingers. "My brother got shot one night outside the club." He still blamed himself for not being there when it went down.

"I'm so sorry to hear that." Instinctively Murda placed her hand on top of Sysco's. Although she didn't know his pain firsthand, she could never imagine losing one of her siblings. As the oldest, there was always of sense of responsibility you felt to protect them. If something like that ever happened to Mya or Donzell, Murda would go crazy.

"Thanks, shorty. I appreciate that, but I'm good." Sysco looked over at Murda and smiled. He couldn't lie, it felt good to open up to someone who could understand his struggle, but he never mixed business with pleasure. Quickly he removed his hand and placed it back on the steering wheel.

Murda was feeling some chemistry between them, but she couldn't tell what it was, so she ignored it. Deciding that the mood in the car was too heavy, she pressed a few buttons on the radio before she landed on a station playing old-school hip-hop and R&B.

Nearly half an hour later, the Impala pulled into Walmart's parking lot. As usual, the place was packed. Sysco didn't need anything from inside, so he opted not to brave the crowd and deal with having to stand in one of the two lines open when it was time to check out. "You go ahead and get what you need. I'll be over there." He pointed across the parking lot to an urban clothing store, Threadz.

"Can I ask you a favor?"

"Damn, another one? I thought the ride was enough. Sike. What's up?"

"Can you grab some gym shoes in a men's size eleven and women's size eight for me? It doesn't matter what kind of shoes they are. Just grab some fly shit for my brother and sister. I promised to bring them some shoes this morning." Murda tried to hand Sysco $200, but again he looked at her like she was crazy. A car behind them blew its horn.

"Go ahead, ma. I got the shoes."

Murdonna couldn't find the words, but she nodded her appreciation. She wasn't used to people being so nice to her, but she was extremely grateful.

Once inside of Walmart, Murda felt like a kid in a candy store. She'd never been able to enter a store with so much money in her pocket that it didn't matter what she was about to purchase. After grabbing a shopping cart, she literally went from aisle to aisle, grabbing some of this and some of that. Within an hour, her cart was filled to the brim with three comforter sets, two blow-up mattresses, a vacuum, bathroom accessories, new dishes and cookware, paint, pajamas, a few groceries, cleaning supplies, several uniforms for Donzell, and a few new things for Mya. Although the clothes weren't name-brand, she knew her sister would appreciate them just the same.

After grabbing everything she thought she wanted, Murda decided to head up to the checkout counter. "Murdonna, is that you?" a woman asked behind her. When Murda turned to see who it was, she almost fainted.

"Mrs. Johnson, what are you doing here?" Her voice was unsteady. She couldn't believe how small the world was. What were the chances of running into her victim's mother, in Walmart of all places?

"I needed to get out and make myself busy to keep from thinking about someone killing my baby," Mrs. Johnson blurted out with a sniffle.

"Oh, my God. When did this happen?" Murda tried her best to act surprised as she inched up closer to the checkout line.

"They sliced his throat some time yesterday." Mrs. Johnson had told the story about two million times already to family and friends, but it still got her choked up just thinking about it.

"Are you serious?" Murda gasped.

"When the police find the person responsible, I pray the same is done to that heartless bastard!"

"Me too!" Murda added before going over to her for a fake hug. "If there is anything you need, please let me know," she lied. Truthfully, Mrs. Johnson could kick rocks with open-toed shoes on for all she cared.

"I appreciate that, sweetheart. I really do." Mrs. Johnson smiled warmly. "Swing by the cleaners next week. I may have a few things for your brother. He and Thomas probably wore the same size."

"Thank you, Mrs. Johnson, but that's not necessary." Murda didn't want anything from her, especially nothing that once belonged to the man she'd just killed. "You look exhausted. You need to go home and get some rest."

"I will. I just came in here to waste time. I didn't want to be alone at home with my thoughts, you know?" Again Mrs. Johnson smiled wearily, then walked off. Murda almost felt bad for the woman, but then she looked down at the cart full of items that she wouldn't have been able to afford otherwise and quickly got over it.

"Wow! Did you just get a new place?" the cashier asked as Murda unloaded everything onto the conveyer belt.

"Something like that." As she continued to unload, it made her heart proud to see everything she was able to purchase.

Once everything had been scanned, the cashier told Murda her total was a whopping $887.03. Without grumbling or complaining, Murda peeled off the money and passed it over. She couldn't wait to get home and show her siblings what they had.

"Have a great night, sweetie." The cashier handed over the change, and Murda took off toward the door. She'd already kept Sysco waiting too long.

As soon as she was outside, she scanned the parking lot for his car, but she didn't see it. Naturally, she thought he left her, and she was beginning to wonder how the hell she was going to get all her bags on the bus. Just then, the Impala flew from across the street to where she was standing.

"My bad. I hope you wasn't waiting long. I got a little caught up." Sysco stepped from the car and popped the trunk to help Murda with her stuff.

"I was just about to say the same thing." She laughed and began to load everything into the already-crowded trunk. "You must have done some serious shopping." She could barely get her stuff inside with all of his bags.

"I did a little something." Sysco forced a few bags in, then closed the trunk, and they pulled off.

The ride back home was much easier than the ride coming. Both Sysco and Murda had relaxed. They joked and talked about life in general. He was surprised that she was so mature for her age. They shared aspirations of being successful, but they had different visions of what it took to get there. Though Sysco's strategies were different, he appreciated hearing a different perspective. Murdonna had a lot to learn about the world she was now a part of, but he knew with the right guidance, she could change the game.

Within one conversation, Sysco had grown on Murda, and she was definitely growing on him. No longer did they feel like the strangers they were yesterday. They now felt like allies. "Thank you so much for the ride." Murda smiled as they pulled back into the projects.

"It was my pleasure. Hell, it was good to get out of the ghetto for a minute." Sysco grinned. It was easy being with Murda. He didn't have to front or be a hard ass all the time. Usually, he didn't let too many people into his world, but he knew she was special. "I'll help you carry your bags in." Sysco stood from the car and popped the trunk. She grabbed two armfuls, and Sysco did the same.

"I think you accidentally grabbed some of your stuff, too." She'd noticed that he had several bags in the trunk of his car when he picked her up from Walmart. Not wanting to lug all his bags back downstairs, she decided to let him know.

"No, it's all yours." Sysco closed the trunk then locked his whip. Chirp!

"I only asked you to grab some shoes. What else did you get?" Murda quizzed.

"A little bit of this and a little bit of that." He chuckled before heading toward the apartment building.

Murda was confused. "Sysco, I don't know what you did, but you didn't have to." She didn't want him to see her as needy, and she didn't want him to act like she owed him in the future.

"It was nothing," Sysco replied without losing his stride. Murda didn't say anything as she followed him.

Upstairs, Sysco set all of the bags down in the hallway. "All right, Murda. I'll catch you Friday." He leaned up against the wall to catch a breather. His arms were tired.

"Thanks again for the ride and the extra stuff and for helping me bring it upstairs." Against her better judgment, Murda went in for a hug, causing Sysco to tense up. Her action had completely caught him off guard. Yet he wrapped his warm arms around her waist.

"Have a good night, baby girl," Sysco whispered. Murda inhaled the peppermint scent coming from his breath. "I'll catch you later." Forcing himself off of her, Sysco turned and headed back down the hall.

With a smile, Murda unlocked the door and started dragging her bags inside. Mya and Donzell were sitting at the dining room table doing homework. "Where the hell have you been?" Mya asked, completely pissed, yet relieved that her sister was okay.

"I'm sorry. I should've called, but I got caught up at Walmart." Murda knew they were probably worried sick. She felt bad, knowing what they'd all been through since her mother went missing.

"You got all this for us?" Donzell quickly forgave his sister when he saw all her bags. Mya did the same.

"Yes, I did. So come on and help me out with this stuff."

For nearly an hour, the siblings went about putting away the groceries and all their new items. It felt good to see everything in the house fresh, and it smelled fresh, too. The fridge was full, and their apartment finally felt like a home. It was too late to start painting the dingy walls, so Murda decided to wait until the weekend. The next thing on her list to buy was furniture. She wanted to get a new living room set and bunk beds for Mya and Donzell.

"Are these for us too?" Donzell asked while looking into the bags Sysco had given to Murda. She'd completely forgotten about them.

"Bring the bags over here. Let me see what's in there," Murda demanded from the sofa, where she was sitting with her feet propped up.

Inside the first bag were two pairs of Jordans, size eleven. Donzell practically cried when he pulled them out to try them on. He'd never owned shoes like this in his life. The second bag held two pairs of Nikes, size eight. Murdonna handed them to Mya, who began dancing all over the living room. The third, fourth, fifth, and sixth bags were filled to the brim with various tops, jeans, belts, hats, and shoes. The clothes were size seven, and the shoes were size seven. Both were Murda's exact size.

"Donna, there is a note on the back of the receipt." Mya handed the paper to her sister. The note on the back of the receipt read:

You looked out for your siblings, so I looked out for you. If the clothes don't fit, take them back.
Sysco

With a huge grin, Murda folded the receipt and slipped it into her pocket. His generosity and companionship during such a difficult time in her life were cherished and much appreciated. For that, she vowed to always be loyal to him.

Chapter Twelve

The remainder of the week went by smoothly. Murda hustled from the time the kids went to bed until the time they had to be up for school. Most days, she walked in just as the alarm clock was going off. She didn't want them to know what she was doing, so she lied and told them she had gotten a night job. The money was rolling in, so they had no reason to doubt her. As soon as the kids went out the door for school, Murda would take a morning nap, shower, and eat, then get back to the grind. As long as she was home when they came in, neither of them was any the wiser.

Today the plans had changed, though. Murda decided to go see Odessa, the hairdresser who lived on the third floor. Although she was a licensed cosmetologist who could do hair anywhere, Odessa preferred to do hair out of her apartment as an attempt to save money. Everyone in the projects went to her for service.

"Shit, Dessa, I didn't know you were booked today," Murda said after opening the door and counting ten bodies in the living room waiting to get their hair done.

"It's the weekend, girl. Everyone is going out tonight." Odessa's Jamaican accent was faint yet still present in some of the words she pronounced. "Take a number, and I'll get you in ASAP." Odessa pointed to the ticket station resting on her coffee table. It was just like the ones at the meat counter at the grocery store. Without a fuss, Murda pulled number thirteen and took a seat.

As she made herself more comfortable in a folding chair resting against the wall, she couldn't help but notice a light-skinned blond girl with green contacts staring at her as if she had two noses on her face. Murda wanted to flat-out ask the bitch what the fuck she was looking at. She knew her attitude always got her in trouble, though, so she refrained from blowing up. With a smirk, Murda returned the glance but remained silent. The light-skinned girl continued to stare, but she too remained silent. It wasn't until Shana came from the bathroom and joined the blond bitch that Murda began to put two and two together.

"Hey, Koko," Shana said while plopping down in the seat next to her friend. "Sysco is going to love what Dessa does to your hair." Although she was talking to Koko, she was looking at Murda.

"Girl, he won't be able to keep his hands off me when I get up out the chair. You know my man in love with that Koko." While speaking, she too looked over at Murda. It was a not-so-subtle way to say that Sysco belonged to her.

"And Koko loves some Sysco." Shana laughed.

"You damn right. I'll step to any bitch trying to come for my spot, no matter how raggedy they are."

"Yeah, these bum bitches been coming out the woodwork lately." Again, Shana looked over at Murda, who was still unbothered. In fact, she found the little skit so comical that she gave them hoes a round of applause.

"The fuck you clapping for?" Koko smacked her lips, causing Murda to step from her seat without missing a beat.

"What did you say, bitch?" she asked while walking up to her. She was in the "wish a nigga would" zone.

"Don't even waste time talking to this lame-ass nobody," Shana jumped in.

The muscles in Murda's jowls tightened as she tried hard to stay cool. Lord knows she didn't need any more bodies on her record, and she wasn't trying to catch a case either.

"If I'm such a lame, how come your nigga cashed me out the other day?" Murda couldn't help tossing the insult.

"He probably did it because he felt sorry for your bummy ass." Koko laughed, and a few others in the makeshift waiting area did the same.

"That's the last bum I'll be before I bust you upside the muthafuckin' head!" Murda was turned up to the max. She wanted to blow both Koko's and Shana's heads clean the fuck off, but then she'd have to kill the other witnesses too.

"If the shoe fits, then wear it, bum!" Koko laughed by her lonesome. Everyone else in the room noticed the fire in Murda's eyes. Shit was about to get real.

By instinct, Murda picked up the gold lamp from the coffee table and smashed it against Koko's head. Dazed and confused, it took Koko a minute to realize what exactly had just happened. Shana sat there, speechless. For one thing, she couldn't believe what she'd just witnessed, and for two, she wasn't trying to feel Murda's wrath. The shit was all fun and games until a bitch went beast mode.

"What else do you wanna say?" Murda asked with a daring look.

"No, no, no." Odessa ran into the living room. "You got to get out of here with all that."

"They started it though," Murda whined.

"I know, me child, but you ended it, and now you've got to go." Odessa pointed at the door. She liked Murda, but she wouldn't tolerate foolishness in her home or place of business. Once Koko got her bearings, she would dismiss her too.

With a smack of her lips, Murda turned and headed out the door. Although she was pissed that she couldn't get her hair done, she was happy to have laid hands on Koko's bigmouth ass. Hopefully that taught both her and Shana a lesson. Murda was not the one to be fucked with.

After being kicked out of Odessa's apartment, Murda decided to head to the mall. She really wanted to get dolled up for a night out with Payro, Sysco, and the rest of the crew. She still hadn't met everyone and wanted to make a good first impression.

After stopping at the makeup counter, getting her nails done, and picking up a new dress from Bella Donna, a premier retail chain, the only thing left undone was her hair. After careful consideration, she decided just to curl it with the heated wand she'd purchased earlier. Her hair was shoulder-length and thick. Usually, she kept it up in a ponytail, but today she wanted to show everyone what this "bum" bitch was really working with.

"What is that on your face?" Donzell frowned when Murda walked into the apartment.

"It's makeup. Do you like it?" Murda knew she looked good. She'd been getting looks all day.

"You look funny." He laughed.

"You look pretty," Mya said after going up to her sister and inspecting her face. "Is that boy taking you on a date?" She raised a brow.

"It's not a date. I'm just going out with a few friends, that's all." Murda smiled, then headed to the back of the apartment. Both Donzell and Mya were on her trail.

"Where are y'all going?" Donzell asked.

"The club."

"What club?" Mya jumped in, wanting to know all the details.

"What's with all the questions?" Murda hung her clothing on the back of the door, then removed the plastic. It was a fitted black dress with navy blue rhinestones and a sheer split across the top of her cleavage. The shoes were wedged heels. They were blue, and her clutch was, too.

"What time are you coming back?" Donzell didn't like letting Murda out of his sight for too long. Silently, he feared losing her the way Sheila had disappeared.

"D, you ain't my daddy." Murda laughed.

"I know." Donzell wrapped his arms around Murda. "Just don't be gone too long."

"I won't. I promise." She crossed her heart. For nearly seven minutes after that, Donzell hung on to his sister's waist. It wasn't until he heard the theme song of his favorite show in the living room that he decided to leave her alone.

As Murda moved about the bedroom, pulling out her underwear for after the shower, she noticed Mya standing in the doorway. She looked as if she wanted to say something. "Spit it out," Murda said without turning around.

"I heard you got into a fight at Odessa's. Is that true?"

"I wouldn't call it a fight. I'd say I beat the bitch's ass. Why? What did you hear?" Murda knew how bitches twisted stories in the projects.

"I heard that Koko is mad as hell. You better watch your back," Mya warned her big sister.

"I ain't worried about her, believe that." Murda smacked her lips, then headed for the shower. She wasn't vexed in the least.

Chapter Thirteen

The remainder of the day went by entirely too slowly. Murda checked the clock every hour on the hour until it was time to get dressed. Payro was picking her up at ten. She was nervous yet excited to get out of the house for a night of fun. For the last few years, her social life had been nonexistent. However, tonight things were going to change.

Slipping into the dress, Murda felt like Cinderella. Tears began to gather in her eyes, but she dared not let them drop and ruin her makeup. The sad reality of the situation was that she'd never owned anything this beautiful in her life. All the ghetto had given her was a crack mom and welfare.

Right on time, Payro knocked at the door. After quickly slipping into her shoes, Murda wobbled all the way down the hall. Instantly she remembered she had never walked in heels, and she wanted to kick her own ass for buying the four-inch wedges. "Here I come," she hollered, trying to make it down the hallway. After tripping over herself a few times while holding the wall for balance, she finally made it.

"Sysco, what are you doing here?" She frowned after swinging the door open to see him standing there in all-black Versace from head to toe. The picture on his shirt and straps on his shoes matched the gold chain around his neck. The medallion was a small replica of Earth.

"Expecting someone else?" Sysco licked his lips and picked an imaginary piece of lint off his shirt, causing Murda's leg to shake. She didn't know why, but his presence made her feel a certain way. Maybe it was his persona, or maybe it was his dope-boy swag. Whatever it was had Murda's full attention.

"I thought Payro was coming, that's all," she replied honestly.

"Well, thanks to you, I didn't have a date for the night." Sysco laughed at the thought of Koko sitting at home with her face covered with a bag of frozen vegetables. Luckily for Murda, she wasn't his girlfriend, or he would've had to check her for that.

"Your girl was getting reckless, so I had to let her know." Murda made no apologies for what she'd done.

"Fair enough." Sysco nodded with his hands raised in the air as a peace indicator. "I'm here because I figured you was flying solo too, and I thought we could ride together."

"I'm a charity case now?" Murda frowned. "How do you know my nigga ain't waiting for me downstairs?"

"I don't know that, but it doesn't even matter."

"And why is that?" Murda asked with a smile.

"Why go with a lame when you can go with a boss?" Sysco extended his arm, and Murda blushed.

"I guess you've got a point." Murda linked her arm with his, then stopped. "Hold up a sec." Quickly she let his arm go, then slipped out of her heels and grabbed a pair of black and navy Jordans from the closet. Murda knew she would look silly wearing gym shoes with a dress to the club, but she didn't care. There was no way she was about to embarrass herself by falling on her face.

Sysco didn't say anything because he dug her style. Murda was who she was no matter what anybody thought, and he was learning to like that about her.

Moments after telling the kids she was leaving, Murda
locked the door, and the duo headed down the hall. In
silence, she tried to calm the nervous flutters in her
stomach while Sysco pretended not to notice the way
her ass jiggled from behind. Baby girl was blessed with
crazy curves in all the right places. "Damn," Sysco mumbled. It was going to be difficult to keep their relationship
strictly business, but he knew crossing the line wasn't
even an option.

Chapter Fourteen

As soon as Sysco and Murda stepped out of the building, all eyes were on them. A few people whistled in their direction, and a few bystanders smacked their lips hatefully. Murda wanted to turn around and address the lip smackers but decided not to let her temper rear its ugly head and ruin the moment. "I'm excited about tonight," she admitted.

"It's just a little something, but I wanted to do right by you and welcome you properly to the squad." He stopped walking.

"Where is your car?" Murda scanned the parking lot.

"I'm not driving tonight." Sysco finished his sentence just as the custom stretch black Denali pulled up in front of them. It was tricked out with neon blue lights beneath the car and triple black tint.

"I can't believe you rented this for just us." Murda smiled from ear to ear. She was in awe that someone would go all out for her like this.

"I told you that I wanted to do right by you, ma." Sys led Murda toward the limo and waited for the driver to open their door. Inside, Murda wanted to scream. Not only was the interior just as custom as the outside, but there was also a bottle of champagne on ice. Her emotions for Sysco were all over the place, yet she remained cool.

The limo hadn't even pulled off before Sysco poured both of them a glass of champagne. Murda was too young to drink, but that didn't stop her from taking a sip.

Honestly, she didn't like the taste of whatever it was, but she continued to sip like it was going out of style.

"Slow down, ma." With a smile, he reached for the glass.

"Sorry, I just wanted to get a nice buzz before we get to the club." Murda stopped drinking and wiped her mouth. She felt silly.

"Having a buzz is cool and all, but you never want to be fucked up in public. Your eyes, ears, and mind need to be alert. Shit can pop off within minutes. You always have to be prepared! Always have your neck on the swivel." Sysco took the time to school his young hitter. She was only a pup now, but one day she would be a full-grown pit bull. He wanted her to know the game in and out. He wanted her to be the best!

"You're right." Murda set the champagne flute down and relaxed on the butter-soft seat. Knowing the night was going to be a long one, Sysco sat back and relaxed as well.

During the ride, he used the opportunity to get in her head and see where her mind was after she had been active in the game for a week now. Some people did it for the street credibility and respect. Most people did it for a few dollars to line their pockets. However, Murda wanted it all!

"I want to give my siblings and their kids something nobody ever gave me," Murda spat.

"And what's that?" Sysco asked while sipping slowly from his cup.

"A motherfucking chance to live life the way God intended for us to live." Murda wasn't big on religion, but she definitely believed in God. She had faith that He was going to remove her family from poverty.

Sysco didn't have a reply. Instead, he speechlessly admired her ambition. Unbeknownst to her, every time they talked, she motivated him to want more and be better at what he did. Murda was the spark he needed to refuel his passion for the game.

By the time the limo pulled up to Club Hennessey, he was more intrigued and impressed with her. Not only was she cold-blooded in the streets, baby girl was beautiful and smart, which was a deadly combination in his book. He believed in her and knew one day she was going to be unstoppable.

"Are you ready?" Murda said when the driver put the limo in park.

"Just a second." Sys reached beneath his shirt and checked his gun. He never left home without it. Murda wanted to show him that she had hers, too. Quickly she reached into her bra to retrieve the new .38 Payro had gotten her and began to check it out. Sysco grinned. Murda was a woman after his own heart, and she didn't even know it.

Hand in hand, they walked up to the door of Club Hennessey. There was a man standing there with a security shirt on. His job was to card everyone who came through the door and frisk them for weapons. However, instead of doing either, he dapped Sysco and held the door open for the couple to enter.

Inside, the club was banging, and everyone was turned up to the max. Although it was early, the place was packed from wall to wall. "This is the Friday night spot! My supplier owns this place," Sysco hollered over the music.

"Really? I want to own something like this one day." Murda took a minute to admire the structure. She liked the way it was decorated with white and silver.

"One day, you will own something twice as good as this, baby girl. The world is yours. Never forget that." Sysco pointed down at the medallion on his chain. "I always wear this to remind me."

Before Sysco and Murda could even make it past the dance floor, their names were being called. Murda looked over to see some of her crew, as well as a few unfamiliar faces. Seemingly everyone was in awe when Murda sashayed up the stairs to the party booth overlooking the club. They couldn't believe she'd cleaned up so well, but they didn't voice their surprise for fear of offending her.

"What's up, Murda? You look nice." Payro was the first to walk up and hug her. Although he was there with a date, he couldn't help but be jealous that she was there with his cousin.

"Thanks, Payro. You look nice as well," Murda said while admiring the casual denim Armani Exchange outfit he was wearing. Payro always dressed to impress.

"Hey, Murda." Lonnie nodded from his seat.

"What's up, Murda?" P-dot said after stepping into Murda and Payro's conversation. "You looking real nice." Although the two enemies had been civil lately, this was the first time P-dot had said anything to her since the day he pulled the gun. Murda was caught off guard by the nice gesture and suspicious, but still, she thanked him.

"Let me get you a drink," Payro said. However, he was a little too late. Sysco had already poured Murda a small cup of Cîroc from one of the bottles on the table and handed it to her. Inwardly, Payro felt some type of way that they were together, but he didn't let on.

"I need everybody to fill your cups, and let's toast the lady of the motherfucking hour." Sysco raised his cup. It took only sixty seconds for everyone in the booth to fill up then raise their glasses as well. "She's a girl who demands respect and doesn't take no for an answer. She always follows through on her word and can out-hustle any hustler! She's the first female in the Detroit City Mafia, and she's here to stay. To Murda, my motherfucking nigga, salute!" Sysco hollered.

"Salute!" half the crowd replied.

"To Murda!" the other half said. Remembering what Sysco said in the limo, Murda took only small sips from her cup, although she wanted to drink more. This drink tasted much better than the champagne. Yet and still, she sipped slowly while surveying the scene.

As the party went on, Murda took the time to remember all the faces and names that came up to the booth and conversed with various members of the crew. Her goal was to become familiar with people who mattered. One face in particular had caught her eye twice that night. His name was Andres, a Mexican American man with a beautiful face, thick black eyebrows, and tattoos on his neck and hands. Though he was dressed in a blue suit and black dress shirt, Murda could tell his body was probably covered in art.

"Who is this?" Andres smiled as he took Murda in with his eyes.

"This is the first lady of Detroit City Mafia." Sysco was proud to introduce the new leading lady.

Andres grabbed Murda's hand and kissed it.

She smiled nervously. "Who are you?" Murdonna had a feeling that he was the plug, but she wanted him to say it.

"This is Andres, the club owner." Sysco wasn't a fool. There was no way he'd use the word "supplier" in a club full of people.

"Andres, I love your establishment."

"I appreciate your compliment. It was a pleasure meeting you." Andres bowed graciously before continuing his chat with Sysco. Murdonna couldn't tell what they were conversing about, but she knew somehow, someway she would need to make her own connection with Andres and get on his good side.

Three hours in and the crowd in the booth had dispersed. Most of the men were walking around the club looking for females to spit game to. Some of them were at the bar ordering more drinks. Sysco was over at another booth, conversing with a group of friends, and Payro was probably in the bathroom. Murda was alone until Shana stepped into the booth and took a seat. By instinct, Murda grabbed the Cîroc bottle and looked at her with a glare that made the hair on Shana's neck rise.

"Murdonna, I ain't got no beef." Shana raised her hands in surrender. "I was coming over to apologize for the little thing that happened earlier."

"Bitch, save your breath. Your apology is no good here." Murda placed the bottle back on the table and dismissed Shana with a wave of her hand. Like a wounded dog, Shana walked away with her tail tucked between her legs.

"Damn, you are a trip." Payro smiled after reentering the booth as Shana exited.

"I don't have room for fake friends or false admirers." Murda smacked her lips. "It's funny the bitch wants to apologize now. But where was her kindness this morning?"

"I completely understand." Payro had heard about the incident at Odessa's. "You look gorgeous, though," he said, completely switching the subject. He'd been wanting some alone time from the moment she'd walked in with Sysco.

"Thanks," Murda said nonchalantly. Payro was full of bullshit, too. A few days ago, he played her like she was a Raggedy Ann doll. Now that she was cleaned up and wearing a tight dress, he thought she was gorgeous.

"I was thinking, maybe we can—" Payro was cut off by the yelling of a drunk man passing by.

"Fuck every DCM nigga in this bitch! My .44 will make sure all y'all kids don't grow!" the man hollered.

Immediately Murda frowned because her gut told her something was about to go down.

"Chill, shorty, he's just drunk. Shit like this happens all the time." Payro could see that look in Murda's eye. He knew she was ready to take action.

"Fuck DCM!" the man hollered again while waving his middle finger.

Murda looked around to see if anybody else had taken issue with the drunk, but it appeared she was the only one feeling uneasy. She didn't know if it was because everyone else was too drunk to notice, or if they couldn't hear him. Either way, her vibe for the night had been killed. She didn't want to ruin it for everyone else by calling attention to the issue, so she decided to excuse herself and take a trip to the ladies' room. Payro offered to walk her over to the bathroom, but she declined.

The club was even more crowded now than it had been when they first got there. Therefore, it took her nearly twelve minutes to squeeze through the packed dance floor and get to the back where the bathroom was. Luckily the line wasn't too bad. As Murda held her spot, she couldn't help but overhear a conversation between the two girls in front of her.

"Juice and them got that whack shit!" the light-skinned plus-sized girl said to her friend. "We took that shit nearly an hour ago, and I'm still not feeling it."

"I was thinking the same thing, Shavonne. I'm going to stop fuckin' with them," the brown-skinned girl replied as the line moved up. "The only thing is, Juice and them are the only niggas on West Grand pushing that shit."

"True," Shavonne replied. "But I'm still done fucking with them. They charge top dollar for these whack-ass bumps, and I'm sick of it. Hell, I would rather drive to the PJs and cop my shit. I heard the DCM got that work!"

"I ain't fucking with the projects. Them niggas crazy."
The brown-skinned girl shook her head. "I heard you
have to know someone who lives there just to get a pass
to go in, and I don't know nobody, so I'll stay my black
ass on West Grand," she said just as her turn came to use
the restroom.

Murda wanted to jump in and plug her business right
then and there but decided against it. Instead, she waited
for her turn to use the restroom and then quickly headed
back to the crew.

Murda couldn't wait to suggest to Sysco that they
should expand their business to West Grand Boulevard
and perform a hostile takeover. However, as she approached their booth, there seemed to be some sort of
altercation going on between Sysco and another man.

"Get your drunk ass on, my nigga!" Sysco barked at the
drunk man who was shouting when she left.

"You bumped into me, nigga," the intoxicated man
slurred. "Better watch where the fuck you going next
time!" he spat.

"You don't even want them types of problems, so I
suggest you shut the fuck up and keep on walking," Sysco
said in a calm tone. He wasn't trying to peel nobody's
shit on such a special night, but it was what it was. For
a second, the drunken man stood there in silence before
deciding to walk away.

"What happened? You good?" Murda asked Sysco, who
was standing down on the floor in front of their section.

"I'm a hundred percent. Are you enjoying yourself?"
Sys completely dismissed the drunk from his mind. "I
noticed you ducked off. Is everything okay?"

"I'm good." Murda smiled. For a brief moment, their
eyes connected, but the moment didn't get the opportunity to go any further.

"Come on, y'all, let's hit this dance floor up one time."
Payro and his date pulled them toward the crowd.

As soon as they joined the dancers on the floor, the DJ switched the pace up from fast to slow. Something by Trey Songz was now playing, and everybody was slow grinding. Murda felt awkward at first and started to turn back. However, the minute Sysco pulled her into his arms, she relaxed and seized the moment by laying her head on his chest. Slowly they rocked from side to side in silence.

For just a moment she pretended he was hers, and he did the same. It felt good to be close to someone. Murda hadn't been in a relationship since the tenth grade. Her boyfriend back then was a kid named Chris Johnson. He was her first love and the only sexual partner she'd ever had. Chris was from the projects, too, and his mother also struggled with addiction. Their lives were so similar it was scary. Chris was supposed to be Murda's husband and save her from the ghetto. However, after the last time his mother got herself clean, she packed up the family and moved to Alabama. It had been two years since Murda had seen or heard from Chris. She often prayed that he was doing well.

"I'm having a good time with you. It's a shame the night has to come to an end." Murda looked up at Sysco with lowered eyes.

"We'll do it again sometime," he replied as the song ended. "Come on, let's get out of here." Sysco never believed in closing the club down. He always left early to ensure he was nowhere around when the parking lot shenanigans ensued.

As soon as he turned around, he stopped suddenly and put his hands up. Murda knew something wasn't right, but she couldn't see what was in front of him. The dance floor was entirely too packed. Thinking fast, she ducked beneath his arms. That's when she saw the same drunk man standing there with a gun pointed at Sysco. Sysco tried to reach beneath his shirt, but the gunman blocked the play by pressing his gun straight into Sysco's chest. The gunman was saying something, but Murda couldn't hear it over the music. It didn't matter, though, because she was about to get the drop on his ass.

Within an instant, she reached into her bra then slid in between Sysco and the assailant. Her swift motion had caught both men off guard. However, by the time the gunman got his bearings, it was too late! Murda had fired all six shots at point-blank range into his stomach and chest, then watched him fall.

Chapter Fifteen

Only those people in close proximity heard the shots. However, once those people started screaming and running, everybody else followed suit. Sysco grabbed Murda's hand and fled the scene too. Payro left his date standing there and was hot on their trail all the way to the waiting limo sitting curbside. None of them bothered waiting for the driver to get out and open their doors. After hopping inside and closing the door, they all yelled for his ass to get them out of there immediately.

"What the fuck was that?" Payro snapped. "You got a fucking problem!" Although he was dancing with his own date, he'd been watching Murda like a hawk. He saw her when she pulled the trigger.

"She saved my fucking life, that's what that was!" Sysco hollered. "I can't believe this nigga got the drop on me in a club filled with my own crew." Sysco was beyond pissed. The people he'd put in position to protect him were slacking. "If Murda hadn't been there, it would have been my blood shed tonight, not his!" The thought of death barely missing his ass had him shaken. "How the fuck you see what Murda did but didn't see the bitch-ass nigga put a pistol to my chest?"

Payro had seen the gunman but decided to let the shit play out. If Sysco had died tonight in the club, he would've taken over DCM. Since Sysco had lived, he would swear on his grandmother's life that he never saw shit coming. Either way, it was what it was.

"Oh, you quiet now?" Sysco barked, knowing that his cotton-soft cousin was full of shit.

Payro didn't have an answer. Therefore, he changed the subject. "Murda, give me the burner. I'll toss it."

"Nah, my nigga, the only thing being tossed tonight is you." Sysco banged on the privacy window, and the driver rolled it down. "Stop this bitch and let this nigga get the fuck out!"

"You gon' just put me out?" By the look on his face, Payro appeared to be in complete shock.

"You put yourself out for not doing your fucking job!" Sysco was smoking hot. Everyone could see the steam coming from his head.

Payro was highly irritated but decided not to get further on Sysco's bad side. Therefore, he exited the limo and walked back toward the club to look for a ride home.

The remainder of the ride back to the projects was silent for Murdonna and Sysco. She nervously pondered having just committed a murder in a club full of people. She couldn't believe she'd pulled the trigger again and was beginning to think this was a newfound habit.

Sysco was doing some reevaluating of the members of his crew. When shit like this happened, you were forced to take a hard look at the people around you. Sysco didn't say a word as he stared out the window, deep in thought.

Murdonna broke the silence. "What if someone identified me? What if the man survived the shooting and gave my description to the police?"

"You're going to be fine, ma," was all Sysco could offer as he tried to process things himself. Up until now, all he'd had were small squabbles with niggas. He'd never really been in a situation where someone would actually make an attempt on his life.

A million thoughts ran through Murdonna's mind just as the limo pulled back in front of her building. Without a word, she grabbed her clutch and slid toward the door. She wasn't even going to say goodbye. However, before she could reach for the handle, Sysco grabbed her hand tight then pulled her close. "Murda, I don't know what to say." He looked through her eyes into her soul. "I ain't never had nobody have my back the way you did tonight."

"We're supposed to look out for one another. I only did what I thought was necessary," Murda replied honestly. Although she regretted pulling the trigger, she knew she would do it again if need be. That was just the way her loyalty was set up.

"You don't know what that means to me." Sysco pulled her face in toward his and pressed his lips against hers. Murda didn't resist, so he continued. "The shit you did tonight speaks volumes. For that, you'll forever have my heart."

"You'll forever be in mine too," Murda admitted. She would never forget the shoes and clothes he bought for her when she didn't have anything. Sometimes it was the little things that meant so much.

"I want you to be my girl, but we can't cross that line." Sysco pulled Murda in again and passionately kissed her lips.

"Then let's not." With a nod of understanding, Murda pulled back. As much as she wanted to know what Sysco felt like inside of her, she wasn't ready to complicate their arrangement. Right now, he was her only drug connect. She didn't want to cut off her supply if things went sideways between them.

"But I want you," Sysco found himself saying as if he were a thirsty nigga. He had never begged for anything in his life, but Murda was something special.

"I want you too, but you and I won't work. What will everybody think?" Murda couldn't believe she was being so strong, especially when she felt so weak.

"Fuck what everybody thinks. Murda, I need you." Sysco was done talking. In one swift motion, he began kissing and caressing Murda's body. His dick was at full erection, and so were her nipples. She wanted to ask him to stop, but the shit felt too damn good. Sysco's massive hands palmed her ass like a Spalding basketball. He rubbed and massaged her shit until her panties practically melted off. Murda was ready to go all the way.

Within seconds her dress was off, and so were his pants. Sysco removed his shirt, then laid Murda down on the side seat. He didn't have much space, but that didn't stop him from going to work on her body. First, he left a trail of kisses from her neck down to her toes. Then he used his tongue to part her pussy lips like the Red Sea. Murda's vagina was so wet the nigga almost drowned. After pleasing her for several minutes, he positioned himself on top of her and slid his nine-inch dick right into her sweet spot. Murda was so caught up in the moment that she forgot to do a condom check. However, once she realized he was raw dogging her, she said a quick prayer that he was clean and continued to enjoy the moment.

For nearly twenty-five minutes, Sysco fucked Murda every which way but in the ass. The chemistry between their bodies was surreal. It was as if his penis were made just for her. She came six times before he had one big explosion. When he finally did climax, Sysco fell over onto his back. Sweat poured down his body as he panted for dear life. Murda was the best he'd ever had.

"Are you clean?" Murda asked quietly. Now that the fun was over, reality set in.

"Hell yeah, I'm clean. What about you?" Sysco watched her scramble to get her clothes on.

"Yeah, I'm good." She looked at the floor.

"What's wrong? I know I wasn't that bad, was I?" Sysco frowned. This wasn't usually the reaction he got after sex.

"You were great." Murda looked up at him.

"What's wrong, then?" Using his T-shirt, Sysco wiped sweat from his face.

"I just want to know what's next." Murda slid the dress back over her head. "Was I just a fuck?"

"I told you. You will forever have my heart." Sysco wasn't lying when he said that.

"What about Koko?" Murda stopped dressing to look at him.

"Koko is Koko." Sysco shrugged.

"Is she your girl?" Murda asked.

"Nah, she ain't my girl, ma." Sysco shook his head, then paused. "Honestly, I'm not quite ready for a relationship with anybody. But this thing we have, whatever it is, it's real." Sysco didn't want Murda to think he was ready to settle down and wife her up, so he kept it 100 percent. "Murda, I fuck with you the long way, and I want to see where this relationship can go, but I'm not looking for love tonight."

"That's cool. Me either." With a smile, Murda lied. Her feelings were hurt because she'd been searching for love since she fell from between her mother's legs. Her father wasn't around to love her, her mother was a piece of shit, and she didn't have any other family besides her brother and sister, who naturally only loved her because they had to.

"Good night, Sysco." Without another word, Murda collected her clutch and stepped from the limousine. She felt deflated, but she wouldn't be defeated. Murda was used to getting over things easily, and this would be no different.

Sysco rolled down the window. "Hey, Murda."

"Yeah." She stopped.

"You left your piece on the seat. Don't worry. I'll handle it, all right?" Sysco whispered.

"Thanks. I appreciate that," Murda replied without turning around. Her mind was not at all on the gun she'd left behind. Instead, she focused on holding her head high as she walked away from the limo.

Chapter Sixteen

Days and then weeks went by after the club incident. Murda hadn't seen Sysco or Payro since that night. It felt strange that both of them had gone missing in action, but Murda wasn't pressed. She decided the night she left Sysco in the limo to never mix her hustle with pleasure again. Therefore, she went on with business as usual. She hustled from sun up until sundown, just as she'd done before, until her supply went dry. Without anything to sell, she went in search of product.

"What's up, Murda?" Lonnie nodded when she stepped from her building. "Where you headed to this early in the morning?" He was sitting on a green electric box, smoking a cigarette.

"I'm doing the same shit I do every day. I'm going to get some money." Murda planned to beat the pavement until her feet got tired. "I'm out of product, though. Do you know where I can cop some?"

"Shit, we all get our work from Sysco." Lonnie shook his head. "In the meantime, everybody decided to close up shop until we hear from him or Payro."

"What?" Murda smacked her lips. "That's stupid," she added, wondering if they knew how much money they would be losing.

"It ain't like we can just pull up on the nigga's plug. We can't go cop from no other organizations either. We're all out of options."

"Man, listen," Murda huffed. "Who said we can't pull up on the plug?" The wheels had already started turning in Murdonna's head. She knew where she was headed.

"I don't make the rules, my nigga. I just abide by them," Lonnie said while flicking the butt of his cigarette to the ground.

"Well, I'm not sitting on my hands waiting to hear from no fucking body." Murda shook her head. She couldn't believe nobody but her was out here trying to hustle. There was no way in hell she could just sit around waiting for orders like these fools. It didn't matter, though, because Murda planned to capitalize on their fuckup.

"I hear you." Lonnie smiled. He liked Murda. She had mad determination. But Lonnie had been around long enough to know that having too much ambition could get you killed. "Do you." Knowing the young, naive girl standing before him wasn't going to last in the game if she kept moving the way she was, all he could do was move out of the way and let her handle her business.

"All right, I'll holler at you later." With a Nike book bag on her back, Murdonna started down the block, headed for the bus stop. While Lonnie and the other niggas in the crew waited around with their dicks in their hands, she decided to make her own moves. She didn't give a fuck about rules and regulations. She needed to keep food on the table.

After her bus had arrived at her stop, Murdonna hopped off and walked four blocks to Club Hennessey. She knew going to the club midday without an invite could prove to be the wrong move, but she didn't care. Lightly she knocked for several moments until the door of the club opened.

"May I help you?" a brown-skinned woman asked after cracking the door.

"My name is Murda. I'm looking for Andres. Is he in?" Murda could sense the woman's hesitation, so she continued. "Tell him that Sysco sent me."

At the mention of a name she was familiar with, the young lady invited Murda in and then asked her to take a seat at the bar. Murda did as she was told and quietly took in the scene. In the morning, with no music or partygoers, the place was less exciting. The mirrors didn't seem to glisten, the lights were not as vibrant, and the place smelled of stale cigarettes.

After keeping herself company for almost ten minutes, Andres finally emerged from the back of the club. Even this early in the morning, he was dressed to the nines in a custom Italian suit.

"*Que puedo hacer por ti?*" He spoke in Spanish, asking what he could do for her. This was the way he tested everyone's knowledge of his language. If they responded, then he knew they were fluent. If they didn't, then he knew he could speak it around them to say things he didn't want them to know.

"*Vine a hablar de negocios.*" Murda had taken Spanish 1 and 2 in high school. Therefore, she knew a little something.

"Okay, what business did you come to talk about?" Making himself more comfortable, Andres took a seat beside her.

Murda proceeded to tell Andres that Sysco and Payro had left without saying a word to the crew, and without them, there was no product. Since Sysco had told her that Andres was his plug, she figured she'd come to the horse and see if she could get some work to tide her over. She didn't have the money up-front that Andres would probably need to pay for the load, so she presented an offer to give him the majority of her profits on the back end if he fronted her the brick.

For several seconds, Andres stared at the girl intently before speaking. He typically didn't do business with anyone as low as she was on the totem pole, but he saw something in her. There was fire in her eyes and passion in her voice. She reminded him of himself when he first entered the game almost twenty years ago. "Murda, if I did decide to work with you, do you think that Sysco would have a problem with that?" Andres knew that if she cared what Sysco thought, then she was in the wrong line of work. The dope game was a dog-eat-dog situation, nothing more, nothing less.

"Honestly, Andres, I can't let what he thinks get in the way of making money. The projects are dry right now. There is room here for opportunity." Murdonna felt like she was on a job interview.

"Okay." He nodded after careful consideration. "I will bless you with a brick on consignment, but there is one condition."

"Shoot."

"You must no longer work for Sysco, but become Sysco's competition. You need to expand your business far beyond the projects." Andres liked competition because he knew it made him richer. If he put Murda against Sysco, the only real winner in the end would be him.

Carefully Murda considered the proposition. On one hand, she hated to bite the hand that had put her on, but on the other hand, it was what it was. She knew if Sysco was given the same opportunity, he'd probably take it. Without remorse, she stuck out her hand and sealed the deal.

Chapter Seventeen

After receiving the brick from Andres, Murdonna went straight home. While Mya and Donzell were at school, she mixed the pack just as Payro had taught her and immediately got to work. Since everyone else in the projects was on break or whatever, Murda's sales skyrocketed. Within two weeks, she was able to sell enough product to save some money and use the rest to make two investments.

Her first investment was a 2008 white Chrysler Sebring. Although it wasn't the flyest whip on the road, it was hers, and that was all that mattered. She'd purchased the used car from a small car lot for $6,875. Though she didn't have a valid driver's license, she was able to slide the dealer an extra $300 to overlook that minor detail, and she promised to get one within the month. Murdonna loved being able to come and go as she pleased. Mya and Donzell loved it too. They thought they were big-time now because most of their friends didn't have cars. Murda wanted to tell them the best was yet to come, but she decided to just show them.

Her second investment had come in the form of rental property. After deciding that she was tired of hustling in the projects, she decided it was time to open up shop elsewhere. Although the money was good where she was, she knew it could be much better if she obtained her own crew and covered a larger territory. She wasn't knocking Payro's or Sysco's hustles, but she wanted more out of life than to just flip birds within a ten-mile radius. The only problem was that Murda had never ventured out of her hood. She didn't know where to go, but then she remembered the girls from the club talking about West Grand Boulevard. It was exactly where she headed to scope out a new location.

By the start of the following week, Murda had responded to an ad in the paper renting part of a two-family flat on Clairmont Street for $450. The price point was perfect, and after scoping the location, Murdonna could practically see the dollar signs dancing on those blocks. She'd met with the owner, Mr. George, to check out the place and was sold. It wasn't a mansion, but it was smack dab in the middle of a very promising area. That same day, she gave him a security deposit and the first and last months' rent.

"Here is your key. Remember, the rent is due by the fifth," Mr. George said as they stood on the front porch. He was an older bald man with a gray beard.

"Thank you, sir." Murda was super excited to be renting the small piece of property. Although it wasn't anything spectacular, she was just glad to see a change of scenery. Inwardly, she pondered moving Mya and Donzell to the new spot instead of using it for a trap. She knew they would be thrilled to leave the projects, but Murda wanted their next house to be special. She also wanted to own it.

"This used to be my sister's house, so be sure to take care of it," Mr. George requested.

"Yes, sir." Murda smiled, feeling accomplished. "How is the neighborhood?" She could tell right away that the block had seen better days, but she just wanted to make small talk with the old head.

"You might not believe this, but back in the day, the Temptations and the Supremes ran all up and down these very streets." Mr. George pointed toward a crowd of young boys huddled on the corner using spray paint to cover the sidewalk. "These hoodlums done took over." He shook his head vigorously. "Speaking of which, let me get the hell out of here before I have to pull off my belt and whoop someone's ass." Mr. George added before making a beeline for his car, "See you next month on the fifth."

Murda waved goodbye then turned to head inside. That's when she was startled by the light-skinned, nappy-headed young boy standing behind her. He was dressed in a dingy white beater and a pair of cut-up jeans. "What's up?" he asked while picking his large, linty afro. His bottom lip was split down the middle.

"You live upstairs, right? Murda asked after remembering she'd seen him on the balcony when she initially came to scope out the place.

"Yeah." He nodded while studying Murda with his eyes. He was trying to get a read on his new neighbor.

"What's your name?" she asked warmly, wanting to make friends with someone she'd ultimately be sharing a roof with.

"You can call me Duck." The young boy in need of a bath smiled back. He was a little ripe under the arms, and his teeth had some butter on them, but Murda smiled again and extended her hand. Although she didn't know much about Duck, she knew enough to never judge a book by its cover. Hell, not long ago, she was dusty too. If nothing else, this drew her closer to him. She wanted to know his story.

"Duck, I'm Murda."

"Nice to meet you, Murda." Duck took her hand and shook it. "Why do they call you that? You must've killed a nigga, huh?" Duck laughed, and Murda did too. She didn't know how else to respond, so she didn't.

"Tell me, why do they call you Duck?"

"Shit, when niggas in the hood see me coming, they duck! They know I don't fuck around." He smiled. He was proud of his reputation. Though he wasn't the biggest or baddest boy in the hood, he was about that action. All his life, he'd had to fight and get niggas off of him.

"I like that." Murda nodded, impressed by what she was hearing. "Who do you live with upstairs?" Murda needed to know what type of neighbors she was dealing with. Before her hustle could get underway, she had to know if they were cop callers.

"I live with my moms and her boyfriend." Duck smacked his lips.

"How old are you?"

"I'm old enough, baby. What's good?" Duck licked his dry lips and chuckled. "I'm just playing. I'm sixteen. How old are you?"

"I'm seventeen." As Murda entered the house, she nodded for Duck to come in. The place was empty, but there were two crates in the middle of the floor. Both Duck and Murda took a seat and finished chopping it up.

"I'm surprised Mr. George let you rent this place. He usually only rents to tenants over the age of twenty-one." Duck looked around at the burgundy and green walls left by the previous tenant and wondered what Murda would do with the place.

"Between you and me, I told him I was twenty-five," Murda admitted. Once she'd given him the first and last months' rent and the deposit in cash, he didn't ask her any more questions or for identification.

"You got any kids?" Duck made himself more comfortable. He liked his new neighbor and felt comfortable in her presence. There was something about how she talked to him and made eye contact with him that made him feel like she wasn't looking down on him like everybody else.

"Nope, no kids, but I do have a little sister and a little brother." Murda thought of her siblings, who were currently in school, and then she frowned. "Hey, come to think of it, why aren't you in school?"

"Those textbooks can't teach me shit that I can't learn on these streets," Duck spat. He'd dropped out of school nearly a year ago after being suspended ten times in two months for fighting. It wasn't his fault, though. Duck was only sticking up for himself when people teased and taunted him about his home life. It was a sensitive subject, and the only way he knew how to deal with it was with his hands.

"Boy, don't repeat that shit to nobody else." Murda smacked her lips. "Knowledge is power. Don't you ever forget that."

"Okay, I hear you, but tell me one time you've used trigonometry since you graduated," Duck quizzed, and when she didn't respond, he continued. "What about calculus or chemistry?"

Murda wanted to tell him that she wasn't supposed to graduate until the end of this academic year but decided not to. How could she be preaching to him about education when she too had given up on her own?

"Your mama just let you drop out like that?" Murda questioned.

"My mama doesn't give a fuck about nothing I do as long as I stay the fuck out of her way." Duck looked down at the floor, embarrassed. "My mother is an alcoholic." This was the first time he'd discussed his mother's habit with anyone. Not even the school social worker could get Duck to expose his mother, though everyone knew she had a drinking problem.

"My mother was a junkie. Trust me, I know the struggle." Murda placed her hand on Duck's shoulder. She wanted him to know that she was no better than he was.

"You said *was*. Did she die?" Duck looked at Murda, who was now staring at the floor the same way he had been seconds ago.

"Yeah, she did," Murda replied solemnly. She hadn't thought about Sheila in a while. Things had been going so well at home that she'd completely forgotten about her until now. Though it still bothered her that she didn't exactly know if her mother was dead or alive, it was easier to think of her as deceased rather than knowing that she willingly just up and left her children to fend for themselves in the cold streets of the ghetto.

"I'm sorry to hear that," Duck said genuinely, then stood to leave. He wanted to give Murda some privacy. However, before Duck could get to the front door, his stomach decided to start growling loudly.

The sound was eerily familiar to Murdonna. Instantly the hair on the back of her neck stood up. "Duck, what did you eat today?" She rose to her feet and walked over to him.

"I had—" He couldn't get it out fast enough.

"Don't you lie to me either." Murda knew that the sounds coming from this boy's stomach were a clear indication that he hadn't eaten in a while.

"My mom missed the appointment to reapply for assistance, so they cut our stamps off. She's going next week, though, to get them turned back on." Duck held his stomach, which growled again.

Without hesitation, Murda reached into her pocket and pulled out two $100 bills and a $50. "Take this, all of it." She practically threw it into his hand.

"No, I'm good, Murda. Your boy doesn't do handouts." Duck would rather starve than let someone think they could hold a favor over his head. Murda seemed cool and all, but he didn't know her like that. Growing up in the hood had taught him to be skeptical of all people, especially those handing out money for no reason. Everything thing came with a cost.

"I promise there is no catch here. I've been in your shoes, and I swear to God I wish someone had been there to help me. Please just take the money." Murda pushed the money farther his way.

"I'm straight, but thanks." Lightheaded and nauseated, Duck walked toward the door with his head held high.

Murda didn't want to force him to take her money, but she did begin thinking of a way she could help him.

Chapter Eighteen

For nearly a month, Murda traveled back and forth between the projects and her new spot on West Grand Boulevard. After making sure the kids were off to school, she cooked up her dope, bagged it, and placed it into a scent-proof duffle bag that was then covered by gym clothes. That way, if she were ever pulled over by the police and the canine unit was called, the scent of cocaine couldn't be detected.

Almost immediately, the new location proved to be a success. In fact, so many people began to come looking for her that she really didn't have to walk the block in search of customers. They liked what she was selling. But some people liked it a little too much, and things quickly began to escalate.

"You got that power pack, right?"

"I think you have the wrong person." Murdonna was standing on the curb in front of the corner store when she was approached by a peculiar character. He was a 30-something heavyset man wearing all black. At first, Murda thought he could've been police, but as the man continued, she realized he was just a customer trying to score. Be that as it may, she wasn't interested in selling to him. Maybe it was the way he fidgeted, or maybe it was the zoned-out look in his eyes, but whatever it was made Murda uneasy.

"Come on, bitch, you just sold to me yesterday."

"Who are you calling a bitch?" As an attempt to calm her nerves, Murda took a swig of the grape Faygo pop she was holding. Out of nowhere, the man slapped the bottle out of her hand. "What the fuck!"

Before she could completely process what was happening, he'd hit her in the face, causing her to fall. Once she was on the ground, the dude started stomping her. Murdonna felt defenseless as she lay on the ground, trying to protect her face.

"Not so tough now, huh?" The man delivered another kick to her shoulder before reaching down and roughly rummaging through the pockets of her jeans. "Oh, shit! You were holding out, little mama." With a grin as large as Texas, he took every last rock she had.

"Hey! I'm about to call the police!" a male patron exiting the corner store hollered from the doorway. His warning was enough to cease the attack and cause the assailant to run away with over $2,000 in product.

"Are you okay, miss? Let me call an ambulance for you." the Good Samaritan was an older gentleman dressed like a pastor or deacon of a church.

"I'm fine. Please don't call the police. That was my boyfriend. He didn't mean nothing." Standing, Murdonna tried to gather her composure. She'd lied because the last thing she needed was the police in her business. The Good Samaritan looked as if he still wanted to call for an ambulance in spite of her protest, but after Murdonna begged him again to leave it alone, he obliged.

Physically injured and emotionally wounded, Murdonna walked back to her car and left. She didn't bother returning to her spot, because she was done for the night. Her pride was hurt. She'd never been hit by a man, but she was grateful it wasn't worse. Her top lip was busted, and her left eye was swollen, but she was alive. Instead of throwing herself a pity party, she reminded herself that this was part of the game. *You win some, and you lose some.* Tonight she'd definitely taken an L.

After arriving home, Murdonna forced herself from the car, through the corridor, and up the pissy elevator. As she approached her apartment, she could hear soft chatter. Her siblings were going to go ape shit once they saw her face. With a deep breath, she opened the door and entered.

"What the fuck happened to your face?" Donzell was the first to speak. Mya didn't utter a word, but she did jump off the couch the minute Murda's face was visible.

"Chill, D. I'll be all right."

"Was it Koko and them?" Mya was slipping into the pair of house shoes she always left near the front door. "I'm about to go fuck that bitch up!" She was hot and ready. In her mind, if anybody came for one of her siblings, they came for them all. This was personal.

"Mya, it wasn't a girl." Murdonna's head was pounding. She spoke in a low tone while heading to the bathroom, where she kept the Tylenol.

"A nigga did that?" Both Donzell and Mya spoke in unison.

"Yes, but it's no big deal. He was just a disgruntled customer, that's all." Murda hadn't lied about that part. Without another word, she walked into the bathroom and closed the door behind her.

As she stared in the mirror, she was thankful that she looked much worse than she felt. With a little makeup and a pair of sunglasses, Murdonna would be back on the block tomorrow like nothing had happened. She knew that was how she had to be. She couldn't let anybody punk her and see her as weak. If word got out that she was a pussy, there was no retracting that. Murda had to take this ass whooping on the chin and use it as a teachable moment. Up until tonight, she'd been out on the streets with no protection, but soon that was all going to change.

Chapter Nineteen

The next morning was a Saturday, so her siblings didn't have school. Therefore, she couldn't proceed with business as usual, but she did need to make an important run. After breakfast, she'd given them each $100 and instructions to walk to the bus stop. Their mission was to head to the mall and do a little shopping.

Once they were out the door and on their way, Murdonna headed out behind them with her old, faithful Nike bookbag on her back. She was on a mission too.

The minute she pulled up in front of Club Hennessey, the door was opened as if she was expected. The young woman who greeted her last time was standing there with a smile. Murdonna was told to have a seat and wait.

Seconds later, Andres entered the room, dressed in a suit and looking as dapper as usual. "*Mi hija,* how are you today?" Andres lovingly referred to Murdonna as his daughter, but he didn't mean that literally. Though he wasn't sure why, he felt a strong connection with her.

"I've been better, but I won't complain." She removed the sunglasses from her face, and he began to inspect it as a father figure would. She pushed him away gently. "Please don't do that."

"I was only trying to evaluate the damage." Andres thought he was doing the right thing.

"If I were a man, would you care that much?" she asked with a straight face.

"Fair enough. Point taken." Andres knew that she was absolutely right. There was no way he'd ever feel compassionate about bruises on another man's face, not even his son's. Therefore, he took a seat on the chair beside her and asked why she was there, since her payment to him wasn't due for several more days.

"I need some protection, and I was wondering if you could put me in contact with someone about purchasing some heat?" There was no need to beat around the bush.

"This is not something a person would usually come to me about. You do know that, right?" Though he did have a gun connection, he was not the go-to guy for guns. Most people in the game just figured out shit like this on their own.

"I know, but I don't have anyone else to ask." With Sysco and Payro still missing in action, Murda was forced to rely on Andres, because she damn sure wouldn't dare ask anybody in the projects.

Andres pondered the situation for a second, then grabbed a napkin from the bar and a pen from his pocket and jotted down an address. He told her to show up and ask for Pete. Once she was alone with Pete, she should mention that she was a friend of his, and from there, it should be smooth sailing. "Now you know this is going to cost you real money. Pete don't do consignment," he teased.

"I got real money." While laughing, Murdonna removed the bag from her back and handed it to Andres, who looked inside and then back up at her in amazement. It was filled to the brim with money, all in various denominations.

Without a word, he grabbed a few bills and inspected their authenticity. Of course, he'd have an employee run the money through a money counter with counterfeit-bill detection, but for now, all looked good. He was very pleased. In one month, Murdonna alone had managed to sell nearly as much as Sysco and the DCM in the past two months. Andres hadn't said anything to anyone, but he'd been looking to appoint someone as the Midwest distributor very soon.

Though Murda had a lot to learn about the game, Andres could see her potential. She was the very thing his business needed to grow to new heights. For that reason alone, he'd secretly vowed to himself to provide anything and everything she needed from him, even if it would piss off the other buyers in his circle, including Sysco.

Chapter Twenty

As soon as she left Club Hennessey, Murdonna headed to the address on the napkin. The small two-story house on Outer Drive and Seven Mile looked so modest she doubled-checked the address to make sure she was at the right place. Casually she stepped from behind the wheel of her vehicle and headed up the driveway. After knocking lightly, she was met by a younger-looking Hispanic man rocking dreadlocks.

"What can I do for you?" He looked like he wasn't for the bullshit.

"I'm looking for Pete," she continued.

"Sweetheart, you got the wrong place." He started to close the door.

"Andres sent me," she spat just before it closed.

After a brief pause, the door reopened, and she was allowed to enter but then was asked to wait in the hallway. The Hispanic man walked up the stairs, and light chatter could be heard from upstairs. Seconds later, a white man with a bald head walked down the stairs toward Murdonna. He introduced himself as Pete and asked how he could be of assistance. Murdonna explained her situation and asked for a weapon that was powerful enough to stop an attack, yet small enough to be concealed on her body.

After careful consideration, Pete took Murdonna into his basement and introduced her to a .38 Special: a silver revolver with a black handle. "This snub nose is just what the doctor ordered." He handed it to her to become better acquainted. She liked the gun. It was substantial but not too heavy, and it fit perfectly beneath her clothes.

"Is it dirty?"

"Not even a little bit." Pete wanted to be offended, but he knew her question was legit. "Baby girl, I deal with only brand-new, authentic merchandise. The only thing I do is scratch off serial numbers," he explained. "I don't care what you do with your purchase, but I don't need shit being traced back to me, do you understand?"

Murdonna nodded her agreement and proceeded to complete the $600 gun sale. Typically, the Smith & Wesson revolver would only sell for around $365. However, Pete added a convenience fee to line his pockets because he knew this girl was too young to purchase a gun from a real store.

By nighttime, Murda was back on the grind with product in her bookbag and her new weapon in tow as she walked the new, still-unfamiliar territory block by block by her lonesome. Although she had her new safety measure locked and loaded on her hip, she wished at least one other person were with her. She wished there was someone else in her circle she could depend on. She wanted to ask one of the niggas from the Detroit City Mafia to come and get money with her, but she knew that without Sysco's or Payro's say-so, the rest of them niggas were too pussy to move, so she went on with business. Time was money, and neither waited for anybody.

The next morning Murda closed down shop a little early and headed to Walmart. She needed to grab a few things for the house, but mostly she wanted to grab some things for Duck. She knew he was probably going to be mad at her, but she didn't care. After purchasing a few groceries and personal hygiene essentials, Murda went back over to the spot and snuck the groceries onto the porch. Quickly she rang the doorbell, then made a mad dash to the car and pulled off.

When Duck got down to the door, there were ten bags of groceries and an envelope with $200 in it waiting for him. Although no one was in plain sight for Duck to see who it was, he knew only Murda would've blessed him like that. Though his pride wanted to leave the money and food on the porch, his stomach begged him to do otherwise.

The first three days back on the block were slow, but once again, they started showing up at her spot in droves. From there, it was on. The response was overwhelming at first, but Murda didn't complain one bit. She was excited that her product was receiving so much love, but what she didn't realize was that with so much love came just as much hate.

Boom. Boom. Loud banging on the side door woke Murda from her sleep on the couch. Instinctively she sat up and grabbed her gun. It was stashed between two cushions on the black sofa she'd had delivered yesterday. She was tired of sitting on the crate all night, so she decided to make the small purchase using a made-up name.

Boom. Boom. The knocking grew louder, which pissed Murda off. She had half a mind not to serve the impatient dopefiend on the other side. With an attitude, she went to the door and cracked it. "Stop banging on my shit before I fuck you up!"

"Bitch, you ain't gonna fuck shit up!" A heavyset man with blond plait braids forced his way into Murda's spot, holding her at gunpoint.

During her nap, she never heard him break the glass on the security door and unlock it. Therefore, she was completely caught off guard when he was able to barge into the house.

"Who the fuck sent you into my territory, bitch?" the man asked after tossing a blow to Murda's face that caused her to fall down. The gun flew from her hand and slid halfway across the floor.

"Nobody sent me," Murda mumbled, trying hard to stay focused, but her vision was now doubled. She was still healing from the altercation a few days ago. To say her shit was rocking with pain right now would've been an understatement.

"Stop lying!" The man sent a few body shots her way before lifting his leg and using his size-thirteen shoe to stomp Murda out. She balled up on the floor in pain, trying hard to block her face and stomach just like she had the last time. "I'm Juice, and this is my turf. Don't nobody move around this motherfucker unless I say so!"

"I don't know what you're talking about. Please stop!" Murda hollered for dear life.

"Everybody knows!" Juice went to raise his foot again but was shot right in the ankle.

Pow! The shot caused both Juice and Murda to look in the direction it had come from. Standing there by the door, with his back in the corner, was none other than Duck. He was on the top porch sneaking one of his mother's cigarettes when he'd spotted Juice approaching the house in all black. In the ghetto, it didn't take a rocket scientist to figure out what was about to go down. Duck didn't want to see anything bad happen to Murda, so he sprang into action and did what he thought was necessary.

"You shot me, little nigga?" Juice glared at him while trying to apply pressure to his ankle.

"Murda, get up." Without breaking his gaze, Duck walked over to Murda and helped her to her feet. The gun was still pointed at Juice.

"I'm going to kill you both!" Even with a bad foot, Juice tried to lunge for Duck, but he was stopped midway. Pow! Pow! Pow! Juice never made it across the room before the three shots ended his life. He collapsed right there on the living room floor with a large thud.

"Oh, shit!" Duck was paralyzed by what he saw. He'd never been so close to death before, and he'd definitely never pulled the trigger.

"Give me the gun." Though Murda was beat up pretty badly, she was relieved that Juice was the one dead and not her.

"I killed him. I can't believe I killed him." Duck began to freak out.

"Listen, you did what was necessary, and I thank you for that, okay?" Murda wiped the tears falling down Duck's face. "I would have been dead if it weren't for you." She wanted to reassure him that he'd done the right thing,

For several minutes, the room was silent. Duck stared at the dead body and tried to make sense of what he'd done. Though he knew it was Juice's life or Murda's, he tried hard to find the reason why he'd inserted himself in something that didn't have shit to do with him. That was when he thought of the other day when she'd blessed him with food and money. It had been a long time since anyone had looked out for him the way she had, and for that, he would always be loyal to her.

Murda finally broke the silence. "Duck, you did good. You saved my life."

"And you saved mine." Though still crying, he wiped his eyes, and then his shoulders relaxed. He was feeling a little better about the situation.

"I told you, bro, I've been where you are. I got you . . . always!" Although she was hurting pretty badly, Murda wrapped her arms around Duck, who chose that moment to begin bawling like a baby.

His tears weren't completely about the act he'd just committed. Instead, he cried for all the times he'd been dealt a bad hand in life. This world was a cold place, and he was brought up to be tough, but right now, in Murda's arms, he felt like a child who was finally made to feel safe.

In silence, Murda held him as if he were her own little brother. She knew his plight all too well and wanted him to know it was okay to let it out. For so long, Duck had bottled up his emotions about his mother. Little by little, the pent-up frustration was killing him internally. It felt good to find a kindred spirit he could vent to.

"Am I going to jail?" Duck finally pulled away from her embrace as the reality of what he'd just done set in.

"Ain't nobody going to jail. I'll handle it. I got you!" Murda assured Duck. She could see how scared he was.

"How can you be so sure?" Duck started nervously pacing the floor. "You never should have come over here without asking Juice first." From his window upstairs, he'd been watching Murda hustle and get money up and down Clairmont Street. He knew she was playing with fire! He also knew that one day Juice would check her for that shit, which was why he had vowed to always keep an ear open and his eyes wide just in case Murda needed help.

Duck was happy he had been able to protect his new friend, but standing there looking down at Juice's corpse made him begin to have second thoughts. "This nigga is the least of our problems." Duck knew there would be consequences coming as soon as Juice's crew realized he wasn't coming home. He was a big dog on the streets.

When niggas like him came up missing, everybody took notice.

"Just trust me, bro." Murda placed her hand on Duck's shoulder. "Even if I have to lie down for this, I got you." In all honesty, Murda had no plans on ever seeing the inside of a jail cell. Therefore, she silently prayed like hell she would be able to find Payro's boy Quan to clean up the mess before the house started stinking.

Chapter Twenty-one

It took nearly two hours for Murda to calm Duck down before sending him home. Once she was alone, she grabbed a few blankets from the closet and tossed them over Juice. There was nothing she could do about him at the moment, so she decided to lock up the spot and head back to the projects before her siblings got up for school.

On the drive home, she rode in silence. She couldn't believe how everything had jumped off, and she scolded herself for not doing better. Everyone had warned her about the rules of the game. Of course, she should've arranged a sit-down with Juice before barging in on his shit. However, Murda was the type of bitch who would rather ask forgiveness than permission. There was no use crying over spilled milk now, so she pushed the "should've, would've, could've" to the back of her mind and pressed on. What she had to do now was to use the hard lesson as a learning tool for the future. Besides, having Juice out of the way meant more business for her. All she needed to do was find Quan, and she'd be in the clear just as she had been with Tricks.

As soon as Murda pulled into the projects, three squad cars were exiting. This was nothing unusual. However, Murda still had an uneasy feeling. Quickly she flew down the street toward her building, where people were gathered outside. Nervously she threw the car in park and jumped out. Before she could approach the scene to ask someone what the hell was going on, she heard someone yell in her direction. "Ay, yo!"

Murda looked down the block to see Payro, and she uncontrollably exhaled a sigh of relief. She didn't know if she was happier to know that he was okay or that he could get her access to Quan. Hurriedly she walked toward him. "What's up? Where in the hell have you been?" Her excitement quickly became irritation at the realization that he'd just up and left without notice.

"Man, my bad. My grandmother passed away, so me and Sysco had to jet to Georgia the day after that shit jumped off at the club."

"I'm sorry to hear about your grandmother, but damn, y'all couldn't let anybody in on what was happening?"

"When shit jumps off with family, nobody is thinking about y'all niggas." Payro said it in a playful way, but he was serious. "What in the hell happened to you?" he asked while conspicuously staring at Murda in a weird way. Something had definitely changed about her since the last time he'd seen her. Although he noticed the bruises on her face and body, she seemed sexier and more confident than he remembered.

"I got into a little altercation. This ain't nothing," Murda replied nonchalantly. "I do need you to hit up your boy Quan for me, though." Murda was about business. There was no time to mince words and play nice when a dead man was on the floor of her trap house.

"I don't even think I want to know." Payro shook his head. "I'll get on that for you ASAP, but right now, Sysco just called a meeting with everybody. You pulled up just in time."

Murda wanted to tell Payro that she had gone solo and was no longer part of Detroit City Mafia, but she told herself that it may be a good idea to see what the competition had up their sleeves before dropping her bomb. "Do the police have anything to do with this meeting?" Murda asked instead.

"I don't know, but we're all about to find out." Payro shrugged his shoulders.

During the walk over to the townhouse, Payro used the time to tell her about his time in Georgia. He made jokes about his Southern family members and reenacted the way some of them had cut up at his grandmother's funeral, but Murdonna didn't say a word. She was too busy thinking about the situation with Juice and the impending beef that might ensue as a result. As a loner, she wouldn't have the manpower to go against anybody's crew. For the first time, she was beginning to regret her decision to split from the DCM.

Ten minutes later, the entire squad was gathered inside of Juan's sister's townhouse waiting for Sysco to arrive like he was the president or somebody. Murda stood near the back door behind the crowd. She liked being able to see the entire room. It made her more comfortable. A few minutes later, Jarvis and Sysco entered through the front. Sysco looked good as hell in a fresh Rock Revival fit and Detroit snapback. Murda was ready to fuck him right there on the spot but remembered the vow she'd made to herself.

Sysco gazed at everyone in the room, including Murda, before opening his mouth. "I've been out of town due to some family shit, and I apologize for not reaching out, but I needed that time to myself." Sysco cleared his throat. "However, I'm back now, and it's time to get shit clarified. Somebody better tell me how the fuck a nigga got the drop on me at the club?" Sysco was still fuming about the situation. "I would have been bodied if it weren't for Murda! What the fuck was y'all niggas doing?"

"Sys dog, I was in the bathroom," one man shouted.

"I was at the bar, big homie," another man responded.

"That shit is irrelevant. I put y'all niggas on the squad for a reason, and now I'm beginning to regret that." Sysco hit the wall. "My life was on the line, and none of you niggas stood tall the way Murda did, not even my own fucking family!" Sysco looked at Payro in disgust. The tension in the room was so thick you could cut that shit with a butcher knife. "In addition to that, I found out today that y'all closed down shop in my absence. What the fuck was that about?" Sysco was highly upset with his crew. If this had been a stress test to see how well their organization would perform under pressure, they would have failed miserably.

"After shit jumped off and y'all disappeared the next day, we didn't know what the fuck was what, so we made the decision to close down shop for a while and let the heat simmer down," Fred, a nigga who ran the Diggs housing projects, answered.

"I understand letting things die down for a few days, but who made the call to stop my money for over four motherfucking weeks?" Sysco was talking to Fred but looked at the whole group one by one.

"We all did," Fred replied nervously.

"So every last single one of y'all sat back and did nothing for over a month?" Sysco shook his head, thinking about how pathetic every last one of his soldiers was.

"Well, everybody except the golden child." Jarvis pointed at Murda. He was tired of little Miss Perfect. It was time to knock her down a few notches, so he called himself throwing her under the bus. "I heard Murda opened up shop on the west side in Juice's territory." Jarvis knew that selling dope on another player's turf was definitely a no-no in the dope game. There were guidelines to the lifestyle they led, and she seemed not to ever abide by any of them. He wanted Murda to be reprimanded.

"Murda, is that true?" Sysco asked aloud with a scowl on his face.

"Look," she sighed, "the projects are cool and all, but there is money elsewhere. I didn't know it was Juice's spot when I barged in, but I know now, and so does he." Murda fudged the truth. You damn right she knew it was Juice's spot, but she couldn't care less. That was just how she operated.

"What do you mean, and so does he?" Sysco needed to know where she was going with this story.

"Juice is dead," Murda replied, and everyone gasped.

"You killed him?" Sysco didn't really mean to ask the question like that, but he was just in disbelief that this young girl could slay such a giant.

"I ain't saying all that." She shook her head. Even if she had been the one who killed him, she was smart enough to never admit that shit, especially in a roomful of people. These niggas weren't her friends.

"Come up here, please." Sysco beckoned her to stand next to him in front of the group. Nervously, she did as she was asked. "I just want these clowns to see what a real hustler is! Ever since Murda showed up, she's been making you niggas look bad."

"No offense, Sysco, but since when is it okay to step on enemy territory, set up shop, and start a fucking war?" Fred was not about to let Murda make them look bad.

"Exactly!" Jarvis added. "The blowback from what Murda did or 'didn't do'"—he made air quotes with his fingers—"is sure to come down on the rest of us."

"And when it does, we'll be ready. Right?" Sysco asked the group. When no one responded, he repeated himself.

"Right!" they replied in unison. Although no one in the group wanted to go to war over the new chick in the crew, they didn't want beef with Sysco either.

Inwardly, Murdonna's stomach turned. She had to tell Sysco that she'd gone solo, but then she'd be fighting two wars: one with Juice's crew and one with her old one.

"The next few weeks might get a little crazy, so everybody needs to get strapped up and prepare for the worst to happen. Keep your eyes and ears open, and Detroit City Mafia will come out on top. For now, you're dismissed. Payro and Murda, I need y'all to stay back."

Chapter Twenty-two

After the meeting, Sysco took a seat on the sofa and waited for the crowd to disperse. Payro and Murda each sat across from him in silence until everyone was gone. Looking at each of them, Sysco leaned forward. "Word on the street is that the police are looking at me for the club shooting last month. I don't know what they have or don't have, but if push comes to shove, I may have to take this one on the chin and sit down for a bid."

"What?" Ro frowned. "What do you mean, take this one on the chin?" His cousin was talking crazy. "You didn't do the shooting."

"How do you know the police are looking at you?" Murda asked. Up until now, she hadn't heard anything about the club shooting except when they first reported it on the news. For all she knew, it was a dead issue. Not even Andres had mentioned it.

"When I got home, I had two business cards in my mailbox. They both belonged to police officers asking me to contact them. My neighbors said they've been by the house once a week religiously since I left. I'm sure they don't have nothing secure because they didn't put out a warrant, but who knows what will happen once they figure out that I'm back?" Sysco sighed. The stress of the situation was evident on his face.

"In the event that I go down, somebody has to take over DCM." Looking from his boo to his cousin, he knew it was going to be a tough decision. Someone wasn't going to like him afterward, but a decision had to be made. "Payro, you're sitting here because I have groomed you from a pup. Though you lack confidence, I know what you're capable of. Yet and still, there have been a few instances here lately when you let me down.

"Murda, you don't truly know the game yet, but you're sitting here because time and time again, you've shown me that you're a stand-up chick. You've shown me that when shit pops off, you're ready to take action. However, you can't be veering off and making moves without getting the okay from me first. While I admire your determination, I can't lie about being upset about the war you've started. When you take a leadership role, you must always think about the greater good of those you're responsible for."

Sysco paused. "For the next few weeks, I will be watching you both to see who is more qualified to lead the Detroit City Mafia in the event that I get hit with murder charges. Word to the wise, Ro, you need to step up more. Murda, you need to calm the fuck down."

"Why would you be hit with any charges when you didn't pull the trigger?" Payro was on ten. How could his cousin even think twice about doing someone else's bid? Though Murda was an asset to the team, she wasn't worth doing time for.

"Look, I don't know the logistics yet, but the way I see it, if there is an eyewitness or something, they'll probably say I was the shooter since the nigga was standing directly in front of me when he was killed. Even if they charge me, there is no way I'll get convicted. There is no evidence to show that I pulled the trigger. At the very least, I could at least plead self-defense." Sysco really wasn't worried about the situation, but he wanted his right and left hands to know what was going down just in case shit went sideways.

"Sys, why would you even consider taking this wrap?" Though Payro was trying to be nonchalant, it wasn't working at all. Murda knew what was meant by this question, and so did Sysco.

"Ro, relax. It's all good. I got my reasons, so just trust me." After standing from the couch, he slapped his cousin's chest. "Trust me," he repeated. Sysco knew that his cousin was making a very good point.

In the past, there was no way Sysco would've ever taken the heat for nobody, but things with Murda were different. It was because of her that Sysco could actually begin to see the small crew he'd started years ago grow into a world-renowned crime organization. With Murda by his side, Sysco could truly conquer the world. She was his ace in the hole. Therefore, it was imperative that she remain free and able to make moves, even if it meant that he had to go behind the wall for a few.

"I'll be in touch with y'all. Until then, Ro will stay with his crew here in the projects, and Murda will start her own crew on West Grand Boulevard. I'll send a few hitters your way just to make sure you're covered all right." Sysco licked his lips and pulled the black hoodie he was wearing over his head. "No matter what I decide, don't forget we're still family." Sysco extended his hand for a pact with both parties.

Although Ro didn't like that his cousin was even considering Murda for a position he'd waited his whole life for, he was still the first to throw his hand in the pile, and Murda followed suit. "All right, I'll check y'all out later." Ro couldn't get out of the townhouse fast enough. He was hotter than fish grease but didn't want to let on.

Murda excused herself for the bathroom, and Sysco watched her but didn't say a word. Instead, he went into the kitchen and made small talk with Juan and his sister.

When Murda came out of the bathroom, she waved goodbye to everyone and headed out the door. Sysco was right on her trail. "Murda, what happened to your face?" He'd noticed the bruising the minute he stepped into the house but decided not to mention it until they were alone.

"It's nothing. Don't worry about it." Without even looking at him, she kept on walking.

"So it's like that! You really aren't going to tell me what happened to your face?"

"Juice is what happened to my face," Murda replied halfheartedly.

"If that nigga weren't dead already, I swear to God I'd kill him myself." Sysco was pissed. "I should've been there to protect you. I'm sorry." Sysco felt guilty that he wasn't able to be there for Murda the way she had been there for him.

"I'm a big girl. I handled it." After turning her back to him again, she continued down the block.

"Why you being so cold toward me?" Sysco was confused. The last time he'd seen her, he was blowing her back out, and now she didn't have any words for him.

"I'm not being cold. You asked me a question, and I answered. What else do you want?" Now Murda did have an attitude.

"Damn, you ain't seen your nigga in a little over a month, and this is how you act when I come back?" Sysco stopped following her down the street and stood there.

"Oh, so now you're my nigga?" Murda turned around and shook her head. "When you left here, Sysco, you said you weren't looking for love, remember?"

"And neither were you," Sysco spat back, throwing her own words in her face.

"Well, I lied." Murda's honesty caught even her off guard. "From the minute you did all those nice things for me, I loved you. The minute I let you enter my body, I wanted you to love me back." Murda began to drop small tears. "It's okay that you don't love me. I'm fine with that, but my heart can't take all this back and forth." Murda wiped her face. "So let's keep it professional from here on out." For the first time, she realized the effect Sysco really had on her.

"When I left you that night, I realized what I said was fucked up, and for that I'm sorry. I didn't think I was looking for love at that time, but when they closed the casket on my grandmother, I realized I was losing the only person who ever loved me enough to possibly kill for me or even die for me. Then I thought of you, Murda." Sysco grabbed her hand. "Although it's pretty quick, I do think I love you, girl. Nah, I don't think. I know. On everything, I love you, Murda," he confessed.

"So, where does that leave us, and where do we go from here?" Murda peered into his eyes. Though she knew what his mouth was saying, she was trying to hear his heart.

"I want to take you to the moon and back! With you by my side, we can take on the world. But right now, let's just go back to my house and chill." Sysco smiled flirtatiously.

"I have to go check on the kids right now, but I'll come holler at you later," Murda gushed. He had her open—wide open.

Sysco nodded his understanding, then went into his back pocket and handed her a gold key.

"What's this?"

"It's a key to my spot. You can use it whenever you want." Sysco had never given anybody a key to his place. However, Murda was different. Sysco already trusted her with his life, so why not trust her with his key?

"I have some things to handle, but I'll be over tomorrow." Murda beamed with joy.

Quickly Sysco leaned in and kissed his girl. He'd waited over a whole month to do that.

"Boy, you better stop before somebody sees us," Murda said, reminding him where they were.

"Fuck 'em!" Sysco replied.

Yet and still, Murda backed away. Although Murda wanted to shout from the top of Mount Everest that she was Sysco's wifey, she decided not to and advised him to do the same. She'd come too far in the game to have people doubting her credibility now because she was sleeping with their boss.

Together they decided to date in the dark and always remain professional in the company of others. Murda didn't want anyone in the Detroit City Mafia to know what was going on, not even Payro.

However, it was too late. Payro was sitting in the parking lot behind the wheel of a rented Mustang watching the whole thing unfold. It was at this very moment that he began to see Murda as a threat instead of an ally. Right then and there, he determined that she needed to be eliminated.

Chapter Twenty-three

The next morning, Murda awoke to knocking at the front door. It was early. The sun hadn't even come up yet. "Who is it?" She was groggy as she squinted through the peephole.

"It's Ro," he replied as Murdonna opened the door to let him enter. Without a word, he entered and roamed the newly remodeled apartment with his eyes. The new paint on the walls, large television, and updated furniture definitely made the space better. Ro could tell that Murda was making money.

"What's up, Ro? Why are you here so early?" She yawned.

"The early bird gets the worm, my baby! That's hustling 101," he teased, but Murdonna didn't laugh. "Anyway, I came by to get the information about Juice so I can pass it to Quan."

"Shit." Murdonna was so excited about Sysco being home that she'd almost forgotten about her problem. Quickly she gave Ro the address to her spot and then grabbed her purse from the table to give him her key and to pay him for his and Quan's services. She knew she couldn't always expect freebies.

"Bet." Ro took the money and placed it into his back pocket. "Your spot should be clean by the time the sun comes up."

"Thank you for saving me yet again. I truly appreciate you always coming to my rescue."

Without warning, Murdonna pulled Payro in for a friendly hug. He was taken aback a bit by her actions, but that didn't stop him from wrapping his arms around her waist. Payro must've held her a little bit longer than necessary, because she pulled back from the embrace.

"Before you leave, I just wanted to say that even though Sysco is trying to put you and me against each other, I wouldn't dare compete with you. DCM is all yours. It's a part of your family legacy, not mine." Murdonna wasn't a fool. She knew Payro was uneasy about Sysco's meeting yesterday, and because she didn't need another enemy, she decided to call a truce. Besides, until she found another way to make a connection with Quan, Murdonna had to keep Ro close just in case she needed him again.

"I appreciate that, but it would mean more to me if you told Sysco the same thing." Payro wasn't a fool either. He knew that an opponent would say anything as an attempt to make him lower his guard. He needed Murdonna to officially decline Sysco's offer.

"I will do that this afternoon." With those words, Murdonna told Payro goodbye, closed the door, and went back to sleep.

As promised, when she woke up from her nap, she showered, dressed, and headed to Sysco's house. She had butterflies in her stomach as she pulled up the driveway and parked in front of his rented two-story brick home in Highland Park. Though she had the key in her purse, she still decided to ring the doorbell after stepping onto the porch.

Within seconds, Sysco opened the door, looking puzzled. "Why didn't you use your key?"

"It didn't feel right. Not yet," she admitted as he slid aside to let her enter.

The place was small but clean. Aside from the large television mounted to the wall and an oversized reclining sofa, the furniture was scarce. There were a few mismatched pieces here and there that looked as if they'd belonged to different living room sets, but all in all, the bachelor pad was quaint.

"Make yourself comfortable. Can I get you something to drink or eat?"

"No, thank you." Murda smiled.

"What are you smiling for?" Sysco grabbed the remote from the table and took a seat beside her.

"I've never seen you in this light, that's all." It was nice to see such a hard ass become vulnerable and expose a different side of himself. Something about that was attractive to Murda.

"I told you, baby, you make me see shit differently. With you, I want to be a better man, a better hustler, a better person. I want to give you all of me, and all I ask for in return is your loyalty." Sysco spoke from the heart. "In this game, I encounter snakes and phonies all day, every day. This is some deep shit that we're into, and I need to know that you will always be solid and keep it a buck with me."

Murdonna hesitated while searching his eyes before she finally spoke up. "Sysco, I want you to know I am solid, and you will always have my loyalty, but I need to tell you something." She didn't wait for him to respond before continuing. "While you were gone, I went to see Andres. He fronted me some product, and I've been doing business with him ever since. He told me that you and I were now on opposing sides."

For several minutes Sysco contemplated the situation. On the one hand, he wanted to be upset that his girl had gone and made a side deal with the plug that didn't include him. On the other hand, he knew why she did and reasoned with himself that he would've done the same. "Don't worry about it. I will go and speak with Andres and get this shit figured out."

"I don't need you speaking to anyone on my behalf." Murdonna was just getting used to being independent and making moves her way.

"What do you want to do then?" Sysco looked confused. "If this relationship ain't what you want, let me know now so I can cut my losses."

"Of course this relationship is what I want. I just want to handle this on my own. I'll go talk to Andres in a few weeks when it's time to re-up. I'm sure it won't be a problem." Murdonna had worked too hard to earn his respect in the game to all of a sudden be reduced to taking a back seat while a man went to fight her battles.

Though Sysco wanted to object to her meeting Andres alone, he had to respect her decision to handle things on her own.

Chapter Twenty-four

Just as Payro had promised, the spot on West Grand Boulevard had been cleaned up impeccably. If Murda hadn't been there when Juice was killed, she would've sworn that nothing had ever happened. For nearly two weeks, the block was quiet. No one in his crew ever mentioned him to her or even questioned her about his absence. Murda thought it was all good, but Sysco knew better, which was why he had put two goons on duty to watch the house damn near twenty-four hours a day. He knew the shit was going to come to a head when everyone least expected it.

Buzzzz. Buzzzz. The sound of Murda's phone sliding across the dresser woke her from her slumber. When she tried to get out of Sysco's bed, he pulled her back toward him. "Just a few more minutes, please." He planted soft kisses up and down her back.

"It could be one of my siblings." Murda hadn't gone home last night. Although she told Mya she would be staying with Sysco, she also told her to call in case of an emergency. When Murda got to the phone, though, it had stopped ringing. There was a missed call from a number she didn't recognize on the screen.

"Did somebody call a cell phone?" she asked after returning the call and placing it on speakerphone. Sirens could be heard in the background. It was so loud that Murda could barely hear anything else. Instantly Sysco was sitting up in bed on high alert.

"Murda, it's me. They shot up the house last night and then set it on fire," Duck hollered over the noise. "My mother was in the house. She's dead! These bitch-ass niggas killed her."

"Calm down, Duck." She could hear how upset he was. "Tell me play by play exactly what happened." Murda looked at Sysco, who was already out of bed and on his toes.

"Last night, my moms asked me to get her some squares. On my way to the gas station, I noticed an old-school black Ford coming down the block. I didn't think much of it, but as soon as I got across the street, these niggas opened up fire on the house." Duck was crying and talking at the same time. It was hard to understand, but Murda didn't miss a beat. "After they shot up the house, they got out and covered it in gasoline, then set it on fire and pulled off. I ran down the block back toward the house as fast as I could, but I couldn't do nothing. There was too much fire. Our neighbor called 911, but it was too late. They killed her, Murda. My mother is gone." He'd seen them carry her body from the house in a body bag.

"Duck, I'm so sorry for your loss. I'm on the way. Give me fifteen minutes." She knew her friend needed her in his time of need.

"Okay. I'll be at the gas station on the corner." Duck sniffed as the call ended.

Murda looked at Sysco. She was completely in shock and trying hard to process what her next move would be.

"Did he say who did it?" Sysco asked, knowing it was go time. This was the very moment he'd been holding his breath for.

"Who do you think it was?" Murda didn't even have to ask the question to know the answer. Juice's crew were the only people who could have that much beef with her that they would shoot up and burn a place where they knew she resided.

"It looks like the war was just started." Sysco reached beneath the mattress and grabbed a double-barrel shotgun and two 9 mms, one of which he handed to Murda. "Let's go."

Although Sysco's house was twenty minutes away from where they were going, he managed to pull up in twelve. Sitting on the curb with his head in his hands was Duck. Immediately Murda's heart broke for the kid. She could only imagine what he was going through and wanted to approach the situation with caution. "Give me a few minutes with him alone," she told Sysco with a smile.

"For sure." He nodded, and Murda exited the car.

"Hey, Duck. How are you doing?" She wrapped her arms around his shoulders. Although it was a pretty chilly day in the D, Duck's body was burning hot.

"I can't believe she's gone." He looked up at Murda with puffy eyes. "It's all my fault. I should have turned around and gone back when I saw that car. Maybe I could have stopped them." For as long as he lived, he would never forgive himself for what happened.

"If you had gone back to the house, you would be dead too. You did the right thing," Murda tried to reassure him.

"The house caught on fire and exploded so fast." Duck wiped his eyes. "What am I going to do now? I don't have nowhere to go."

"You're coming with me." Murda helped him stand. "I told you I got you, little bro, and I mean that shit." She knew from the minute Duck called her with the news of his mom's murder that she would take him in and raise him just the way she was raising Mya and Donzell. She'd grown to love him just that much.

"I don't want no handouts. Let me at least work for it." Even in the midst of tragedy, Duck's pride was still stronger than ever. Murda admired that about him. Honestly, it was one of his best characteristics.

"You're family. This ain't about handouts. It's just what we do for one another." Murda wrapped her arm around him and guided him toward the car.

"I still want to work for it. Let me join your team at least." He looked up into her eyes.

Murda pondered his proposal for a second. This could be the start of something big for her and Duck. They were both two kids from the ghetto whom society tried to throw away. However, they were fighters, both hungry and destined for great things.

"Do you think you have what it takes? This shit ain't for the weakhearted."

"I ain't ever been weak," Duck replied while wiping his face.

"Then welcome to the team." Murda smirked. "Now, let's get you out of here." The block was still swarming with spectators, fire officials, and news reporters. Duck didn't need to be around all of that.

"I got your back, Murda." Duck stopped midstride. "On my mama, I won't let you down." He wiped his eyes again.

"I know you won't." Murda saw in Duck the fire that burned inside of her. She knew that once he learned the game, he would be dangerous, and with him under her wing, she would be powerful. In no time, they would rise to levels that many dreamed about but only few had conquered.

Just as Sysco put the car in gear, Murda made introductions. "Duck, this is Sysco. Sysco, this is Duck, my right-hand man." She knew if she could trust anybody in the game, it would be Duck. He'd already proven himself in her book.

"Young'un, I'm sorry to hear about your moms." Sysco turned around to look at the young boy. "I swear on my life we gon' ride on them niggas tonight!" Sysco was putting the whole crew on go mode.

"When we do find them, I'm pulling the trigger my motherfucking self," Murda assured him. She'd killed three people for less already. This one would be easy. Besides, if she let someone else do it, it wouldn't mean shit. Murda wanted to be the one to even the score in this situation.

"I appreciate you for that." Duck double-tapped the spot on his chest over his heart. His young mind had a lot to process, but he was happy to have found a friend in Murda. Although they were close in age, she was still more like the big sister he always wanted.

"Do you know where these niggas stay at?" Sysco asked. Although he'd heard of Juice a time or two, he didn't know shit about the fuck nigga except his name.

"Yeah, his crew be at 1022. That's an after-hours joint a few blocks from here on Woodward," Duck replied.

"All right then." Sysco nodded. "We're going to hit up the spot tonight and lay all these niggas down for taking your moms."

Chapter Twenty-five

During the ride, Sysco called all members of the Detroit City Mafia for an emergency meeting at Juan's sister's house. He told them to come strapped and prepared for battle. Murda wanted to come too, but Sysco thought it was best that she head home for now and look after the kid until he called. Duck needed to get some rest, and Murda needed to get her head in the game for what he was going to ask her to do later. Murda obliged.

Once Sysco dropped them off in the housing projects, Murda and Duck walked silently up to her building. They both had a lot on their minds, but Murda decided to break the ice. "Do you want me to call anybody for you and tell them what happened?" She felt silly assuming he could just come and live with her. If he had any other relatives, then they would have more right to take him than her.

"No, I'm good." Duck shook his head. He had an aunt who lived in Chicago, but she never called or visited anyway, so why would he call her?

"Would you like to give your mom a funeral service?" Murda was willing to foot the bill.

"No. We didn't have no family, and she didn't have any friends for real. Nobody would even show up."

"You got family in us. If you want to have a service for your mom, we'll be there for you." Murda pressed the button for the elevator.

"Can I think about it and let you know?"

"Of course you can." Murda nodded and stepped on the elevator after the doors opened. Thank God she didn't have to wait for it today.

"Do you think your brother and sister are going to like me?" Duck asked nervously.

"Oh, they're going to love you," Murda assured him.

The remainder of the ride up to her floor was quiet. Murdonna was thinking about what was going to take place later, while Duck was thinking about how different his life was going to be from here on out. Though often-times he was frustrated with his mom for what she lacked in the parenting department, he had never imagined life without her. All he wanted right now was to be able to tell her that he loved her, and the fact that he couldn't made him sick to his stomach.

Within seconds, the elevator arrived on their floor, and they stepped off. "Are you sure I can stay?" Duck blurted out, beginning to let his nervousness get the best of him.

"Don't be silly, boy." Murda laughed. "You're more than welcome to stay with me. It's not much, but soon I'll be able to upgrade to something bigger." Murda couldn't wait to start house shopping. Now that there were four of them, she really needed more space.

"Just give me a blanket and a spot on the floor. I don't want to be in the way, and I promise not to be a burden," Duck said while following Murda down the hall.

"Stop it." She laughed, then paused as her apartment door opened. Two men in uniform had just stepped out, and Murda's heart froze midbeat. It was the police.

"When your sister returns home, please have her call us." One of the men gave a card to Mya, who looked over and saw her.

"That's my sister right there." Mya pointed.

"Ahh, Ms. Carter, may I have a word with you for a minute?" one of the men asked.

"First, can you tell me why the fuck you came out of my apartment just now?" Murda was hotter than fish grease.

"Well, this young lady said it was okay," the other man interjected.

"That young lady is fifteen years old. You cannot talk to a minor without an adult's consent." Murda knew her rights.

"Sorry, Ms. Carter. We thought there was an adult in the house. As soon as we found out there wasn't, we left." He raised his right hand to indicate that he was telling the truth. "We were only inside for two minutes."

"Is that true, Mya?"

"Yeah. I'm sorry, Donna." Mya knew she was in trouble. Her whole life, she'd been told not to open the door for strangers, yet here she stood, breaking the cardinal rule number one.

"Go inside and take Duck with you, please." She pointed to the door, and both Mya and Duck went inside. "Now, what can I do for you, Officers?" She folded her arms.

"We were hoping to get you to come down to the station to discuss the shooting at Club Hennessey last month," one of the officers said.

"You do realize I'm a minor too, right?"

"We just need to ask a few basic questions. There is no need for you to have an adult present."

"Am I under arrest?" Murda knew how shady officers could be. *They tell you whatever you want to hear just to get you to talk.*

"No," both officers replied.

"All right, then we can talk right here." Murda wasn't about to go anywhere. She knew the game.

"Okay." The main officer cleared his throat, then pulled out a notepad. "Have you ever been to Club Hennessey?"

"Isn't that a twenty-one-and-older club?" Murda raised a brow. "I'm only seventeen."

"Ms. Carter, we don't care about your age. All we need to know is if you have ever been to Club Hennessey."

"Well, in that case . . ." Murda smiled. "Yeah, I've been there once or twice with my fake ID." She only told the truth about being there because she knew they wouldn't have been standing here if they didn't already know she was there.

"Do you recall being there around the twentieth of last month?"

"Sir, I don't know, maybe." Murda shrugged. "Did something happen?"

"A man was murdered inside the club." The second officer was growing impatient because he knew she was playing games.

"Wow! I'm so sorry to hear about that." Murda paused. "But I'm still confused about why you're here. How did you get my name? I know y'all aren't just randomly knocking on people's doors." Murda was tired of playing games too, so she cut to the chase.

"We received an anonymous tip that you were in the club the night of the shooting with Sysciano Nelson, the alleged triggerman," the first officer admitted.

"Is that true?" the second officer asked.

Murda stood silent for a second while evaluating the situation. She knew the tip had to come from someone inside of DCM, because up until recently, she was a nobody. Therefore, she knew no one at the club would've given up her name, because they didn't know it. Though she wasn't really friends with any of the niggas in the Detroit City Mafia, she knew Fred, Jarvis, and P-dot especially had no love for her. Maybe the tip had come from them, or maybe there was no tip at all and these fuckers were pulling her leg.

"Were you at Club Hennessey with Sysciano Nelson on the night in question, Ms. Carter?"

"No, I wasn't, Officers." Murda decided to lie. After all, if they had any real evidence proving that she was there, they would have said it.

"Thank you for your time. We'll be in touch." The first officer nodded, then proceeded down the hallway. They both knew she was lying. Now all they had to do was prove it.

Chapter Twenty-six

"Donna, what was that all about?" Donzell asked after Murda came inside the apartment. He was sitting on the sofa playing Xbox with his new friend Duck.

"Nothing," Murda replied on autopilot, although her mind was racing. She couldn't believe that someone in the camp had given her name to the police. Whoever did was going to pay severely, that was for sure.

"Who is he, and what is he doing here?" Mya pointed across the room at Duck.

"Oh, shit! My bad. This is my friend Duck. Duck, this is Mya, and you've already gotten to know Donzell, I see." Murda smiled. "He is a part of this family now and will be treated as such. Does everyone understand?"

"But—" Mya started. She didn't like new people in her space.

"Do you understand?" Murda interjected.

"Yes," Mya mumbled.

"I know it's a little cramped in here right now, but I will find us something bigger soon. Everyone, please let's try to coexist in the meantime." Murda went to the back of the apartment. She needed to call Sysco, but Mya had other plans.

"I don't want him here," she whispered after boxing Murda in the bedroom and closing the door. "He is a stranger."

"He is not a stranger. He's my friend, and he needs a place to call home. Enough said," Murda snapped.

"Why can't he stay wherever he came from?" Mya wasn't backing down.

"His mother was just killed. He has nowhere else to go! Any more questions?" Murda paused when she noticed the look of horror on her sister's face. "Look, I know this is a big change, but it will all work out, trust me. Besides, he won't even be here. He'll be with me most of the time working anyway."

"How can that young boy be going to work with you? He looks like he's my age." Mya folded her arms. She knew something in the milk wasn't clean.

"Please get out of my face. I need to make a call." Murda was over this conversation. She didn't need to explain anything.

"You may as well tell me the truth, because I already know."

"Tell you the truth about what?" Murda smacked her lips.

"I already know you're a drug dealer, so you might as well confirm it." A few kids in the neighborhood had told her a couple of weeks ago.

"Mya," was all Murda could say because she was at a loss for words. Although she knew they would find out eventually, she hadn't really thought about what she would say when the time came.

"How could you sell something that has already destroyed our family?" Mya shook her head, disappointed. "Drugs took our mother away. Have you ever thought that your actions may take someone else's mother away too?"

Her words hit Murda like a Mack truck. Though Murdonna hadn't ever thought about it like that, it did make sense. Yet and still, the drugs that had taken Sheila away was the very thing that put money in their pockets.

"I'm doing what I can to keep this family afloat." Murda looked her sister in the eyes. "This may not be ideal employment, but I'm bringing food to the table, keeping a roof over our heads, and a whole lot of other shit. When I get where I need to be in life for us to live comfortably, then I will go legit. Until then, I've got to hustle. It's all I know how to do right now."

"I just want you to be safe. I don't want you to go to jail or worse," Mya sighed. She may have fussed and given Murda a hard time, but she knew she would be lost without her big sister.

"I'll be all right. I promise." Murda crossed her heart. "Does Donzell know?"

"I don't think so." Mya shook her head.

"Good. Let's keep this between you and me for now." Murda held out her pinky finger. Mya took it, and they shook on it.

Chapter Twenty-seven

Just as the clock on the cable box struck 3:00 a.m., Murda's phone buzzed. She looked down at the screen to see a text from Sysco. Quickly she yawned then opened the message.

It's go time. We're out front. Come outside.

Although Murda was lying across the bed half asleep, she was already completely dressed down to the shoes. Therefore, all she had to do was grab her gun, cell phone, and keys then be out the door.

Quietly she tiptoed down the hallway trying not to wake Donzell, who had school in the morning, or Duck, who she thought had gone to sleep an hour ago.

"Can I go?" Duck was sitting at the dining room table in the dark. He'd been sitting there for hours.

"I don't think that's such a good idea." Murda shook her head as if the boy could see her.

"I have to be there. I need to see the look in their eyes when they see death coming." Duck stood from the chair. "Please, Murda," he begged.

"Are you sure this is something you want to get into?" Murda sighed. "Once you step over to the dark side, there ain't no turning back." This was something Murda knew first-hand.

"I crossed over to the dark side when I did what I did to Juice, remember?"

Even in the dark, Duck's eyes met Murda's, and the decision was made. If the young boy wanted to draw down on the niggas who had taken his mother's life, who the hell was she to stop him?

"Let's go then." She proceeded to the door with Duck on her trail.

Once they got downstairs, both Duck and Murda were surprised by how many members of the Detroit City Mafia had actually shown up. There was a fleet of ten cars lined up behind a black motorcycle. Sysco was standing near the bike, wearing a black bandana around his mouth.

He waved for Murda to come over to him. "What's the boy doing here?"

"He wants to be there, and I respect that," Murda insisted.

"Do you trust him?" Sysco hated when plans went awry, but he knew if Murda said the boy was good, then the boy was good.

"Yes, I trust him with my life." Murda found no reason to divulge that Duck was the one who actually killed Juice to save her. All Sysco needed to know was that she vouched for him.

"Okay, then we on." Sysco nodded, then walked over to where the young'un was standing. "Duck, have you ever pulled a trigger before?"

Nervously Duck looked to Murda before nodding slowly. "Yeah."

"Bet, take this." Sysco placed a .45 in his hand. "When the car stops, you shoot until you don't have no more bullets, all right?"

"Got it." Duck nodded.

"You can ride with CeeLo in the red van." He pointed to the van parked behind the motorcycle.

"Who should I ride with?" Murda asked anxiously, ready to play her position.

"You're riding with me." Sysco walked over to the bike and grabbed a helmet off the seat. "Put this on."

"Let's ride then, baby." Murda's adrenaline was racing. She was ready for action.

Three minutes later, after everyone was in position, the caravan of cars took off down the block with Sysco and Murda leading the way. Payro was three cars back, sitting on the passenger side of a stolen Maxima. A 9 mm rested on his lap as he and P-dot passed a Dutch back and forth.

"You quiet, nigga. What's good?" P-dot asked after inhaling the sticky.

"Just trying to get focused, that's all." Payro reclined in the seat and closed his eyes. Truthfully, he wasn't feeling what was about to go down, but he would never say it out loud. Payro was a hustler! He wasn't a killer, but in the dope game, it seemed that the two almost always went hand in hand.

"You see how Sysco got Murda up there in the front?" P-dot asked. "I don't know how I feel about that shit."

"What do you mean?" Payro opened his eyes.

"You're his right-hand man and cousin, right? Seems to me like you should be the one taking the lead on this, fam."

"This is Murda's beef. That's why she in the front of the pack." Payro tried to justify the situation. However, he already knew what was up.

"Man, fuck that! The bitch is taking over. We need to get her up out of here." P-dot passed the blunt. Although he'd been playing it cool lately, he still couldn't stand Murda ever since the incident at the bus stop.

"She ain't going nowhere." Payro shook his head. Now that Murda was involved with Sysco, her position in the Detroit City Mafia was solid. Even if Sysco chose to make him head of the organization, as long as he was alive, Murda would always have a seat at the table.

"If we don't do something fast, this bitch is gonna be the goddamn boss!"

P-dot's words hit Payro in his gut as he replayed the conversation Sysco had with him earlier tonight. He'd told Ro that he needed to step up if he wanted the throne, and tonight he planned to do just that. Payro was gonna be on some Tony Montana shit, even if it cost him his life.

Chapter Twenty-eight

Murda held on to Sysco for dear life as they flew down the freeway. It felt good to let the wind blow through her hair, but the way the nigga was speeding and taking curves had her stomach doing backflips. After a while, though, Murda relaxed and took the time to enjoy the moment. She leaned her body in closer, then laid her head on Sysco's back. Although they were rushing into harm's way, Murda couldn't have felt any safer.

Within twenty-five minutes, Sysco pulled off the freeway with all of the squad right behind him. He'd done a dry run earlier and cased the joint. Therefore, he knew exactly where he was going. Raising his hand in the air, he flashed five fingers. This was a signal to let CeeLo know they'd be arriving in five minutes. CeeLo hit the brakes five times to signal P-dot, and so on and so forth. "This is it!" Sysco tapped Murda's leg in case she couldn't hear him with the helmet on. On cue, Murda reached inside her jacket and retrieved her gun. It was cocked and loaded.

After pulling up to the light in front of the after-hours spot, both Murda and Sysco smiled. There had to be at least ten people standing outside engaged in conversation. "Sitting ducks!" Murda laughed as Sysco revved the engine on the bike. By the time the crowd looked up, it was too late.

Zooooooooom! Sysco hit the gas, and Murda started dumping. Next, the side door of the van opened up, and all you could see was fire. People starting dropping like flies. However, two of the men pulled pistols of their own and started busting back.

"Stop the car," Payro hollered.

"What?" P-dot frowned. He wasn't stopping shit until they got back to the projects.

"Stop the fucking car." Instead of waiting, Payro opened the door and got out. It was now or never to prove himself. Bang! Bang! Bang! He squeezed the trigger for dear life and watched one of the gunmen fall to the ground. Bang! Bang! He turned his gun on the second one. The bullets caught him in the neck and chest.

"What the fuck is he doing!" Sysco hollered before turning the bike around and going back for his cousin. Murda couldn't believe the stunt Payro had just pulled.

"You take one of ours, so we're taking ten of yours! Be down with us, or get laid down by us! DCM for life!" Payro beat on his chest like a gorilla, but his gloating came just a tad too soon.

Just then, an armed man came from behind the building with his gun pointed at Payro's back. Murda had exactly one bullet left. Thinking quickly, she pulled the trigger and prayed like hell it hit the intended target. Pow!

As the bullet whizzed past Payro's ear, he turned his head just in time to see the man behind him fall. Instantly he was shaking! Not only had Murda's bullet barely missed his head, but he was about to be sniped from the back. The situation shook him to the core and quickly deflated his Tony Montana ego.

"Get the fuck in the car, Ro!" P-dot screamed, but Payro's feet were stuck in place like they were being held by cement. He couldn't believe how death had missed his ass twice in two seconds.

"We are leaving with or without you!" Sysco hollered.

That's when Ro saw the door of the club begin to open. Like magic, his feet were set free from the invisible hold, and he ran like hell all the way to the waiting car.

Pow! Pow! Ting! The bullets from another gun ricocheted off a light pole as shots were fired in his direction. Lucky for Payro, the guy behind the trigger was a bad shooter, or else he would've caught two slugs in the back.

Screechhhhhh! P-dot pulled off, leaving a trail of smoke behind him. "What the fuck was that about!" P-dot was beyond pissed. Not only was Ro playing Russian roulette with his own life, but he was also playing with P-dot's as well. "I got a son, B! You trying to get me killed?"

"I'm sorry, man." Ro felt extremely embarrassed about his actions. In his head, the plan had gone a lot smoother.

"Goddamn!" P-dot hit the steering wheel. "You just made this shit ten times worse. You do know that, right?" P-dot looked over at Ro. "You said, 'DCM.' Now they know it was us."

Immediately Payro's heart sank. In the heat of the moment, he hadn't even realized he'd made such a deadly mistake. Carelessly he'd just put targets on the backs of all the members in camp. Shit was about to get real!

Chapter Twenty-nine

Pulling back into the projects, everyone was silent. They all knew Payro had fucked things up royally. What they didn't know was how Sysco was going to handle it. Some thought he would hit his cousin with some slugs, because he'd killed niggas for less in the past, while others thought he would be kicked out of Detroit City Mafia for good. Even though everyone had thoughts and opinions, no one said a word as they parked and entered the townhouse, not even Sysco. He couldn't believe Ro was tripping like that. He had definitely taught him better.

"I just want to tell everybody I'm sorry. I don't know what I was thinking. I got caught up in the moment, and for that, I—" Payro stood in the middle of the living room, trying to address the elephant in the room. However, he never got the opportunity to finish his sentence before Sysco's fist went flying into his mouth.

"I should kill your ass, nigga!" Sysco sent another blow to Ro's body before being pulled off of him by Jarvis and P-dot.

"Look, man, emotions are running high right now. Let's leave this shit right here and pick it up in a few days," Jarvis tried to reason with Sysco, who was seeing red.

"Y'all are cousins," Fred chimed in with his two cents. "Yeah, he fucked up, but let's not forget we wouldn't have even been there if Murda hadn't fucked up first." He looked over at Murda, who was standing next to Duck.

"Like you said the other day, we are a family." Fred sighed. "Right, wrong, or indifferent, family sticks together. We just gotta stay strapped and see this thing through until the end."

Fred made all the sense in the world, and Sysco appreciated the old head for kicking knowledge to him. "The OG is right." Sysco looked around at the crowd of faces. "We're in too deep now, so there ain't no turning back. I need everybody to stay on high alert! Be on your p's and q's. We cannot have any more fuckups." Sysco balled his fist up, then extended his arm. "All for one." His eyes met Payro's.

"One for all," everyone said after placing their fists in the pile. Payro was the last person to add his hand, but Sysco let it slide. He knew his cousin was probably pissed with him, but the feeling was mutual, so it didn't even matter.

"Get a good night's rest. We're back to business as usual in the morning." Sysco dismissed the group.

The next few days went by in a blur. Although things had been quiet, everyone was still on guard. Since Murda no longer had a trap house, she went back to flipping vials on the corner in the projects. Naturally, she didn't like it, but without any other options, she did what was necessary. Besides, her mind was preoccupied with a whole lot of other shit. For starters, she was trying to teach Duck the game while simultaneously planning a private service for his mother. Mya had been suspended from school for fighting, and Donzell was home, sick. Things were chaotic, but Murda didn't miss a beat. She tended to the house by day, and by night she was back on the corner. Ironically the corner was where she found peace.

"Do you like it here?" Murda asked Duck, who was sitting on the green electric box.

"Hell yeah." Duck hawked some spit onto the grass. "Why?"

"I was just asking." Murda shrugged. He'd been with her for almost a week. She'd wanted to give him time to adjust before she asked the question.

"Can I be honest?" Duck looked up at Murda.

"Always," Murda replied.

"I like being here better than I liked living with my mom." Duck hopped off the box. "Don't get wrong, I love my mother. But being here with you, Mya, and Donnie is like having a real family."

Murda thought it was sweet that Duck had given Donzell a nickname. "We are a real family, and don't you ever forget that." Murda looked at the boy who would always hold a special place in her heart. "I got you no matter what." She placed her arm around his neck, and he smiled. Although they had only become friends a short time ago, their bond was unbreakable.

Just then, a black Nissan with tinted windows bent the corner and came down the block on a slow creep. Both Duck and Murda noticed it. Instantly they broke their embrace and reached for the heat that each of them had tucked into the front of their jeans. "I'm about to just start blasting." Duck cocked his shit and pointed.

Murda placed her hand over his gun and pushed it down. "It could be a customer. It could be the police," Murda said while straining her eyes to see down the block. However, it was useless. She couldn't see a damn thing. "Go get behind the green box. I'll stand right here," she instructed.

"I'm not leaving you." Although the box was a mere few feet away, he didn't want to leave Murda exposed by her lonesome.

"Duck, do what I said," Murda yelled as the car got closer. "If it's the police, take the shit and run. If it's an unwanted visitor, then you'll have the drop on them."

Reluctantly Duck did as he was told. As soon as he was in position, the Nissan pulled up, and the driver rolled down the window. Murda gripped the handle on her piece for dear life. She wasn't prepared to die tonight, but if the reaper came calling, she was going to take the shooter out with her.

"Excuse me, can you tell me where Mack and Gratiot is?" a white man asked before he noticed the gun in Murda's hand. "Oh, dear Lord!" He gasped and tried to roll up the window while pulling off at the same time.

Duck fell out laughing hysterically behind the electric box because the look on the man's face was priceless. Murda couldn't help but laugh too as she wondered how in the hell he'd gotten lost in the projects in the first place. "Come on, let's go inside. We've had enough action tonight."

Chapter Thirty

The remainder of the week finished off just as fast and quiet as the week had started. Murda thought it was suspicious that none of Juice's crew had tried to retaliate yet. However, today was the private ceremony she had arranged for Duck's mother, so she was too preoccupied to worry about it.

Though there was no fancy singing or funny remarks from friends, the service was still nice. The minister delivered the eulogy as if he'd been personal friends with Duck's mother, and there were several pictures on display. Duck held his tears in and his head high the entire time. Murdonna commended his bravery.

"Thanks for coming. I know Duck appreciates it." Murda hugged Sysco, Payro, Juan, and even P-dot as they all exited the small church. Mya and Donzell were sitting in the car waiting for Duck, who was having a private moment to say one last goodbye to his mom. She was to be cremated in the morning.

"It ain't no thang. I'm glad we could make it. I like the little nigga." Sysco smiled. Duck reminded him a lot of Murda and himself. All three of them had risen from the very ashes meant to destroy them.

"Yeah, I'm glad we could come." Payro nodded. Although he was still pissed with his cousin for what had gone down the last time they were together, he knew the whole thing was his own fault.

"Excuse me, miss, may I have a word with you?" a black man in a cheap suit asked after exiting the church.

"And you are?" Murda had seen him sitting in the back of the sanctuary earlier but thought he was possibly a family member Duck had called. The man looked around at the small crowd before responding.

"My name is Detective Casey. I'm with the homicide unit." He opened his suit jacket to reveal a badge. "I was assigned to the case of Ms. Rhonda."

"What can I do for you, Detective?" Murda asked nonchalantly. Noticeably all the fellas in the crew became uneasy.

"Well, her case was just one that tugged at my heart-strings, you know?" He smiled, but no one returned the gesture. "I asked around the neighborhood, and no one really knew her, so it's hard to believe that she had any enemies." Detective Casey cleared his throat. "I heard there was some drug trafficking going on in the rental property below Ms. Rhonda. Didn't you rent that property?"

"I did." Murda looked him square in the face.

"Can you tell me about the drug trafficking claim?"

"Did you find any drugs in the house?" Murda raised a brow, already knowing the answer. Every time she left the spot, she took all the work she had in her possession just in case a fiend wanted to break in and rob her.

Detective Casey decided to switch up the line of questioning. "Do you have any enemies or know of any party who may have done this?"

"Nope," Murda replied.

Detective Casey knew he wasn't going to get anywhere with her, so he decided to fall back but keep a close watch on her from a distance. Something wasn't adding up. "Here is my card. Call me if you think of anything." He tried to hand her one of his cards, but she didn't take it.

With a nod, Detective Casey put his card back into his pocket and headed over to his car in the parking lot.

"I'm sure he spoke with Duck while they were alone in the church. Make sure he kept his mouth closed," Sysco said as the group watched the detective walk away.

"I will." Murda nodded.

"Tell the little homie I'll catch him on the flip. I got to meet my son and his mother at the mall in a few. He's getting his first-year pictures taken." P-dot beamed. Having a child in high school wasn't an easy task, but he took pride in being a father. He loved little P with everything he had. He couldn't wait to teach him things like playing ball, pulling the girls, and being a man.

"Tell my godson I'll lace him with a few dollars at the party next week." Payro smiled. Although he was in no rush, he looked forward to becoming a father himself. He loved the bond P-dot had with his son. It was a bond Payro wished he'd had with his own father.

"For sho'. I'll catch y'all later." After chucking up the deuces, he headed toward the parking lot.

"West Grand Crew in full effect!" someone screamed as a blue Dodge pulled up in front of the church. By the time Murda, Sysco, Payro, and P-dot could even process what was going on, it was too late.

Pow! Bang! Pow! Shots rang out from the front and back passenger windows. Boom! Boom! The last one sounded like a canon.

Immediately everyone hit the ground. "Fuck!" Murda screamed as she remembered her siblings were in the car. Pop! Pop! More shots sprayed the area, but Murda didn't give a fuck. On her knees, she crawled all the way to the parking lot. Her heart damn near leaped from her chest when she saw the back window of her car completely shattered. Fearing the worst, she paused for a second before crawling to the other side of the car and opening the back door.

"Donna, what's happening?" Donzell was tucked down on the floor of the car with his head buried under his arms.

"Are you guys okay?" Murda could see Mya on the floor in the front of the car.

"Yeah, are you?" Mya asked.

"Thank God." Murda began to cry with joy. However, her relief was short-lived.

"Somebody, help me! Please call an ambulance!"

Murda noticed the shooting had stopped, so she stood. She could see Payro kneeling over a body that didn't appear to be moving.

"Call the fucking ambulance!" he hollered. "Get up, man. Get up." Payro viciously shook P-dot.

"This is Detective Morgan Casey. I need a bus!" After Detective Casey told dispatch the address of the church, he looked back at Murda, who was standing in a huddle with her siblings. "Ms. Carter, someone here has enemies. I won't stop until I find out who."

Chapter Thirty-one

Sadly, P-dot lost his fight for life just moments before the ambulance could arrive. With his dying breath, he told Payro to look after little P, then closed his eyes. His body shook one final time, and then it was over.

Payro lost both his best friend and his mind that day. As if it weren't bad enough watching the coroner throw a sheet over his homie, he had to be the one to deliver the news to P-dot's family. When they arrived on the scene, all hell broke loose. Payro and Sysco had to control the crowd. Murda took her siblings and got out of there. She felt bad for P-dot, but he wasn't her bestie, so honestly, she wasn't too bothered. Detective Casey decided to stick around, although it wasn't his district. He tried to interview people on the scene, but no one would give him the time of day.

A few days later, Payro called a meeting at the town-house. Attendance was mandatory. However, no one knew what the meeting would be about, not even Sysco. Usually, he was the one to schedule things like this, but he didn't gripe, as he was sure his cousin had a good reason.

"First and foremost, I called y'all here today on behalf of my brother P-dot," Payro slurred. He was obviously intoxicated. "He didn't have any insurance. His mom needs help burying him, and I told her that we got her." Payro removed the Detroit snapback cap from his head, then turned it over. "Everybody in this bitch better hit your motherfucking pockets and place some money in my shit."

He waved the hat in the air before handing it over to Jarvis, who reached into his pocket, then placed a twenty inside.

"What the fuck is twenty motherfucking dollars gonna do?" Ro smacked his lips.

"Ay, man, I feel bad for P-dot, but I still got mouths to feed," Jarvis defended himself.

"Fuck that!" Payro spat. "We hustlers, remember? Everybody in this bitch should be able to toss two hundred and fifty dollars in the pot at the very least."

"Ro." Sysco tried to get his cousin's attention, but Payro was too far into his feelings.

"Jarvis, you got five fuckin' seconds to find two hundred and thirty more dollars," Payro demanded.

"Or what?" Jarvis was now up out of his seat. He wasn't one for being disrespected.

"Sys, get this nigga," Fred chimed in.

"I don't need him to get shit!" Payro flexed. He was sick of being in Sysco's shadow. He was tired of being treated like a child.

"All right, Ro, that's enough." Sysco didn't want to embarrass him in front of everyone again, but he would if Payro continued being belligerent. "I understand P-dot was your nigga, but this ain't no motherfucking stickup. You can't just put a price on how much a person should donate." Sysco sighed before pulling his cousin aside. "After you get what you get from these niggas, just come see me for the rest."

"Thanks, man. I appreciate that." Payro pulled his cousin in for a hug. "DCM for life."

"DCM for life," Sysco replied before stepping back into the center of the room. "Now that that's out of the way, does anybody want to bring anything to the table before we call this one a wrap?" Sysco hated that Payro had pulled everyone from their post for some shit that could have been sent via text message. However, they were there now and might as well make good use of their time.

"Um . . ." Duck cleared his throat after Murda nudged him. "I was in my old hood the other day. Some of Juice's niggas rolled up on me, talking about they wanted me to arrange a sit-down with you."

"A sit-down for what?" Sysco smacked his lips. "It's a little too late to be holding meetings."

"We took one of theirs, and they took my moms. We shot up their spot, and they shot up the church." Duck's eyes roamed the room nervously. He didn't have everyone's attention but continued anyway. "They want to call a truce and stop the violence."

"Fuck out of here with that bullshit," Payro hollered. He didn't know the young boy like that, but he knew the boy must be stuck on stupid to even repeat that dumb shit. "There ain't truces in the hood."

"I think they are trying to join forces, and honestly, that's not a bad idea," Murda said, backing Duck up. However, Sysco didn't agree, which was apparent by the way he shook his head. Yet and still, Murda continued, taking the floor.

"Listen, how many more soldiers do we have to lose before you will consider it? That could have easily been Jarvis, Fred, Juan, me, or hell, even you, Sysco." She looked at each of them as she spoke. "I don't know about y'all, but I'm tired of watching my back and seeing bloodshed."

"But you started this war, Murda," Jarvis said, pointing out the fact.

"And now I'm ready to finish it so we can get back to what we do best." Murda looked at Sysco with puppy dog eyes that no one in the room but him seemed to notice.

"Do you think this truce is legit and not a setup?" Sysco looked over at Duck.

"I think it's one hundred. It came from a good source." Duck's mother's ex-fiancé, Xavier, had reached out to him when he found out she was murdered. Though it had been years since they were together, he still held a spot in his heart for Duck. As luck would have it, he was now in charge of running Juice's old crew. Therefore, Duck approached him about calling the truce. Xavier agreed that he was tired of losing people on his watch, and he wished he could sit down with the head of DCM. At the time, he was just venting to who he thought was a neutral party. Xavier had no idea that Duck was now riding for the other side.

"All right then." Sysco exhaled. "Call your source and arrange the meetup."

"Fuck that. Are you serious?" Ro was irate. "We're making friends with the enemy now?" He peered into his cousin's eyes.

"This is business. Nobody is trying to make friends." Sysco attempted to calm Ro down, but it was no use. The boy was turned up to the max. In fact, he had actually broken the knob.

"They killed our brother, our friend, and this is what we do?" Ro was utterly disgusted. "How can we call ourselves family? This ain't no fucking family."

"I feel bad for P-dot. He was like a little brother to me," Sysco hollered. "I watched both of y'all come up since kids. You think I'm not hurt behind this? We all hurt, Ro, but niggas in the dope game die every day!" Sysco's voice echoed off the wall.

"You right, Sysco." Ro laughed. "You always know what's best, don't you?" Without another word, Payro headed for the door.

Chapter Thirty-two

By the time Saturday came, Duck had managed to arrange the meeting with Xavier at a Coney Island on Davidson. Although Sysco wasn't 100 percent sure he'd made the right decision, he trusted Murda, and that was all that mattered.

"You ready?" he looked over to his passenger seat and asked, then checked his rearview mirror.

"Before we get out of this car, I need to know if you're ready." Murda could sense that something was bothering her man. He wasn't his usual self today, and he hadn't been himself since Payro stormed off the other night.

"I'm good, ma," Sysco lied with a smile. What he failed to realize was that the proof was written all over his face.

"What are you going to do about Ro?" Murda cut right to the chase. She knew that was what was on his mind, and she didn't want it getting in the way of this meeting with Xavier.

"What do you mean?" Sysco frowned.

"The nigga is getting reckless, Sysco," Murda said, stating the obvious. "You need to put his ass on ice for a minute." She liked Payro, but he was becoming a liability to the organization. Murda knew Sysco would never kick his blood out of the crew, which was why she suggested the time-out instead.

"It ain't that simple. That's my fucking family." Sysco shook his head. "Look . . ." He sighed, then checked the rearview mirror again. "I'm really not in the mood to be discussing this right now." He didn't tell Murda, but he'd sent Payro a message earlier asking him to attend the meeting. He wanted his cousin to be a part of this moment to show him how real bosses do things. Never in the history of the D had two rival organizations sat down together in hopes of ending the violence and mending fences.

"Are you looking for someone?" Murda asked after he checked the rearview again.

"No. Can we go now?" Sysco snapped. Payro had told him he would be there after asking for the time and location, but he had yet to pull up. Secretly Sysco was beginning to regret sending the message.

"Fine, we can go." Murda raised her hands in the air. "But sooner or later, you're going to have to deal with him, or the shit is going to get out of hand."

"Let's go." Sysco hopped out of the car like it was on fire. Murda shook her head in disgust while following suit.

Together they headed across the street toward the restaurant like Bonnie and Clyde. Standing outside were three men. One of them leaned against the exterior of the building. The other two men were engaged in a sports conversation on the sidewalk. "What's up?" Sysco nodded. "Do one of y'all know where I can find Xavier?"

"That depends on who wants to know," the man up against the wall said in a raspy baritone.

"Duck sent us," Murda replied. There was no need to drop their names if they didn't have to.

On cue, the other two men stopped talking and turned their attention to Murda and Sysco. "Are y'all strapped?" the deep-voiced man asked.

"No," Sysco and Murda replied in unison. They had been instructed by Duck to leave all weapons in the car at Xavier's request.

"Frisk them," the deep-voiced man instructed his goons, and they went to work searching the couple because he didn't trust them.

"Man, watch my nuts!" Sysco hollered when one of the men got a little too close to the family jewels.

"He's clean."

"She is too."

"Now that that's out of the way, let's go inside and talk." The deep-voiced man turned to head inside.

"Hold up." Sysco shook his head. "You've got to be out of your rabbit-ass mind if you think we're going in there unstrapped. The shit could be a setup. It's best if we talk right motherfucking here, out in the open."

"If I wanted you dead, my brother, I would have killed you and your old lady while y'all was sitting in the car across the street." Xavier nodded at the car.

He had a good point, but Sysco was nobody's fool. Once they went inside of that building, they may never walk out again. At least they had better chances of escape out in public.

"We speak right here, right now, or we just don't speak at all," Sysco flexed.

Murda could see that there was about to be a pissing contest between these two alpha males. Therefore, she stepped in. "Sir, we've come to your turf unprotected at your request. The least you can do is talk with us right here. We've shown good faith. Now it's your turn."

Xavier considered what the girl was saying. She was right. This was his turf, and they weren't strapped. What was the worst that could happen?

Chapter Thirty-three

"Grab us some chairs," Xavier instructed one of his goons. Immediately the man headed inside and was back in seconds.

"Is this your spot?" Murda asked after noting that the sign read XAV'S CONEY ISLAND.

"Yeah. It's my first one. The other one is on Outer Drive." Xavier was proud that he'd used his dope money to go legit. His father had taught him to always have a legal way to prove where his money came from should the Feds come knocking.

"It's nice." Murda smiled.

"It's a little something-something I would like to leave my children." Xavier looked back at the building that meant so much to him. "Speaking of my kids, all this killing has to stop!" Xavier looked from Sysco to Murda. "Back in the day, we settled beefs with our dukes." He held up his fists. "Y'all young motherfuckers only know how to pull pistols." He laughed lightly. "I'm only forty-two years old, but a nigga is trying to see eighty, you feel me?" Xavier wasn't trying to insult the young bosses before him, but he knew that compared to him, they were still wet behind the ears. "My young'uns want blood, but all I want is an understanding." Xavier paused. "Y'all stay on y'all side, and we will stay on ours."

"That's fair enough." Sysco nodded.

"Xavier, we want the same thing," Murda added.

"It sounds like we got ourselves an agreement then." Xavier stood from his chair. "Detroit is small. If our paths should cross again, I need to be assured your crew will keep it moving."

"As long as your crew does the same, there shouldn't be a problem." Sysco stood from his chair and extended his hand. With a grin, Xavier extended his, and they shook on it.

"Can I get y'all something to eat on the house before y'all go?"

"No, thanks. We're cool." Sysco wanted to get back on his side of the city ASAP. Although they'd just called a truce, his stomach was doing the Watusi. It was almost like he knew something was about to go left.

"What's wrong?" Murda mumbled as they crossed the street. Sysco didn't have time to respond before a gray Mustang came barreling down the block at full speed. Both the driver and passenger wore Halloween masks.

"Fuck!" Sysco pulled Murda toward the car for cover. With shaking hands, he tried to unlock the car before the bullets started flying. However, it was too late. On cue, they started. Murda bowed her head and closed her eyes. Payro was right. This was a setup. She and Sysco were sitting ducks, and it was her fault.

Seconds turned into minutes as both Sysco and Murda waited for the shooter to approach them. However, he never did. The car sped off, leaving a trail of smoke and a cluster of confusion. Murda raised her head, then stood up. "Oh, my God!" she screamed.

"What?" Sysco stood up and stared across the street. Lying deathly still on the sidewalk were none other than Xavier and his two goons. "Oh, shit!"

"We need to do something."

"Fuck that! Get in the car and let's go!" Sysco hollered before unlocking the car and jumping into the driver's seat. If they didn't get out of there now, they would be up shit's creek for real. There was no way to explain what happened when the police showed up. Even worse than that, they were now in deeper shit with the West Grand Crew. Sysco already knew they would be pinned for this.

"Who was that?" Murda couldn't believe the ambush.

"The hell if I know," Sysco said while peeling out of the parking space.

Murda could sense that he was lying. "Did you arrange that shit?" She held her breath for the answer.

"No." Sysco kept his eyes on the road.

"If I find out you organized that, I swear on everything that I'm leaving you!"

"I said no, didn't I?" Sysco raised his voice to match hers.

"Let me out of this fucking car." Murda opened up the door, fully prepared to jump out, but Sysco pulled her back.

"Do your crazy ass wanna die?" He looked at her briefly before returning his eyes to the road.

"If you pulled that shit, then I'm already dead anyway." Murda hit the dashboard. She was beyond pissed.

"What I got to do to prove that I didn't have no part of that?" Sysco lowered his voice. He'd never seen Murda this upset.

"Swear on your grandmother's grave you don't know nothing about that." Murda peered at him.

"I swear on my grandmother's grave," Sysco spat, then paused before telling the truth. "I told Ro about the meeting, but I swear on everything I love I did not tell him to do that." Sysco knew Murda would find out sooner or later. It was best he drop the dime now.

"What did you think he was going to fucking do?" Murda smacked her lips. "You are too damn smart to be so goddamn stupid!" She had never talked to Sysco like that, but her blood was boiling. "Do you realize the danger he put Duck in?" Murda couldn't care less that her life was on the line, but when it came to Duck, that was another story. "He used his relationship with Xavier to mend the fences between our crews, and this is the shit Payro pulls." Murda looked over at Sysco, who was speechless. "If that nigga weren't your family, I would kill him my goddamn self!"

Chapter Thirty-four

As soon as they pulled back onto their turf, Murda sent word to the crew that the beef was back and everyone should be on high alert. Sysco, on the other hand, went on a solo manhunt for Payro, who had seemingly vanished into thin air. He wanted to wring his cousin's neck when he found him, but he had to find him first.

After going to all his hangouts and known locations, Sysco returned to the hood empty-handed. He didn't want to deal with questions and the other bullshit that came along with being the boss, so he decided to head home instead of to the projects.

Murda blew his phone up until it finally died. He thought she would end up using the key he'd given her to pop up on him, but she didn't. In fact, after that day, Murda never called back.

After three days of no contact, Sysco could sense that he was losing her, but he was torn between her and Payro. He had to fix things but didn't know how. By the time he'd cooled off and was ready to talk, he was now the one being ignored. Sysco had called and had even gone to Murda's apartment today, but no one answered the door. Unfortunately for him, he'd just missed her by an hour.

It was time for her to go and re-up with Andres. As per usual, she headed to Club Hennessey and was met at the door by the same woman as always. Without being asked, Murdonna took her same seat at the bar and waited.

"Good to see you, *mi hija*." Today Andres wasn't dressed in a suit. Instead, he was dressed for the round of golf he was about to go play with a few of his entrepreneur friends.

"I've got your money, and I need a re-up, but I've got to tell you something first." Nervously, Murdonna looked into his eyes and began explaining the situation between her and Sysco. In so many words, she told him that they were in a relationship and that it would be complicated to be his competition. Murdonna still offered to move the same weight as usual. She would just do so under the DCM instead of her own shit.

Andres listened to Murdonna speak her piece, and then he spoke up. "Relationships and this lifestyle don't mix. In fact, there ain't even a place for love in the game. If you love something or someone, you'll begin thinking irrationally if ever that thing or person were put in harm's way. Love will get you killed, and I guarantee Sysco doesn't love you. He loves the idea of you." Andres broke it down further. "Until you came around here, he was content ripping and running in the projects. His dreams were small, too small. Yes, Sysco has been a very consistent buyer, but he ain't going to the next level with me. In fact, our ride together is about to end."

"What does that mean?"

"I am about to be promoted to head of the Garcia Family, which means I call the shots and will control all of the distribution for the entire brown and black population in the Midwest and Southern states. Murdonna, this right here is a powerful position to have. I can change lives, and I want to start with you! I promise to propel your game to the next level. You will be a multimillionaire before you're twenty-five. All you got to do is get rid of Sysco."

Murdonna's heart was racing, and her hands were sweaty. Not only was she being offered the position of a lifetime, but she was also being told to kill her man. She knew the game could be treacherous. She just didn't know how treacherous.

"What's it going to be, kid? Are you in or are you out?" Andres extended his hand. It dangled in the air for almost a full minute before Murdonna shook it.

"I'm in," she agreed.

"You won't regret it!" With a smile the size of Texas, Andres headed toward the back of the club to get Murdonna's package, leaving her alone with her thoughts.

As she pondered how exactly she would get rid of Sysco, he started blowing up her phone. She declined the calls. He needed to be put on ice until she could figure out her next move.

Within minutes, Andres was back with a small duffle bag. It felt different. She knew it wasn't cocaine. Curious, Murdonna looked inside and gasped when she saw all of the greenbacks. He'd given her back a little over twice the amount she'd just given him. "Why are you giving me all of this?"

"This small gift is a sign of good faith, *mi hija*. I want you to know there is more where this comes from."

"Okay, but where is my package?" Murdonna was extremely grateful for the money, but she still needed cocaine to conduct business.

"Take care of your competitor, and then we'll discuss our ploy to conquer the world further. You will be my secret weapon! With my position and your persistence, we will be unstoppable." In other words, he was telling her that she would be cut off until Sysco was out of the picture.

Chapter Thirty-five

By day five of being blocked, Sysco was losing his mind. Part of him was pissed that she was being so stubborn, and part of him was concerned for her safety. However, today was P-dot's funeral. He had to put on his game face and show support for the family of his fallen soldier and deal with Murda's shit later.

"Hello, Ms. Walton. If there is anything you need, please don't hesitate to ask," Sysco said when he approached P-dot's mother, who was standing near her son's casket.

"I want my son back. Can you do that?" Ms. Walton glared at the man who'd introduced her baby to the streets.

"No, ma'am, I can't." Sysco remorsefully put his head down, then looked at P-dot resting peacefully in the brown casket. He was wearing a white Lacoste shirt and jeans. His right hand rested over the left. The tattoo of DCM was dull, yet visible. Sysco smirked while looking down at his own tattoo. He could still remember the day they all went and got them. P-dot was the last person in the chair because he was afraid of needles.

"What the hell are you smirking for?" Out of nowhere, Ms. Walton hauled off and slapped the shit out of Sysco. The sound was so loud that it captured everybody's attention. Sysco's immediate reaction was to hit her ass back, but he refrained. "You think it's funny that my baby boy is gone? He would still be here if he never got involved with you."

"Ms. Walton, I'm sorry you lost your son, but he wasn't no saint when I met him." Sysco smiled. "He was already selling your pills, remember?"

"Boy!" Ms. Walton went to raise her hand again, but this time Sysco caught her by the wrist and forcefully squeezed. He leaned in real close so as not to make a scene in front of the other mourners.

"Bitch, I was trying to be respectful, but if you ever raise your hand to hit me again, I will put you with your son. I'm sure it's not too late to order a double plot." Sysco gritted his teeth then walked away.

Although Sysco was ready to leave the funeral immediately after the altercation, he knew it wouldn't sit right with his crew. Therefore, he took a seat near the back of the church and counted the minutes until it was over.

"Hey, stranger." Koko took a seat in the pew next to Sysco. She was so close that her leg was practically resting on his.

"What up doe?" Sysco nodded. He hadn't seen Koko since the night he'd come back from his grandmother's funeral. As soon as he returned to Detroit, he stopped by her apartment and told her they were through fucking around. Naturally, she turned on her sexual charm and tried to change his mind. As much as Sysco liked what Koko was offering to do to him in bed, his mind was made up. The time away had given him clarity that Murda was indeed the woman for him.

"That's all I get?" Koko opened her arms for a hug.

Sysco looked around the church quickly before obliging. Even though he had yet to speak with Murda, he knew she would show up today.

"Damn, that little bitch got you gone, huh?" Koko sat back in her seat, then folded her arms. Her ample breasts practically exploded from the tight black dress she was wearing.

"Chill with that language. Don't forget you in God's house," Sysco scolded her.

"My bad, Sys. I'm sorry." Koko exhaled. "I just get so mad when I think about someone having something that was once mine."

Sysco wanted to advise Koko that he never belonged to her, but he saw no need to ruin her moment. Instead, he changed the subject. "Have you seen Ro?"

"Yeah, he was outside when I pulled up," Koko replied halfheartedly. She didn't miss the way Sysco was dismissing her.

"I need to holler at him before the service starts. I'll catch you later." Sysco tried to stand, but Koko placed her arm out to stop him.

"I'm pregnant," she whispered.

"What?" Not sure he'd heard her correctly, he asked, "What did you just say?"

"I'm almost four months pregnant," Koko repeated with a hand over her belly.

"Fuck!" Sysco mumbled. It was almost like all the wind had been knocked out of him. Although Koko didn't like the way he'd just responded, she understood that he was just as shocked as she was when she took the home pregnancy test. Therefore, she let him slide.

"You're going to be a father." Reaching over, Koko grabbed Sysco's hand and placed it on her belly.

Sure as shit, it was round and firmer than he remembered. Sysco didn't know whether to rejoice because he always wanted to be a father, or cry due to the circumstances. However, the latter seemed more appropriate when he looked up and saw Murda coming down the aisle of the church.

Chapter Thirty-six

Murda was hotter than fish grease when she saw her man rubbing the belly of a bitch she couldn't stand. She knew what it meant, and she was devastated, no doubt. Instantly, she turned around and made a beeline for the door. Sysco was hot on her trail, and Koko sat back in her seat to enjoy the show.

"Murda, wait up!" Sysco called, but Murda paid him no mind. She wasn't in the mood for the bullshit today. "Wait up!" Sysco put on his jets and caught up with her. "Don't do me like that, please." He was out of breath.

"Don't do you like what, Sysco?" Murda hollered. The stragglers coming from the parking lot were all into the drama unfolding before them. "You were the one cuddled up with your old bitch!"

"It's not what it looks like!" Sysco tried to defend himself, but he knew there was no ground for him to stand on.

"You're saying she's not pregnant? Because that's what it looked like to me." Murda folded her arms tightly as an attempt to restrain herself. She really wanted to lay hands on Sysco. "How far along is she?"

"Almost four months." Sysco felt bad even uttering the words.

"Congratulations." With a tear in the corner of her eye, Murda managed to smile.

"This doesn't change anything between us, baby." Sysco grabbed her arm, but she snatched away.

"Are you crazy? This changes everything." Murda was hurt beyond belief. Her head started pounding so loud she could practically hear it. Her soul ached inconsolably. Here stood the man of her dreams telling her he was having a baby with someone else. As much as she wanted to be mad at him, she knew she couldn't. The baby had been created before Murda and Sysco made their thing official. Yet and still, the news rocked her to her core. It was too tough of a pill to swallow. Therefore, she decided right then and there not to swallow it. "Sysco, I think it's best we go our separate ways."

"No." Sysco shook his head. He raised his voice. "We will get through this. I can't lose you." He felt like he was going crazy. Too much was happening too fast.

"Lower your voice." Murda shushed him as a reminder that no one knew about their secret relationship.

"Fuck them!" Sysco spat. "I'll tell the world if that's what it takes. I love you, Murda."

"Hey, Sysco, I see trouble at three o'clock," Jarvis hollered. He was standing on the sidewalk with Ro and Fred. Both Sysco and Murda looked up to see three police cars parking. One of the officers waved him over. Sysco wanted to finish the more important conversation with Murda. However, he didn't have any beef with the police today, so he obliged.

"May I help you, Officer?" he asked after approaching the window of the first squad car.

"Sysciano Markell Nelson. Long time no see, my man." The black officer's face was partially covered by mirror-tinted glasses.

"Do I know you, my nigga?" Sysco rarely told anyone his full government. The fact that this motherfucker knew it meant their paths had to have crossed at some point.

"I'm Officer Rollins. Cassie's father."

Right away, Sysco's memory was jogged. Cassie was a carefree girl he'd dated in the ninth grade. Even at such a young age, she lived life on the edge. That was what Sysco liked most about her. In fact, Cassie was the one who introduced him to cocaine. She used to sell for a guy by the name of Rollo. Sysco was impressed by the amount of money he watched her make, and he wanted in. Needless to say, Cassie set the meeting up, and the rest was history.

Sadly, by the twelfth grade, Cassie began to get high on her own supply and was now a full-time cokehead. Although Cassie was the cause of her own downfall, Officer Rollins needed someone to blame, and for him, it was Sysco. It had been years since they'd had any contact, but Rollins would never forget the hate he had for the young thug.

"Is there any reason you're down here?" Sysco asked.

"We're here to ensure there won't be any drama today." Rollins removed his shades and peered at Sysco.

"You know the old saying, right?" Sysco adjusted the black tie around his neck. "Don't start none, won't be none."

"Keep fucking with me, smart-ass, and you'll be seeing the pen a lot sooner than you think." Officer Rollins smirked. "We've got your ass almost dead to rights on that club shooting a few months ago." Every time Sysco's name or anyone affiliated with him came through the precinct, Rollins was all over it like flies on shit. He was hell-bent on bringing the young dealer down.

"If that's the case, why haven't I heard about it?" Sysco knew the boys in blue were barking up his tree, but he hadn't heard anything substantial lately.

"Don't worry, boy." Rollins laughed. "Once we're done processing the witness statements, I'm going to nail your ass to the cross."

"Witness?" This was the first time Sysco had heard this information.

"You'd be surprised what people do when they want you out of the way."

Officer Rollins laughed, but Sysco didn't. He didn't know if the old cop was pulling his leg or if someone in his camp had actually snitched. Either way, he was going to get to the bottom of it.

Chapter Thirty-seven

Shit had not been going right at all for Sysco today, but at least he'd managed to keep Murda by his side a little longer and make it through the funeral in one piece. Luckily Koko kept her distance, and Payro too. Sysco told his cousin they needed to take a ride after P-dot's repast. There was so much he wanted to say and ask, but Sysco damn sure wasn't going to hold the conversation in the presence of everybody.

"'Although we've come to the end of the road still, I can't let go,'" a heavyset male sang over P-dot's casket as they lowered it into the ground. Murda watched from behind a pair of large shades as the mother of his child stood over the hole in the ground with her son. Although Murda couldn't force herself to drop a tear for P-dot, she did get emotional when the baby tossed a single rose into the hole and said goodbye to his daddy. It was a sad scene that made Murda really think about her own life. How would she be remembered? What legacy would she leave behind?

"Are you ready to split?" Sysco leaned over and whispered into her ear.

"Yeah, let's go." Murda nodded. When the couple turned around to head back to the car, they both spotted a black Lincoln riding up slowly.

By instinct, they both went for their pieces, but it didn't matter. When the back window on the Lincoln rolled down, an AK-47 assault rifle popped out. Bullets sprayed the air like a thunderstorm. Sysco dove on top of Murda, who was still trying to let off her own shots.

"West Grand Crew for life!" one of the shooters yelled as the Lincoln sped past. The shooting only lasted for seven minutes, but the damage was irreversible.

"My baby!" P-dot's baby mother yelled over her son's lifeless body. He had taken one of the bullets to the neck.

Murda couldn't believe it! Her heart immediately went out to the woman. For the first time since joining the DCM, she wanted out. Although she knew bloodshed and turf wars came with the territory, Murda never signed up to see babies catching bullets.

"You did this!" She sprang from the ground like a jack-in-the-box and charged at Payro. "You did this, didn't you?"

"Did what?" Payro glared at her.

"We went to end this shit, and you made it worse!" Murda clutched the gun, then pointed it right between Payro's eyes. She no longer saw him as anything other than her enemy. She despised his worthless ass and was ready to end his life right then and there.

"What are you doing?" Sysco hollered.

"You better call off your pit bull." Payro grimaced.

"Or what?" Murda pushed the nose of the gun against his temple. She was so close to pulling the trigger it wasn't even funny. Payro was their downfall. Murda wanted badly to sever all ties with his ass.

"Murda, put the goddamn gun down!" Sysco barked.

"I'm done playing with this weak-ass nigga. It's me or him. You call it." Murda was on one today.

"Yeah, you call it, Sysco," Ro repeated without moving an inch. "Blood or a bitch!" He knew Murda was the wedge between them. It was time to pull rank and get rid of her ass once and for all.

"Both of y'all are on y'all way out. This is not the time or the place for this. We got a dead baby over there." Although Sysco spoke the truth, he was trying to buy time. Both Ro and Murda knew it, yet only one of them was real enough to call bullshit.

"Sysco, apparently you like playing games, but I don't." Murda lowered her weapon. "You keep him. I'm out."

"Don't leave, please." Sysco grabbed her arm, but she snatched away.

"Look, you got to do what's best for you, and I need to do what's best for me. If our paths cross again, then cool. If they don't, just promise me you'll take care of yourself." Murda looked back at the scene with tears in her eyes. The cemetery was in complete disarray. She knew the beef with the West Grand Crew was about to escalate to another level, and she wanted no part of it. There was already too much blood on her hands.

Without a word, Sysco looked from Payro to Murda and then watched her walk away. He wanted to chase after her and beg her to stay, but he couldn't. Payro was his blood. No matter how bad he'd fucked up, Sysco was required to have his back.

Chapter Thirty-eight

Thirty minutes later, Murda and Duck pulled back into the projects. She was mentally exhausted and deflated. Things with Sysco were done for good on account of several things. Not only would Payro forever be a thorn in their side, but she knew Koko and her baby would be, too. Murda wasn't mentally prepared to deal with any of that. Therefore, she had to accept the facts and move on with business as usual. It was time for her and Duck to go independent.

"When the dust settles, I'm going to get us back on our feet. For now, we need to lay low and get out of the projects." Her plan was to use the money given to her by Andres to do so. Once she and Duck got squared away, she needed to assemble a crew and prepare for the work she was about to put in for Andres and the Spanish mafia family.

Duck silently nodded in agreement. After the stunt they'd pulled at the cemetery, he knew the West Grand Crew didn't play. They were wild and crazy. He wasn't trying to become a face on a shirt.

As soon as Murda unlocked the apartment door, she saw that something was amiss. She heard three voices from inside the house. At first, she couldn't catch familiarity in the third voice, but when she did, her heart nearly stopped.

"Donna, look who came home." Mya pulled her mother from the bathroom.

Sheila stood in the hallway nervously, not knowing whether to hug her oldest daughter.

"Where the fuck have you been?" Murda asked with a trembling tone.

"I took a little trip down South with my friend to clear my head and get myself clean. I'm sorry for being gone so long," Sheila replied.

"They don't have phones?" Murda frowned.

"Donna, I'm sorry." Sheila tried to approach Murda with open arms, but she wasn't in the mood.

"Bitch! Do you know what you did to us?" With a shaking hand, Murda reached into her bag and pulled her gun out. "You left us here to die!" Instantly she placed the gun to her mother's head the same way she'd just done to Payro. Murdonna could only see red as tears fell from her face.

"Murda, calm down," Duck begged while standing behind his friend.

"Donna, what are you doing?" Mya hollered.

Donzell didn't say a word. He was scared to death.

"Are you going to shoot me?" Sheila asked nervously.

"I should," Murda barked. "Do you know what we went through?" Her blood was boiling as the flashbacks of having no food, money, or parental guidance hit her all at once. Then she thought about killing Chains for money and killing Tricks because she had to. Murda cried silently as thoughts of being alone in the trap house invaded her mental space. Although she never said it aloud, she was scared shitless every time she left the house, not knowing if she would return.

"I'm sorry," Sheila cried. "I know I left a lot on you, and I'm sorry."

"Sorry didn't feed us! Sorry didn't keep the goddamn lights on. I did!" Murda hit her chest. "Do you know what I had to go through to make sure we stayed alive?"

"I know I left a lot on you, but I was sick then." Sheila wiped her eyes. "You have to believe me when I tell you that I'm better now." Sheila's eyes desperately searched her daughter's face for any sign of forgiveness the way the younger kids had forgiven her when she showed up bearing gifts an hour ago.

"You weren't sick! You were a junkie. There's a big difference." Murda wiped her eyes with the sleeves of her shirt. "You got five seconds to get the fuck out!"

"Please don't make her leave!" Mya begged. She'd missed her mother so much. She wasn't ready to let her go just yet.

"Either she's leaving, or I am." Murda couldn't believe she found herself giving two ultimatums in one day.

"Donna had our back when Sheila didn't, remember?" Donzell finally used his voice to speak on his sister's behalf. Even though he had love for his mother, his loyalty would forever be with his sister.

Mya did remember. Although she wanted more time with her mom, she couldn't forget how she'd left them hanging. She backed away a little from Sheila.

"Mya, I've changed," Sheila said, trying to appeal to her youngest daughter, but Mya was no fool.

"Maybe you can come back and visit some time." Mya sniffed.

"I birthed all of y'all, and this is how you do me?" Sheila was irate, although she had no right to be. "You can't put me out of my shit."

"You can leave voluntarily or involuntarily. The choice is yours." Murda gripped the gun.

Sheila studied her daughter's face. The coldness in her eyes caused a chill to come over her. Murdonna had changed and not in a good way. Long gone was the little girl who always had her nose in a book.

"I guess I'll be staying at a friend's house." She turned to face her other children. "I love you both very much." She kissed both of their foreheads, then grabbed her suitcase and headed for the door.

Chapter Thirty-nine

Things around the apartment were tense among the siblings for a few days following Sheila's visit, but slowly they went back to normal as the week came to a close. While Mya and Donnie were in school, Murda and Duck went house shopping. Although they were working with a small $60,000 budget, they'd managed to find a four-bedroom fixer-upper on the west side. It needed a few things like new windows, updated appliances, and eventually, a new roof. Murda had depleted her savings to purchase the property, but it was hers, and she could move in tomorrow. That was all that mattered.

With no real money in hand, she knew it was time for her and Duck to get back on the grind once they touched down on the west side. However, without product, they were at a standstill. She knew she'd ultimately have to handle Sysco, but for now, she concentrated all her time and energy into moving.

Knock! Knock!

"Come in," Murda yelled from the back of the apartment, where she and Duck were breaking down the bedroom set. She thought it was the landlord coming for the scheduled inspection.

"Can we talk?" Sysco stood in the doorway of the bedroom.

Murda was surprised to see him. "I'm busy," she replied calmly, although her heart raced for many reasons at the sight of him.

"Please just give me ten minutes." Sysco rubbed a hand down his full, disheveled beard. Murda could tell by the bags under his eyes that whatever was on his mind was getting the best of him.

"Okay, ten minutes," she relented and told Duck she'd be back. She followed Sysco out of the apartment and into the hallway.

"You look good." He looked down at her.

"You don't. What's up?" she asked.

"I miss you," he replied honestly.

"Let's not do this." Murda tried to turn around and head back into her apartment, but he stopped her.

"My time ain't up yet. Please just hear me out, damn." Sysco reached into his pocket. "Put this on." He handed her a blindfold.

Murda looked skeptical, but she trusted him, so she put it on. "Where are we going?" Murda asked as they began to walk up the stairs.

"We're almost there." Sysco laughed while trying to guide her. She looked like a mime feeling around an invisible box.

"This isn't fun. I'm about to take it off."

"We're almost there." He wanted to surprise his boo with a romantic gesture, but she was ruining it. "Okay, now you can take the blindfold off," he said once they made it to their destination.

"Oh, my God! Is this all for me?" Murda smiled from ear to ear after looking around at the sight before her. There was a picnic blanket, picnic basket, balloons, roses, and a small box. She couldn't believe Sysco had gone to such lengths to set up this romantic rooftop scene on her building. As grungy as the projects were, they currently served as a stunning backdrop for their impromptu date. "This is beautiful."

"You're beautiful." Sysco pulled Murda in close and planted a wet, sloppy kiss on her lips.

"What's this all about?" Murda felt so special. As much as she hated to admit it, she was overjoyed to be in his arms once more.

"I appreciate the way you stepped up to the plate in such a short time and held me down. Without you, DCM wouldn't be able to stand tall right now." Sysco peered down into Murda's eyes. He loved the girl standing before him to death.

"What can I say?" Murda shrugged. "We were a team, Sysco." Though she was struggling to act cool on the inside, outwardly, she was doing fine.

"We *are* a team," he corrected her.

However, Murda shook her head. "Unless you've let Payro go, we ain't shit." She looked up at him. As much as she loved Sysco, she couldn't be a part of the chaos Payro always seemed to create. He wasn't made for this life, and everybody knew it.

"That's my family, Murda. He ain't going nowhere." Sysco wasn't one for sugarcoating things. The truth was the truth, no matter how you sliced it. "That's my mother's sister's son. Payro is my first cousin, my blood. As long I live and breathe, he will be a part of Detroit City Mafia. He practically helped me build this shit down here in the projects, and with your help, we've grown to want more for the organization."

"I understand what you're saying, and that's why I removed myself from the situation." Murda nodded.

"Baby, I need you back now more than ever." Sysco sighed. "I know the team has hit a few bumps in the road, but Detroit City Mafia is a family, our family. Let's take over the game."

Murda wanted to tell him that with Andres' deal, she didn't need him or DCM to reach new heights, but instead, she saw this as the perfect opportunity to put her plan in motion.

"Murdonna Carter, will you be my Bonnie?" Now down on one knee, Sysco proposed with the nicest ring Murdonna had ever seen. It wasn't a rock, and it wasn't super clear in clarity, but it was beautiful.

"Yes, baby, I will marry you, but on one condition."

"Anything." After placing the ring on Murda's hand, Sysco stood.

"If we're going to get married, I don't want to wait. I want to do this tomorrow," Murdonna insisted.

"I don't think now is the best time. You know, I still got that Club Hennessey shooting hanging over my head, and I got the baby on the way. I say let's give it a year and see how everything pans out." Sysco was speaking rationally. His points made sense, but still, Murda pushed.

"It's now or never. I don't have a year to give anybody."

Though Sysco didn't like ultimatums, he knew that if he let his good thing go this time, she'd never come back. "I love you, Murda. If you want to get married tomorrow, then we'll be getting married tomorrow."

Chapter Forty

As soon as the agreement was made, both Murda and Sysco went to work. Since there were still a few months left until Murdonna turned 18, Sysco was in charge of using his connections to find someone to authorize a marriage license. He also had the tasks of securing the church and minister. She was in charge of ordering a cake, which was to be served in the fellowship hall of the church, and she had to reserve a limousine that would drive them away from the church and to the Marriott for the night. They decided not to go overboard on the wedding and keep things simple.

The news of their coming nuptials spread like wildfire through the projects. Needless to say, not everyone was happy that Sysco and Murdonna were about to make it official. When Koko saw Sysco that night heading to the townhouse, she tried to stop him by making it known how she felt, but it didn't matter. Sysco reached into his pocket and pulled out a few bills.

"This wedding is happening, whether you like it or not." He handed her the money. "I will always take care of my seed, but me and you will never be a thing. You will respect my wife, and I will make sure my wife respects you. In the meantime, take the money and go shopping for the baby or get your hair done." Sysco knew that having a wife and baby mother was bound to have its challenges, so he wanted to nip this shit in the bud now before the baby got here.

Once he was done with Koko, Sysco headed into the townhouse where everyone was waiting. The cat was already out of the bag, he could tell by the silence in the room, but that didn't matter either.

"I know y'all have already heard that Murda and I will be tying the knot tomorrow. I didn't come here to ask permission, and I didn't come here to hear your thoughts on the matter. I came here to ask my brothers if y'all would do me the honor of at least attending."

For nearly a minute, no one said a word. Fred was the first to speak up. "Man, if you like it, I love it. I'll be there for sure."

"Me too," a few others added, but Payro hadn't uttered a word.

"Ro, I need you to be there because a wedding ain't shit without a best man." That was his way of asking.

"How would your wife feel about that?" Ro huffed.

"It's not about what she thinks. This is about me and you. I've been there for you your whole life, and now I'm asking you to be there for me." Right, wrong, and indifferent, Sysco needed his cousin by his side on such a big day.

"Yeah, I'll be there for sure!" Payro embraced his cousin for a hug. "Do you think Murda would care if we took you for one last soiree." He laughed, and the other men laughed too. Sysco knew it was about to be a crazy night, but he was with all the bullshit.

"Let's ride!"

The next morning flew by like a breeze. Murdonna had risen early to take Mya, Donzell, and Duck to get dress clothes. Luckily there was a David's Bridal in the plaza where they were, so she was also able to grab a wedding dress along with a pair of shoes to match. After dropping

Donzell and Duck off at the barbershop, she and Mya headed to the last-minute appointment she was able to make with Odessa.

After getting her makeup done by Kelly J, a prominent up-and-coming makeup artist, Murdonna felt like a million bucks. She couldn't believe today was the big day. Bzzzzzz. She looked down at the phone dancing on her nightstand and picked it up. "Hello."

"*Mi hija*. I heard the news, and I was a little bit confused," Andres said cautiously into the receiver. "I thought we had an agreement, and now you're getting married?"

"We still have an agreement, don't worry. I'll be in touch." Without another word, Murdonna ended the call and walked over to the mirror. Though she was all made up, looking like a princess, the reflection she saw looking back at her was that of queenpin on the rise. It was game time, and she was ready for war by any means necessary.

Right at 2:30 p.m., Murdonna and her family made their way into the church through the back door being held open by the secretary. She didn't want Sysco or anyone to see her. "Right this way, ma'am." The secretary led her down a hallway toward the pastor's office. "You look stunning."

"Thank you. Is my fiancé here?"

"Yes, he's in the office next door. He's just waiting on his groomsmen to arrive, but we should still be all set to start at three." She looked at her watch.

"Can you give him something for me?" Reaching down into her bag, Murdonna handed the lady a box.

"Aw, how sweet. I'll go give it to him now." With a smile, the lady left the room with Duck on her tail.

"I'll go too. That way, I'll see what his reaction is and let you know how it all went down."

"Thanks, Duck." Nervously Murdonna began to pace the office floor because she knew what was about to happen. Instinctively she wanted to go after Duck and call the whole thing off, but she couldn't. She knew this had to be done.

Chapter Forty-one

Duck and the secretary made small talk as they walked the short distance to the office where Sysco was currently rehearsing his vows. Though Payro and the boys were late, he knew they'd be there.

"Do you want to give the gift to him?" the secretary asked with a smile.

"No, ma'am. I'm going to record it for my sister if you don't mind." Duck made a show of getting his cell phone ready.

"Okay." Without a second thought, the lady knocked on the door.

Seconds felt like minutes as Duck waited for it to open. When it finally did, the secretary presented the box, and Sysco smiled, already knowing who it was from. His smile soon faded the second he felt the piercing bullet sent to his midsection. He couldn't see the shooter but instinctively knew it wasn't the church secretary. Frantically he tried to get past her. He needed to see who had come for him, but his legs gave out, and he fell to the ground.

Due to the silencer on the weapon, there was no sound of gunfire. Yet and still, as soon as the secretary saw the groom fall to the floor with blood pouring from his body, she started to scream, but it was too late. From behind, Duck placed the silencer toward the lady's head and pulled the trigger. She dropped like a bag of potatoes. Knowing he couldn't be seen in the church now with blood splatter on his clothes, he decided to make a mad dash for the back door.

Once he was out of the building and safely behind the wheel of Murdonna's car, he sent a text message: Sorry, sis, I'm running late. I spilled something on my shirt and had to turn around. Be back shortly. This was his way of establishing his alibi. Should the police check his phone records, they would know he was in the area by checking the cell phone towers.

Duck, hurry up. I need you here, Murdonna responded with sweaty hands. She knew the message meant that the deed had been done. Now all she had to do was wait for someone to discover the body. Unbeknownst to her, Sysco was next door still clinging to life.

"911. What's the emergency?" the young operator asked after the second ring. She sounded perky and cheerful, like the heaviness of her job hadn't yet weighed her down.

"Help! I need help!" he screamed as loud as he could into the blood-covered phone he was clutching for dear life. "Please, help me." Using what felt like his final breaths, he begged this stranger with every ounce of energy he could muster to send help his way. Internally though, he could sense the end was near. His toes were turning cold, and it was becoming harder and harder to get air.

"Everything is going to be okay. Calm down, please, and tell me what your emergency is," the operator said.

"I've been shot in my stomach, and I . . . really . . . can't . . . breathe." As Sysco ended the sentence, he started to cough up chunky bits of blood. On cue, his body began to tremble. He knew death was around the corner.

"Help is on the way. Just hang on. Keep talking to me. Are you alone?" Now, fear had consumed the young operator's voice. Gone was the perkiness. Now she was panicked. "Hello. Are you there? Stay with me."

Although he wanted badly to reply, he just couldn't. His attention was focused on the large hole in his stomach. There was so much blood you'd swear he'd been covered with gallons of dark red paint. This shit looked like the scene of a horror film, and he was the unlucky victim.

"Hello. Please say something," the 911 operator begged frantically. She wanted him to give her some indication that he was still alive, but he just didn't have the strength.

As he tried to press a button on his call screen to at least let her know he was still alive, the room started to spin. His eyelids opened and closed uncontrollably. Suddenly he felt extremely tired. Fighting with everything he had, Sysco forced himself to stay awake. He knew if he closed his eyes now, they would probably never open again.

Fuck! This was really it. The curtains were finally about to close. All his life, he thought he would die of old age, in a hospital, surrounded by his loved ones. Yet, here he lay, dying young and all by himself. Silly him for thinking that God would look out for him this one time. *Shit!* His life had been hell for as long as he could remember. Why would today be any different?

Right on cue, the phone slipped from his bloody grasp into the large pool of blood flowing from his midsection. He tried hard to reach for it, but it was no use. *Fuck!* He couldn't believe today had turned into such a tragic occasion. It was his wedding day, and to make matters worse, he was expecting his first child soon. How would his seed survive in such an ugly world without him? Nobody would love his son or daughter like him! No one could teach his child the game like him! *Fuck!* he thought again as the severity of this situation hit him like a ton of bricks.

Just then, he heard the sirens approaching from outside, and things began to look up. Maybe he was going to be all right after all. Silently he prayed the Lord would spare him. God knows he'd done some dirt! Nevertheless, he was just beginning to figure his life out, and then some shit like this happened. He'd heard the saying, "Tomorrow ain't promised," plenty of times. He just never knew how true the shit was until this very second.

Knowing that help was only seconds away, he used the time to ponder the situation. He needed to keep his mind focused on something to prevent himself from closing his eyes. Who could've done this? Who was that fucking crazy? Not only had the bastard sniped him in the church, but they had also come for him in a venue filled with all of his soldiers. Whoever did this shit was brazen. They had no idea of the war they were starting, or maybe they did. Either way, there was going to be some smoke in the city once word got out that this shit had happened to him.

In addition to being on the rise as one of the top narcotics distributors in Detroit, he literally had the projects on lock! Once his niggas found out the hand that was feeding them had been laid to rest, they were bound to go bananas. No doubt, shit would be dry on the streets without him for a while.

As these thoughts ran through his mind, he began to transition from feeling helpless to pissed off. Impulsively, he wanted to get up from this cold floor and grab his gun to retaliate. He knew the perpetrator was probably still in the church, hiding among his family and friends who were waiting in the sanctuary for the wedding to start. If he had to die today, he at least wanted to take that bitch-ass nigga with him. Yet when he tried to move even his fingertips, his body betrayed him, forcing him to lie still and wait for assistance to arrive.

Finally, he surrendered and closed his eyes to calm his rapid breaths. While doing so, he decided to go ahead and make peace with God. They had never really seen eye to eye, but he knew things were out of his hands and now in His. Quickly, he recited a short prayer in his head that he'd learned in Sunday school and decided then to let the chips fall where they may. If he died, he died, but if the Lord saw fit to let him see another day, he promised to give up the game, but only after he'd gotten revenge on the person who tried to end his life. It sounds crazy to think about killing someone as you're dying, but that was him: a hothead from the east side of Detroit, with a trigger finger that was always on go.

His days on earth hadn't always been the easiest, but instead of seeing himself as a victim, he always saw himself as a victor. He had fought many battles and slain several giants in his short life, and today was no different. Seconds felt like days before he finally heard the sound he'd been waiting for.

"My name is Bryan, and this is Elizabeth!"

Sysco opened his eyes to see an older male EMT introduce himself as he and his partner dropped down to the floor beside him. After they ripped his clothes off and poked him with several needles, he was wrapped with some gauze, then lifted onto the gurney and rolled toward the waiting ambulance. With weak eyes, he caught a glimpse of a few spectators in the hallway of the church. They all had tears running down their faces. He knew they could see death riding shotgun with him on the stretcher, because he saw his punk ass too! Still, he fought.

"It's going to be okay. You will pull through this," someone yelled out.

He wanted to encourage everyone not to worry. He wanted to tell them that it was all going to work out in the end, no matter which way it went, but he was way too feeble. Instead, he managed to muster up the strength to at least give the onlookers a halfhearted smile. If he had to go out like this, he at least wanted the last thing on his face to be a smirk. He needed niggas to know that he wasn't scared and that nobody could get the best of him, even in death.

"What happened, baby? Who did this?" his fiancé asked while running up to the stretcher. This caused a tear to form in the corner of his eye. Not for him, though. He was too G for that shit. The tears he was shedding were simply for the loss of what could've been and the loss of love unexplored to its fullest potential. These tears were falling because they were losing the forever that they'd promised each other.

"Please step back! We need to clear a way to the door. Our patient needs to get to the ambulance," Bryan hollered.

"Don't you fucking die on me! Do you understand? I love you. I need you. Baby, I need you!"

"I love you too." He tried to mumble the words for what he felt would be the last time. His heart began to break into a million pieces. Death for him was inevitable, and he knew it.

Finally, they made it outside into the cool April air and into the waiting emergency vehicle with flashing lights. Elizabeth jumped behind the wheel and took off, pushing the large vehicle to at least eighty miles per hour. Sysco shrieked in pain as they hit several unavoidable potholes. Unfortunately, these were a permanent fixture on all Detroit roads.

Bryan placed an oxygen mask over his face and hooked him up to some white machine. Sysco listened as he called over to the local hospital, telling them about his grave condition. He advised them to assemble a surgical team and to have them at the door stat.

"Elizabeth, drive faster!" he yelled. She punched the gas so hard that Bryan must've lost his balance. Sysco saw him fall toward the back door then quickly regain his footing. "Stay with us. We won't lose you tonight." Bryan sounded like he felt confident, but Sysco didn't feel the same. He knew his time was up.

Within twenty minutes, they had arrived at Detroit Receiving Hospital. It was the number one trauma center in Detroit. Bryan and Elizabeth pulled his gurney off the back of the ambulance and flew through the emergency room doors like it was their lives that were on the line. From there, he was then handed off to a team of doctors and nurses. At this point, all he could see were blurs of faces. He couldn't make out anything. They anxiously went to work on his body all the way into the operating room, which was lit up with so many white lights it could've almost been mistaken for heaven.

"Come on, people, we have a life to save here!" someone yelled. Sysco assumed he was the doctor in charge.

The operating room was freezing cold. He was numb yet shivering uncontrollably. When the staff transported him from the gurney to the table, his entire body went limp. He couldn't feel a thing, not even his face. The light above his head was so blinding that he had to ponder if it was the surgical lamp or the Lord Himself.

"Who shot me?" He randomly mumbled while peering at the anesthesiologist, who was injecting something into his IV line. Naturally, she didn't respond, but it didn't matter. Out of nowhere, an array of scenes began to play out in front of him like the movie of his life. Maybe this was God's way of giving him the answer to his question before he took his last breath. Maybe He wanted his soul to have eternal peace . . . even if he was going to hell.

"Goddammit. We're losing this patient!" the doctor screamed.

Beeeeeeeeeeeeeeeeeeeeeeeeeeeeeeeeeeeeeeeeeeeeeeep! Right then, right there, he flatlined.

Epilogue

Sysco's life ended that day on the operating table. He'd lost too much blood, and the damage was irreversible. Surgeons had done their best, but Sysco just didn't have the strength left to fight any longer. Minutes after he was removed from the church, the DCM arrived and took Murdonna to the hospital. They all sat on pins and needles for over an hour until they were delivered the dreadful news.

As expected, everyone went crazy when the doctor confirmed that Sysco was deceased. Of course, Payro took it the hardest. Immediately he felt guilty for what had happened. In his mind, this shit had stemmed from when he shot up the truce between the DCM and the West Grand Crew. For as long as he lived, he would never forgive himself for allowing this to happen to his cousin, his brother. Payro would also regret not being at the church on time. For that reason, he vowed to find the person responsible and settle the score in the worst way. Losing his cousin had lit a fire within him that he didn't even know was there. Payro knew it was time to go into beast mode.

Silently Murdonna sat with her head in her hands as the tears fell big and hard. Though she knew what she'd orchestrated was necessary, that didn't make it any less painful. She truly loved Sysco with all of her heart, but like Andres said, love had no place in the dope game. With that lesson in mind, she wiped her face and stood from the chair. One by one, she walked over to each of the guys and offered them a hug or a handshake. Ro was the last one. When their awkward embrace was over, she gave one last look at the crew, knowing their run together was over. It was time to activate her inner boss and elevate her game. Pulling out her cell phone as she walked away, she dialed Andres.

"*Mi hija,* do you have good news?"

"It's done. I'm on my way." Without another word, Murdonna ended the call. She walked away from the hospital lobby and into the night air with more clarity now than ever. From that day forward, she would be determined to get to the top no matter whose toes she had to step on. Come hell or high water, she would be the biggest goddamn drug dealer in Detroit, even if it killed her.

"Murda, wait up!" Ro called out, stopping her in her tracks.

She didn't know how long he'd been behind her, but she decided to play it cool. "What's up?" She turned around slowly. The train of her dress dragged on the ground.

"Just tell me, why did you do it?" Ro asked with tears falling from his face.

Initially, when he saw her leaving, he chased after her to see if she wanted to go back with him and say a few words over Sysco's body before he went to the morgue. However, as he got closer, he heard her say it was "done," and he knew then she was the culprit.

"Ro, I don't know what—"

She never got the opportunity to finish her lie before Payro pulled a 9 mm handgun from the waist of his slacks and sent one shot to the center of her forehead. He didn't care one bit that he was right outside of the hospital. All that mattered was that Sysco's killer was brought to justice—street justice.

"Detroit City Mafia until I die, bitch! I am my brother's keeper." After sending one last shot to Murdonna's chest, Payro tucked the gun back into his slacks and ran off under cover of night.